ON THE REBOUND

"You always make me feel great on the rebound," Jacy said.

"Yeah, as long as I remain single."

She stiffened, wide-eyed with surprise. Releasing his hands, she turned to face Risk, a bit pale and somewhat unnerved. "H-have you met someone? Are you seriously involved?"

He was head-over-heels involved. With her. "There's no one in my life at the moment, babe. But when the right woman comes along, she's mine."

"Yours." She drew in a breath. A breath that hitched in her chest. "I never thought…"

"Thought *what*, Jacy?"

Her hand fluttered as she waved off the thought. "Never mind. It isn't important. You're here with me now." She ran the tip of her finger down his bare chest and belly. "I plan to enjoy you."

Squeeze Play

KATE ANGELL

LOVE SPELL NEW YORK CITY

*Squeeze Play is dedicated to
fans of baseball, summer, and romance.*

LOVE SPELL®

June 2006

Published by

Dorchester Publishing Co., Inc.
200 Madison Avenue
New York, NY 10016

ISBN 0-505-52667-0

The name "Love Spell" and its logo are trademarks of Dorchester Publishing Co., Inc.

Printed in the United States of America.

Visit us on the web at www.dorchesterpub.com.

ACKNOWLEDGMENT

Alicia Condon, vice president and
editorial director, you are appreciated.

PROLOGUE

"Welcome to game seven of the World Series. This is Mickey Calloway at Carver Park in Tampa Bay. It's the bottom of the ninth. Tampa Bay Bombers four. Richmond Rogues three. Rogues have two outs with one man on base. The on-deck hitter, center fielder Risk Kincaid, is headed for home plate."

Cheers and boos, clapping and stomping erupted outside the commentator's booth. The plate glass shook. In his thirty years of broadcasting, he'd never heard anything like it. The noise was deafening.

Calloway stood, sat, then stood again, as restless as the crowd. "Aaron Grayson is throwing major heat," he continued his commentary. "A southpaw with a clocked speed of ninety-eight miles per hour, he'll raise the hair on Kincaid's forearms."

He reached for his glass of water and took a quick sip. "Kincaid's digging in, taking a few practice swings while staring Grayson down. The men have been competitors since the minors.

"Catcher signals. Grayson drops his head, rocks

1

back, and . . . *strike one!* Backdoor slider. The pitch appeared out of the strike zone, but broke back over the base.

"Kincaid shares a few choice words with the umpire, knocks the head of the bat against his heel, then takes his stance. If anyone can pop it out of the park, Kincaid can, given the right pitch. Grayson has no plans to oblige him."

The noise of eighty thousand fans built around Calloway as the crowd grew wild, so wild he could see the whites of their eyes clear across the field, mouths moving as they screamed and begged the Bomber's pitcher to bring the pennant home.

Mickey Calloway was about to hyperventilate from the excitement. "Kincaid's set, and Grayson winds up, throws . . . *strike two!* He swung on the curve, fanned it. His lack of expression says it all, folks. Kincaid's in his own zone. A look toward the runner on third, and Zen Driscoll extends his lead off the bag. Kincaid plans to bring his teammate home."

Calloway narrowed his eyes along with the fans as Kincaid raised his left hand and slowly drew it from right to left field. "A change in the wind?" Calloway grew watchful before slowly shaking his head. "I wouldn't have believed it if I hadn't seen it with my own eyes. Kincaid's jabbed his finger toward left field, telling the fans where he plans to stick the next pitch. Arrogance or confidence, folks? He's promised a home run."

The crowd went ballistic. Calloway motioned to the cameraman to pan the left-field crowd for the fans' reaction to the batter's boast. Amid the bouncing, jostling bodies in Rogues jerseys and faded jeans, the cameraman zoomed in on one young woman in a bright yellow T-shirt and hip-hugging red jeans. Short, spiky Valentine pink hair was complemented by aviator-style sunglasses.

Her hand gestures had Calloway agreeing to flash her on the big screens displayed throughout the park.

"Bring it on, baby," the announcer interpreted her outstretched arms, the wiggling curve of her fingers. "I'm not certain if she's encouraging or daring him."

He couldn't help chuckling. "Kincaid's spotted her on the Jumbotron. A second jab of his finger toward left field just warned our fan to duck."

Tension thickened in Calloway's throat. "Two practice swings, and Kincaid digs in. Catcher signals, and Grayson sets up, ready to throw. Hearts are hammering. Everyone's holding his breath. Grayson sends a cutter—*slam-bam*. The ball is long and gone! It lands two rows above the lady with pink hair, bounces off the bleachers, and nearly knocks her in the head. Kincaid takes the bases while fans scramble for the winning ball.

"Congratulations, Rogues! This is Mickey Calloway handing over coverage to my colleague, Gary Swift, who's down on the field."

Two heartbeats, and Swift took over the commentary. "Rogue fans are shouting, embracing, and dancing in the aisles." The cameraman scanned the stands. "Bomber supporters have settled into tears and a five-month wait until next season. Security circles Risk Kincaid as he's surrounded by teammates and press."

Fireworks exploded overhead as Swift jabbed his microphone between two reporters and under Kincaid's nose. Risk backed up a step. "You pointed and delivered," Swift yelled, struggling to be heard over the barrage of questions fired like bullets.

"I connected with the sweet spot," Kincaid returned easily.

"What if—"

"I never recognize failure," Kincaid said, cutting Swift off.

"You've never played better." A woman reporter had gained his attention. "A double, two triples, and a home run."

Kincaid glanced toward her. "Total team effort."

"What about the girl with the pink hair?" someone called.

"What about her?" he shot the question back.

"You nearly slammed the ball down her throat."

A corner of his mouth turned up slightly. "She needs to learn to duck."

"Where are you headed after the series?" Swift shouted. "Disney World?"

Kincaid tipped back his baseball cap and stared directly into the camera. "Frostproof, Florida. I owe my hometown a visit."

CHAPTER 1

"Damn, Opie, are we in Mayberry?"

Risk Kincaid cut Zen Driscoll a look. "Not funny, man." Downshifting his Lotus to a crawl along Wall Street, he cleared his throat, then directed, "You can release the dashboard now."

Zen shook out his cramped fingers. His death grip was imprinted in the black leather. "You drive like a bat out of hell."

Sleek and dangerous, the Lotus shot through traffic like a silver bullet. Team management had encouraged him to drive his Hummer from Richmond to Frostproof. A big vehicle with lots of protection on the highway. He'd debated between his Harley and the Lotus. Deciding to kidnap Zen for company on the drive, Risk had settled on the sports car. They'd arrived in record time.

"Quaint little town," Zen commented, looking around at the tree-shaded sidewalks that banked brick storefronts, all aged and faded. Globe streetlights flanked black-pole traffic lights on every corner. A two-pump gas station was wedged between Wall and Third. "Goober?" Zen pointed to a mechanic working on an Astro van.

"Still not laughing."

They passed two city police, sitting on a cement bench outside the courthouse, drinking coffee, eating doughnuts. One of the men was broad-shouldered with a full head of hair, the second thin and wiry. Barney Fife wiry.

"Say it, and you can walk from here," Risk warned.

His threat silenced Zen. His friend had pulled his hamstring during his sprint from third to home during the World Series. He was still walking stiffly.

Hitting on a safe subject, Zen asked, "How long has it been since you've been home?"

Risk shrugged. "Two, maybe three months." *Two months, one week, and four days*. Jacy Grayson had called, down in the dumps after ending a six-month relationship with local pharmacist Mel Colburn. Hearing the sadness in her voice, he'd hopped a plane in between road trips, arriving in Frostproof to heal her heart.

He had stayed all of five hours.

He wondered if Jacy was involved with someone now. Or if they'd have a month of great sex ahead of them. More than a booty call, he was her rebound lover. Totally into her, he delivered both pleasure and comfort until she forgot the man who'd broken her heart. They shared a history of friendship and sex, a closeness envied by many married couples.

A smile curved one corner of his mouth. Jacy had one fine body. She'd fleshed out sweet and curvy. Playful, seductive, uninhibited, she drove him crazy in bed. Thoughts of her naked shot from his head to his groin. He shifted on the leather bucket seat, uncomfortable as hell. If he wasn't careful, the press of his sex would pop the buttons on his denim fly.

"I'm going to stop for coffee," Risk told Zen.

"You don't drink coffee," Zen reminded him.

"I do today."

The Cornerstone Building claimed a full block along Wall Street. The five stories housed a pharmacy, several retail stores, doctors, lawyers, architects, and Jacy's Java.

"Damn, there's no place to park," Zen muttered, scanning the street for a spot.

Risk found a space six blocks north of their destination. "Can you hobble or should I call a cab?"

"I'll make it, as long as I don't have to run."

Companionable silence stretched between them as they sauntered along cracked sidewalks beneath bright blue canopies. Their reflections flashed in the windows, two tall men, casually dressed, without a trail of press, fans, or groupies.

"Are you glad you came along for the ride?" Risk eventually asked.

"Did I have a choice?" Zen returned. "My Navigator's in the shop, waiting for a new carburetor. When you offered to drive me to the grocery store, I didn't know we'd be shopping in Florida."

"Freshest citrus in the country."

"I'll fly a crate back to Richmond."

Risk slowed his stride. "I couldn't let Aaron down."

Zen came to a stop. "I barely know the man."

"He'll appreciate your participation in the weekend events."

Zen shrugged, pushing forward. "That's yet to be seen."

Risk saw a great weekend ahead.

Aaron Grayson sponsored a charity event each year, attended by players throughout the major league. An auction, golf and softball tournaments, along with a country club dance, brought in spectators and fat donations for the expansion of Frostproof's parks and recreation facility—a facility Aaron and Risk had established as their second home during their teens.

"You can ride in my golf cart," Risk offered.

"Not if you drive the cart the way you drive your Lotus."

"Carts barely make five miles per hour."

"Yeah, right, and the Lotus maxes at fifty."

"We were cruising."

"We were *flying*. The tires never touched the pavement."

They passed Walter's Meat Market and Marla's House of Hair. *Big* hair from the look of the woman who came through the door.

Risk nodded. "Mrs. Moreland."

The woman in the plain tan housedress and brown flats was pushing eighty. She peered at him through thick glasses. "That you, Richard? Ben and Carrie's boy?"

"Ben and *Mary's*," he gently corrected.

She looked up at him through her bifocals. "What grade you in now? Senior?"

"I, uh, graduated several years ago."

"Where are you working? Still packing oranges at Temple Groves?"

"No, ma'am. I'm playing ball."

Pity creased the corners of her eyes and mouth. "No money in that, boy. You need to find a real job."

"Duly noted, Mrs. Moreland."

She turned slowly, all big hair and thin, frail body. "Greet your parents for me."

"Yes, ma'am," Risk replied. He caught Zen's stare. "What?"

"You're a real hometown hero, *Richard*." Zen chuckled.

Risk grimaced. He hadn't been called Richard for twenty years. Not since the day his Little League teammates tagged him Risk for all the chances he took both on and off the field. "Here, I'm Ben and Mary's boy," he explained. "Here, the World Series takes second place to the new fire truck."

"You should have arrived with flashing lights and a siren."

They pressed on down the sidewalk. Overhead signs swung in the light breeze, in need of paint and fresh lettering.

Another block, and Zen slowed. He shaded his eyes with one hand. "Is that a line up ahead? What's drawing the early morning crowd? Flu shots?"

"No, coffee."

Zen stopped, bent, rubbed the back of his leg. "Is Juan Valdez making a guest appearance?"

Risk grinned. "It's all in the sugar."

"I drink my coffee black."

9

"You won't today."

Thirty minutes of inching forward landed them at the door. A bright red door with gold paisley swirls. Another ten, and Risk held the door for Zen to pass ahead of him. He wanted to catch his friend's reaction to the coffee shop.

Zen didn't disappoint. His eyes widened, then narrowed. His jaw dropped. "Damn, Kincaid, I need sunglasses."

Jacy's Java defined *bright*. Prior to the grand opening, Jacy had decorated like a wild woman. Free-spirited and flamboyant, she'd tossed buckets of paint onto the walls, laughing when the colors mixed and ran like a box of melted crayons.

The colors reflected like a kaleidoscope off the shiny black-tiled floor when the morning sun shot through the windows along the east wall. Hung from the original gilt ceiling, gold fans stirred the air. The scent of strong coffee blended with freshly baked sugar-and-spice cookies and gingerbread men. Red chili pepper Christmas lights glowed against the cappuccino machine all year round.

An eclectic scramble of chairs from red leather and honey-toned rattan to retro pub stools were pushed up to cherrywood, tubular steel, and mosaic-tiled tables. Sunflowers bloomed in cranberry vases. Beside each table, silver water buckets displayed a selection of newspapers and magazines. The atmosphere was one of contentment as the morning regulars took their first sip of coffee, closed their eyes, and collectively sighed.

Zen studied the crowd and nudged Risk with his elbow. "Major babe at one o'clock."

Risk recognized the babe. "That's Jacy Grayson."

Zen's interest was piqued. "You know her?"

As intimately as Adam knew Eve. "She's Aaron's second cousin."

"Introduce me?" Zen requested.

"Maybe, if you're lucky."

From his vantage point, Risk watched Jacy work the coffee crowd. While her other employees were identifiable in khaki slacks and pale blue polos imprinted with Jacy's Java curving around the rim of a coffee cup, Jacy reinvented herself every day of her life. To Risk, it was all part of her charm.

Her now lavender hair curled softly about her heart-shaped face. Violet contacts colored her normally blue eyes. Flashes of a fuchsia tube top and coral slacks appeared beneath a long, black velvet equestrian jacket. Turquoise earrings and a chunky bracelet pulled her outfit together.

She rounded the corner of the counter and slipped through the swinging doors that led to the kitchen. Zen choked. "She's wearing combat boots."

She certainly was. On Jacy, the boots looked *almost* feminine. Despite the boots, she walked lightly, as if she wore ballet slippers.

When she returned from the kitchen, a lanky older man perched on a stool at the counter gently grabbed her wrist. Risk recognized him as Frank Stall, owner of the largest orange grove in the county. "Little sugar for my coffee, Jacy," he requested.

Jacy smiled at the man. "One lump or two?"

"Two, please."

She produced an English wildflower sugar bowl

from behind the counter, and with sterling silver tongs selected two cubes of sugar decorated with purple pansies. Dropping the cubes into Stall's black coffee, she followed with a perfectly manicured fingertip, slowly stirring the brew. The sugar cubes melted, and the pansies floated to the top.

"Sweet enough?" she asked.

Stall's weathered face broke into a grin. "Until my refill."

"My coffee's too hot to drink," said the man beside Stall. He was Walter Tate, the developer responsible for the Cornerstone Building.

Risk watched as Jacy picked up Tate's bone china cup, puckered her lips, and blew lightly on the opposite side from where he'd sipped. After several seconds, she took her own tiny sip, leaving a trace of pink lipstick on the rim.

"I think it's ready to drink," she said, handing the cup back to Tate. "Let me know if it needs another blow."

Tate's Adam's apple worked as he tried his coffee. "Still too warm. Another blow, please."

Jacy obliged with a second soft blow. After satisfying Stall and Tate, she worked her way down the counter, pleasing the row of males vying for her attention. More sugar. More cooling blows. A sampling of homemade cookies. A second cappuccino.

She gave damn good attention, Risk noticed as the line slowly moved forward. Even at ten in the morning, a line of customers was wrapped around the building, standing three deep before the counter to make their purchases. Jacy gave each a smile and a kind word. She flirted, teased, and tempted them to try the new pumpkin or eggnog latte. The peppermint hot chocolate. The green tea frappuccino. Risk enjoyed watching her work.

"Well, well, look what the World Series dragged in." Frank Stall was the first to recognize Risk and Zen. With his comment, every person in the coffee shop stopped what he was doing and looked their way.

Jacy was slow to look up from counting back change on a sale. When she did, she looked straight at Risk, her stare open and honest and glad to see him. His heart hitched, and his body warmed.

"What, no cutting in line?" she asked, raising one eyebrow.

No one but Jacy dared call him on the carpet. Countless times throughout high school, college, and into his major league career, he'd used his star athletic status to gain the best seats in a restaurant, sports event, or at a concert. Yet here at Jacy's Java he'd stood in line for forty minutes. All for her.

"You're worth waiting for." His voice was deep and a little husky.

Frank Stall and Walter Tate cleared their throats and nodded their agreement. Jacy blushed to the roots of her lavender hair.

"Sweet talker," she managed.

"I'll take a little of your sugar any day," he returned.

"Think he's hinting at more than a pansy sugar cube," Frank Stall chuckled.

A whole lot more than a sugar cube. His welcome home would include a trip to the walk-in cooler if he had his way.

When it came time for him to order, Risk requested black coffee and a cinnamon bun.

Jacy shook her head. "Sorry, we're all out of cinnamon buns."

"Caramel roll?"

"Might be one in the cooler."

He jerked his head toward the back of the shop. "How 'bout we take a look?"

"How about we do," she agreed.

Leaving Zen to fend for himself, Risk shouldered his way through the crowd, following the sweet swing of Jacy's hips.

Small town gossip clucked behind them. "Think there's caramel rolls in the kitchen?" Frank Stall's question rose loud enough to reach Risk's ears.

"I'd say Jacy's his sugar fix," Walter Tate returned.

Damn if Tate wasn't right.

The kitchen was deserted. Jacy's foreplay came in the sashay of her hips as she enticed him to the cooler. Lolita Lampeka drifted in her wake. The vanilla fragrance was as deliciously warm as her skin. He couldn't wait to touch her.

A flick of the cooler latch, and Jacy Grayson held the door for him. He stepped around her, their shoulders brushing. She followed him in and threw the deadbolt.

He eyed her speculatively. "New security, babe?"

"I'd hate to have someone walk in while I'm hunting for caramel rolls."

So would he.

He leaned against the door as she moved among shelves of fresh fruit, eggs, milk, cream, and cookie dough. Puffs of cold air burst from the blower; the motor sounded overly loud in the silence that separated them.

She finally held up her hands. "Sorry, no caramel rolls."

A heartbeat of silence. "You know what I want, babe."

A flick of her tongue to her upper lip. "I do, do I?"

"Damn straight."

He moved in on her then, a man of midnight dark hair and a sexy smile. Cut and solid, Risk could pack a polo and a pair of jeans. Seductively tangible, his arrogance and strength embraced her. When he cupped her chin, then grazed one corner of her mouth with his thumb, her lips parted, anticipating his kiss.

A kiss that never came. "I *want* my baseball, Jacy," he breathed against her mouth. "The game ball of the World Series."

She scrunched her nose. "What makes you think *I* have it?"

He leaned back slightly. Looked her in the eye. "I *know* you do. Replay on the television monitor caught you taunting me, then scrambling for my slam."

"A *lot* of people scrambled."

"You're scrappy, babe. You'd have pulled hair and bitten ankles for that ball."

She rubbed her lower back. "I was kidney punched. And"—she held up her hand, her knuckles bruised—"a three-hundred-pound man stomped on my hand."

"Poor baby." He drew her hand to his mouth and

kissed it all better. "How did you like my prediction? My point to left field?" he asked.

"You bragged your balls off."

"It's not bragging if you deliver." He kissed the tip of her nose. "I hit the home run for you."

"You hit it *at* me."

"Couldn't miss you in the crowd, *Pink*."

She hooked her arms about his neck. "You'll get your ball."

"When?" he wanted to know.

"When I'm ready to give it back." She stroked his dark hair, which was in need of a haircut. Then the stubbled jaw in need of a shave. "Can we forget the baseball and concentrate on me?"

His gaze narrowed. "Are you seeing anyone?"

Jacy knew he wouldn't touch her if she was involved with another man. "I'm still reeling from Mel Colburn," she white lied. "I haven't dated since your last lecture on my poor taste in men."

A crooked smile cut a dimple in his cheek. "Horny, babe?"

"I have ten minutes to be a woman before I turn back into the owner of a coffee shop."

Risk made her feel every inch a woman. Sliding his hands inside her equestrian jacket, he skimmed her belly, her sides, locking his fingers at her spine. Man against woman, the delicious cut of his muscles, along with the thick ridge of his sex, left her wet. And wanting him madly.

Judging from the size of his erection, the most valuable player of the World Series wanted her as badly as any home run.

Rising on tiptoe, she kissed him with the hunger of having missed his big, bad body. He responded, mating with her mouth with the force of ravishment. His lips were warm. His tongue hot. His French kisses deep and devouring.

His hands rose, worked the equestrian jacket off her shoulders. He pushed up her tube top. The soft, creamy swells of her breasts spilled onto his palms. Her nipples rose as red and puckered as raspberries. Kneading and squeezing, he drew a low moan from her.

Jacy touched him in turn, her fingers working their own erotic magic. Shoving up his gray knit shirt, she traced his pecs and abs, scraped her nails down his sides. Then went for his button fly.

While she worked the buttons, he loosened the drawstring on her slacks. He shoved the coral cotton over her hips and down her thighs with the force of his need. Her red v-string followed. A single touch of his finger, and she was slick for him.

Having unbuttoned his jeans, Jacy tugged both denim and navy briefs low enough to free his sex. His arousal was hard and huge like his body. Jutting and oh-so glad to see her.

His sex twitched when she skimmed a fingernail down his *happy trail*, the line between his navel and the base of his shaft. In bold black across his groin ran his *Bad to the Bone* tattoo.

Jacy traced the tattoo, remembering his recent photo shoot with *Playgirl*. "Did you flash *Bone* during your layout?"

"Unzipped for the tattoo, but nothing lower."

"Female fans will be disappointed."

"There were ten 'Men of the Outfield' photographed." He flicked his tongue against her lips. "Nine dropped their drawers."

Jacy was relieved he'd unzipped, yet kept his pants on. A part of her wanted to keep his package private. The tattoo was a turn-on. A totally naked Risk would cause a nationwide riot. He was that impressive. Jacy didn't want to share him.

She sighed when he slid his tongue into her mouth, then slowly pulled it out. "There's a condom in my wallet."

The man had impressive muscles in his butt, Jacy thought admiringly as she felt around in his back pocket until her fingers touched leather. Removing the condom, she tore it open and sheathed him quickly. "Ribbed?" She stroked him.

"High sensation, babe." Splaying his hands beneath her bare bottom, he grunted when he lifted her. "One too many sugar cookies?"

She squeezed his hips with her thighs. "It's the combat boots."

"Real feminine, Jacy."

"I felt kick-ass today."

He probed her with his erection, and she parted for him. He penetrated her with a push of his groin and a growl low in his throat.

The shelves of the cooler pressed against her spine. A container of strawberries tipped, as Risk Kincaid rocked forward, ground deep inside her. Their kisses were as wild as their pounding hearts and pumping hips.

She came with six strokes of his sex.

He climaxed seconds thereafter.

"Hot and fast and feeling eighteen." His words stroked a chord deep within Jacy.

They had first made love at eighteen. A memory that had grown up with them, as she'd become a woman and he'd become a man.

A sexually competent man who always satisfied.

She kissed his neck, his shoulder, and left nipple before sliding off his body. She then tugged down the tube top that was wrapped around her neck. She panted. "The elastic nearly choked me."

Risk gave her breast a final squeeze. "Here I thought I left you breathless."

Clothed or naked, the man stole the breath from her lungs. He always had, always would. He was the only constant in her life. After drawing up her slacks, she straightened her equestrian jacket and fluffed out her hair. "I need to get back to work before I'm missed."

Risk buttoned his fly. "I'm still short one caramel roll."

"Would you settle for an oat bran muffin?"

He made a face. "When I'm sixty."

"How about a blueberry scone?"

"Too English." He brushed a parting kiss over her lips as she eased around him. "I'll live with black coffee and a little of your sugar."

She pulled the deadbolt, then pushed the cooler door open. "Grab a screwdriver from the counter drawer when you return to the coffee shop."

"You advertising what we just did?"

"Tsk tsk, Risk." She shook her head. "Screws need to be tightened in the retro stool with the aqua vinyl cushion."

"I'm your fix-it man?"

"You give good screw."

He smiled at her retreating back, then sought the men's room. After cleaning up, he stepped into the hallway. Sated and relaxed, he leaned against the wall, let his mind momentarily wander. His thoughts drifted over the years, clear back to high school. To his senior year. To a day that began with Sherry Sherman and ended with Jacy Grayson. To the time that set them up as lovers. When he'd become her rebound man. . . .

After-school detention sucked. To his disgust, Risk Kincaid would be reporting to detention for an entire week. All because Sherry Sherman had made him late for school. She was such a girly-girl. Damn, she could primp. He'd parked his Cougar at the curb in front of her house at seven-fifteen, then waited and waited for her to get her makeup just right.

Just right was the natural look. So why the hell was she even wearing mascara and blush? At five minutes before the bell was due to ring, Sherry of the blond hair, brown eyes, and the biggest breasts of any girl in the senior class strolled down the sidewalk and slid into his car, all flashing teeth and hot lips.

Their kisses had turned deep, their breathing heavy, and after thirty minutes of feeling her up be-

neath her skimpy tank top, first period class was half over.

Sherry's English teacher didn't give a rat's ass if she was late. Unfortunately for Risk, his physical education teacher was also his baseball coach. Coach Donahue believed in punctuality. He cut Risk little slack, sending him to the office for an admittance slip. Each tardy cost him time after school.

Risk broke up with Sherry following his third detention. He had more important things to do after school than sit in a classroom with sixty other students tapping their pencils and feet as they counted down the longest hour of their lives.

Sherry had begged him not to dump her. When he'd refused to take her back, she'd spread the rumor she'd dumped him. Whatever.

Now, hitting a jog, he cut across the baseball field and headed toward his Cougar, the last car in the student parking lot. The black car looked damn fine on the asphalt, the sun's own reflection in its polish.

As he kicked dust past home plate, he caught a flash of violet and red, and snatches of turquoise from the top bleacher behind the right field dugout. He slowed and squinted against the sun. Seated, slumped over, her fists balled at her eyes, sat Jacy Grayson, second cousin to his best friend, Aaron.

He slowed and caught her soft sob on the breeze. Damn, this couldn't be good. Changing direction, he bounded up the bleachers. "Jacy?" he called to the girl who was one year behind him in school. And in his opinion, the prettiest girl in the junior class.

She didn't look up when he dropped down beside her. "Get lost, Kincaid," she sniffed.

"Fine, I'm gone." He stood and took a step to leave.

"Leave and die."

Her words made him smile. Through Aaron, he'd known Jacy all his life. She often said one thing, but meant another. His gut told him Jacy needed to talk. She looked vulnerable and broken.

Seated once again, his hip bumped hers as he wrapped his arm about her shoulders and pulled her close. "Who do I need to kill?" he asked, the feeling to protect foreign, yet strong.

She sank against him. "He's a teammate of yours."

Great. The members of his baseball team were close as brothers. "Give me a name."

"Danny Rhodes."

The Road Runner. *"I can do upper body damage, but can't break his legs. State tournament starts next week. No one steals bases better than Danny."*

"You need him."

He looked at her closely. Sadness misted her eyes; her mouth turned down. "Apparently so do you."

"I really liked him, Risk," she confessed on a sigh. "I thought we'd make it through the year together. We just broke up. And he doesn't want to take me to the prom anymore."

Asshole. *"Did he give a reason?"*

She sniffed. "He thinks I draw too much attention to myself."

Risk understood. Danny was brown-and-tan

bland. A good student and star athlete, he flew under everyone's radar. While most people knew his name, few could pick him out of a crowd.

In comparison, Jacy was jarringly visible. Totally unforgettable. She was pure sparkle and pizzazz.

"I'm not color blind as Danny accused," she said between sniffs. "I like mixing plaids and stripes; paisleys and prints."

Today was no exception. She made the sun blink in her violet silk blouse, red-flowered denim mini, lime green high tops with yellow star laces, and a ton of turquoise jewelry.

A fan of different and daring, Risk liked her look. Beyond her clothes, she had incredible blue eyes, fragile cheekbones, and flawless skin.

"I prefer you blond," he ruffled her burgundy hair with its platinum highlights. "But don't change the color for me or for any man."

Her chin quivered and a tear escaped. "I like the way I look."

He threw back his head and groaned. "Damn, girl, I don't do tears."

She cut him a look, the tear drying on her cheek. "What do you do, Risk Kincaid?"

The words that spilled forth were light and teasing, and more heartfelt than he'd ever admit. "Rebounds. I could kiss you until you forget Danny Rhodes."

She plucked at the hem of her skirt. A skirt that rode high on her thighs. "Could be a long make-out session."

He shrugged. "I'd make time."

"Me . . . too."

They'd fooled around until their lips were numb. Somewhere between giving her a hickey on her neck and brushing her firm, little breasts beneath her silky blouse, he'd helped Jacy forget Danny Rhodes.

The very next weekend, Risk took Jacy to the prom; then in the backseat of his Cougar, he took her virginity.

At the end of the summer, he made the only promise a young man bound for college and then onto the major leagues could make: he promised to be her rebound lover.

Anytime, anywhere, anyplace.

She need only pick up the phone and call.

Risk Kincaid drew his hands down his face as the memory faded. He felt damn lucky to be in Jacy's life. Whenever her world fell apart, he picked up the pieces. She would die laughing if she knew her power over him. For all his super-star status, for all the women available to him, he held himself back. Only with Jacy did his heart get involved.

He was whipped. Had been whipped for thirteen years. He could count his lovers on one hand. His sex life centered around Jacy's breakups. He could live without other women knowing Jacy's poor choice in men would land him in her bed within six months.

With each breakup, she poured out her heart and he listened. Then, they made love. He took her beyond the men who bruised her heart and drew her as close to him as he dared.

Over the years he'd set up boundaries to keep himself sane. He never spent the entire night. Never stayed in town more than two days. However, this trip to Frostproof was different. He planned to spend the entire month of November. Planned to take a serious look at their friendship and intimacy and see if there could be more between them than hot, fast, rebound sex.

Pushing off the wall, he went in search of a screwdriver. The least he could do for Jacy was tighten a few loose screws.

Tool in hand, he moved toward the kitchen door. Before he could push through, Jacy came flying back at him. Her face red, her fingers adjusting her tube top.

"Why didn't you tell me my top was on backward?" she demanded.

He'd noticed her breasts and belly, but not her top. "Didn't know there was a front and back." It all looked the same to him.

She pointed to a tiny row of roses that split her cleavage. "Flowers go in the front."

His brows pulled tight. "Who asked about the roses?" *Who'd been checking out her breasts?*

"Frank Stall noticed. He always compliments my clothes."

Dirty old orange grower. A bachelor at the age of fifty-five, Stall believed himself in contention for Jacy's affection.

"What did you tell him?" Risk asked.

"I told him the top must have twisted while I searched the cooler for your caramel roll."

"Did he believe you?"

"Frank winked, then whispered I had a red stain on the back of my left thigh."

"Turn around."

She twisted about and brushed at the spot. "Looks like a squished strawberry."

"A container toppled while we were in the cooler."

She scowled. "Next time don't pump so hard."

He reached out, curved a wide palm at the nape of her neck, and pulled her on tiptoe. "You like it hard," he reminded her, then kissed the scowl from her lips.

"Hot and horny, get a room."

Risk hadn't heard the door swing open, but before him now stood Stephanie "Stevie" Cole, Jacy's closest friend and part-time employee. When not at the coffee shop, Stevie worked as a sports coordinator for the department of parks and recreation. Auburn-haired and athletic, she'd once excelled in track and field. Stevie's zest for life had inspired Jacy to coach a little girls T-ball team. The six-year-old Bluebells practiced twice a week, all year round.

Releasing Jacy, he wrapped Stevie in a bear hug. "Good to see you, sweetheart."

"Good to be seen," Stevie returned as she ran her hands over her hips. "Even if I have put on a few pounds."

Risk grinned. "I like curvy."

"More like plump," Stevie said on a sigh. "Working at the coffee shop has packed on the pounds."

"You don't have to sample every new treat," Jacy teased her friend.

"I do to recommend them," Stevie defended her weight gain. "*Decadent* best describes your chocolate-cherry brownies. *Heavenly*, your lemon-mint cookies."

"Her caramel rolls?" Risk asked.

"*Better than sex*. When Jacy bakes, it smells so good I could lick the air and gain weight." Stevie's gaze cut to Jacy, the hint of a smile playing on her lips. "Heard there was a problem with the cooler."

Noticing the screwdriver in Risk's hand, Jacy quickly fabricated, "The door wouldn't close all the way, so Risk offered to tighten the screws."

Stevie's smile broke. "By the color in Jacy's cheeks, I'd say nice work, Tool Man."

Risk took the heat off Jacy. "Trivia, Stevie?"

"Hit me with your best shot."

Jacy always admired Stevie's baseball IQ. The players invariably tried to stump her, but her friend kicked butt.

"Which Yankee pitcher got the final out in the World Series with game seven on the line, two years after giving up the game-losing homer in the seventh game of the 1960 World Series?"

Stevie rolled her eyes. "Elementary, Risk. You're talking Ralph Terry."

"Impressive," he praised before turning to Jacy. "I'll fix the retro stool; you go change your slacks."

He disappeared, leaving Jacy to face her friend. A smiling, I-know-what-you-did-in-the-cooler friend. "I heard Risk's been in town less than an hour, and ten of those minutes he had you in the cooler."

Frank Stall and Walter Tate gossiped like girls. "Nine minutes, actually." Jacy couldn't help grinning. "Risk's already turned my life into a twisted tube top and strawberry-stained slacks."

"Mmm. Gotta love the man."

"I do."

"When do you plan to tell him?"

Jacy shrugged. "Not today. But someday."

"Someday needs to come soon."

"I wouldn't know what to say."

"Try the truth."

"That my lovers are as imaginary as my breakups? That I fake heartbreak so I can call Risk to make it all better. That he's not my rebound lover, but my *only* lover." She shook her head. "He would feel used if he ever found out."

"A *good* used," Stevie assured her. "I think he'd be flattered you've only wanted to be with him."

"He's played my rebound man far too long to seek anything permanent. As far as he knows, we come together for sex only. It's not his fault we fooled around and I fell in love."

"How long will Risk be home?"

"An entire month."

"A long time to hide your true feelings."

"But I will. I do free and easy better than anyone."

"That you do." Stevie drew in a breath and worked up the courage to ask, "Any sign of Aaron?"

"He telephoned earlier," Jacy told her. "He's due in town within the hour."

"I hope he comes by the coffee shop. I want to go over the details of the auction with him one final time."

Jacy caught the expectation in Stevie's eyes. Stevie and Aaron had dated throughout high school and college. Stevie had loved him with a passion that promised forever. She'd thought Aaron felt the same. Yet over the past year, Aaron's once-a-month visits had faded to six weekends a year. One of those weekends included the charity auction. He was so committed to the success of the event, he'd gone as far as to hire a professional event planner.

When an unexpected bout of flu left the coordinator bedridden, Stevie volunteered to take her place. As chairperson of the committee, she had unlimited access to Aaron. For three whole unlimited days. Jacy knew her friend planned to make the most of her time with the man.

Slapping her hands against her thighs, Stevie said, "I'm on the clock. Guess I'd better get to work. Do you want me in the kitchen or out front?"

"Out front," Jacy directed. "Push the plum-date bars."

Stevie lifted a brow. "You baking?"

"Caramel rolls. Risk's favorite. The man always had a sweet tooth."

Gazing down at her stained slacks, Jacy decided to slip into a pair of kitchen whites she had in her office. Whites she had tie-dyed in a psychedelic print. The rental uniform company had yet to complain. In a small town, business was business.

She rubbed her hands together, ready to blend the ingredients, roll and slice the dough, and get sticky to her wrists from the caramel glaze.

She knew the scent of baking caramel rolls would draw Risk to the kitchen. She could already feel the warmth of his mouth, the moist sweep of his tongue, the delicious tug of his lips when he licked her fingers clean.

Her body melted like the butter on the stove.

CHAPTER 2

Stevie Cole French-braided her auburn hair before entering the coffee shop. The place was still packed. The line still stretched out the door. She caught sight of Risk repairing the retro stool at a corner table, and wondered as to the identity of the man supporting the aqua vinyl against his thigh while Risk tightened the screws. The man was clean cut, well put together, smart-looking, and, somehow . . . familiar.

So intense was her scrutiny, she slammed smack into the edge of the counter. The sharp edge jabbed her hip. She winced.

Casting a second glance his way, she had to admit he was as attractive as she'd first believed. The thought shook her. She'd never looked at another man. Aaron was her life. Her focus. Yet a strange flutter in her belly caused her to sneak a third peak.

Brown hair. Broad shoulders. Tall, considering the stretch of his legs blocking the aisle between tables. White-and-blue striped button down shirt. Collar turned up. Navy slacks. Loafers without socks.

He must have felt her eyes on him. Glancing up from the *New York Times,* he met her stare over wire-rimmed reading glasses and held it for fifteen heart-pumping seconds. A quick once-over and he nudged Risk, then nodded her way.

Risk looked up, smiled and motioned Stevie to their table. Her legs refused to move. Had another employee not bumped her from behind, she might have stood there like a statue until the coffee shop closed.

The man's brown gaze, so dark it was nearly black, tracked her progress until she stood next to Risk, who was still kneeling on the floor. Stevie found herself wishing she was ten pounds lighter and a whole lot prettier.

"Stevie Cole, meet Zen Driscoll," Risk said casually.

Zen took her in. "Stevie, huh? You don't look like a boy."

"Her real name's Stephanie," Risk explained.

Zen understood. "A tomboy at heart?"

"I love sports," she returned.

"Zen was traded from the Bombers. He came on as shortstop with the Rogues this season," Risk finished the introduction.

Recognition hit hard. Driscoll was a traitor. He'd left Tampa Bay for Richmond beneath the cloak of darkness. The media had begged an explanation. Zen, however, had remained closemouthed. Her feelings cooled considerably toward him.

"Einstein," she said, calling him by his player nickname. A man known for his intense strategy both on the field and as a financier. He'd stolen more bases than anyone else in the league—seventy to be exact—and laid claim to six Gold Gloves. "You were the one who started the ninth inning rally that brought Risk to bat."

He creased his newspaper and laid it on the table. "I admit to the triple, but Risk hit the home run that brought us both in."

"Lucky hits."

"Luck had nothing to do with it. In every at-bat, a hitter will get at least one pitch that's hittable." He eyed her over the rim of his glasses. "I gather you're not a Rogues' fan."

"Gather you're right."

"Stevie's into the Bombers," Risk injected from the floor. "Aaron Grayson to be exact."

"I know Shutout." Zen referred to Aaron by his nickname. "Decent pitcher."

"*Decent?*" She rolled her eyes. "You've slid head-first into one too many bags if you don't believe he's the best."

Zen looked at her thoughtfully. "In the grand scheme of life, win or lose, it's only a game."

Only a game? Was the man from Mars? " 'Baseball, it is said, is only a game. True. And the Grand Canyon is only a hole in Arizona. Not all holes, or all games, are created equal.' "

"*New York Times* columnist George F. Will." Zen surprised her by recognizing the quote.

"Zen's a bit of a trivia buff," Risk said from the floor. "He might be the one to stump you."

Stump me, my ass. " 'Baseball is more than a game to me, it's a religion,' " Stevie was curious how much Zen truly knew.

"Umpire Bill Klem," he replied easily.

Too easily for her liking. The competitive look in his eyes told her he could match her every challenge. She hated that look and wanted him and his baseball brain gone. "In town long?" she inquired as sweetly as she could manage.

A smile pulled at his lips. "You in a hurry to see me go?"

"I could point you toward I-4 North."

"Point me there after the weekend."

Three whole days. The town was too small for their paths not to cross.

He rested his elbows on the table, steepled his fingers and asked, "Are you taking coffee orders?"

She nodded toward the line of people at the register. "Ordering is done at the counter."

"Long line, and it hurts to stand. Pulled hamstring."

She was aware of his injury. She hoped it pained him to death. Looking down her nose at him, she drew a resigned breath. "Latte, breve, cappuccino?"

His gaze lit with interest. "Do you give sugar?"

"That's Jacy's specialty."

Zen nodded. "Jacy's one hundred ten pounds of sweetness."

While Stevie tipped the scale at one-thirty-six, ten of those pounds lacked sinew. Brownies and cookie dough had stolen her cheekbones. Her pants wouldn't zip. Her thighs now rubbed together.

"If you don't give sugar, how do you satisfy your customers?" he asked.

"I blow—" Heat shot to her hairline. She'd give her life to recapture those words.

Zen folded his hands on his lap. Right over his zipper. His fingers were long. His nails clean. "Blow *what*, exactly?"

She couldn't breathe. Couldn't swallow. "Blow on hot coffee until it cools," she rasped out. "Same as Jacy."

"I'll have a double cappuccino. And a blow."

She stepped back and straight into another server carrying a full tray of gourmet coffees. Stevie grimaced as froth sloshed over the sides of the china cups. She then escaped as fast as her legs would carry her.

"Play nice, Zen." Risk pushed himself off the floor, then righted the retro stool. The legs were no longer wobbly. Rolling the screwdriver between his palms, he added, "Stevie's sweet and incredibly loyal. She's shaken her pom-poms for Aaron Grayson since high school."

Zen's chest squeezed for a fraction of a second. When he'd caught her staring, he'd sensed her curiosity. A curiosity that bordered on interest. An interest that left her irritable once she'd recognized his name. As far as she was concerned, he played for the enemy. "There's no ring on her finger," he noted.

Risk shrugged. "Aaron has yet to propose."

"Stevie hasn't heard the league rumor, then?"

"It's strictly a rumor until Aaron makes a formal announcement," Risk returned.

Zen hoped for Stevie's sake the rumor was false. Catching her by the cappuccino machine, he watched as she chatted up customers with a quick smile and an easy laugh. Although a confirmed bachelor, he was a sucker for hazel-eyed women with freckles. He admired her fire and loyalty. Found her soft breasts and rounded hips womanly. He'd had his fill of stick chicks.

And Stevie's baseball IQ fascinated him. He'd never met another person who tracked facts, remembered and recited them.

Beside him, Risk inhaled deeply. So deeply, he drew Zen's full attention. The man's nostrils flared, his gaze fixed on the kitchen door. "Jacy's baking caramel rolls." Male hunger for more than Jacy's culinary skills darkened Risk's eyes. "I'll be in the kitchen if you need me."

Zen tracked Risk's swagger, around tables and through the kitchen door. Whispers followed the major league player. A few chuckles, followed by raised eyebrows.

"Kincaid's going to delay the caramel rolls," Frank Stall complained.

Walter Tate agreed. "Jacy's sweet. The man's after her sugar."

"All I've ever gotten is a pansy cube and a swirl of her finger," Stall muttered.

"You're lucky to get that with Kincaid in town," Tate stated.

Zen stared at the kitchen door until Stevie stepped into his line of vision.

"Your cappuccino." Stevie delivered his double in

a blue-and-white wedgewood cup. Steam crested the rim. A sucker for a sexy mouth, Zen stared as she puckered her pink lips and gently blew on his cappuccino.

The longer he stared, the shorter her temper seemed to get. Her final blow sent froth over the rim and onto her wrist, blotching her skin. Her hand jerked, and the wedgewood tilted on its saucer.

Zen jumped to his feet and made a grab for the cup. "You've burned yourself."

Stevie clutched the cup to her chest, steadier now.

Zen, however, was shaken. He'd nearly grabbed her left breast in his haste to right the cup. Even now, his fingers lingered over her nipple. A nipple that puckered from the mere suggestion of his touch.

Stevie Cole's entire body tightened. Tightened and blushed. With her free hand, she furtively plucked at the front of her blue polo in hopes of hiding the twin peaks. Beneath Zen's stare, her breasts swelled even more, as if seeking the brush of his fingers.

Zen dropped his hand and balled his fist. His face was as red as her own. "How much for the cappuccino?" he asked, his tone as tight as her breasts.

Utterly mortified by her body's response, she quickly set the cup and saucer on the table and informed him, "Four dollars."

He pulled a money clip from his pants pocket, peeled off a twenty and pressed it in her palm. "Keep the change."

"A sixteen-dollar tip? For what?" *Puckered nipples? Nearly laying my breast in your palm?*

"The blow, Stevie," he said as he dropped onto the

stool and rubbed the back of his leg. She caught the flicker of pain in his eyes before he straightened and reached for his cup. His forefinger was too thick to slide through the handle, so he cupped the base as he took his first sip. "Good coffee. Good service."

Stevie knew different. Her service had been poor. Her attitude unprofessional. Her body unpredictable. She'd embarrassed them both when her nipples beaded beneath his hot stare. She didn't deserve a tip.

Guilt prodded her to suggest, "How about a butterscotch brownie on the house?"

He shook his head. "I don't eat sweets."

"Never?" She couldn't imagine life without sugar.

He patted his flat abdomen. "Need to stay at the top of my game."

Which meant she was at the bottom of her own. Feeling fat and vulnerable, she took her leave. "Let me know when you need a refill."

"Will do." He returned to his newspaper. His expression turned serious as he scanned the financial section.

Stevie kept an eye on Zen. While waiting patiently for Risk, he covered the *Times* and *Miami Herald*, then selected *Forbes, Fortune,* and *Newsweek* from the silver bucket and read them cover to cover. Several of the female servers stopped and spoke to him, flirting a little, but getting no more than a polite nod in return.

The afternoon coffee crowd—those in need of a caffeine kick to see them through to five o'clock— filtered in slowly. Amid the crush, Stevie recognized the Bat Pack. Three Rogues power hitters Risk Kincaid had introduced to her over the years. Though Risk held the highest batting average on the team, the Bat Pack came out swinging strong every season. They were young, hot, and full of themselves.

Right fielder Cody "Psycho" McMillan led the pack. All lean and tan; wild and crazy. And a known nudist. Jesse "Romeo" Bellisaro came second. He bore the all-American blond of his mother with the Italian fire of his father. He was one hot third baseman. During spring training, women threw their panties onto the field to gain his attention.

Catcher, Chase "Chaser" Tallan, brought up the rear with the tightest ass known to man. Chaser's advertising contract with Wrangler flashed his butt on billboards and in magazines around the world. Dark sunglasses hid his eyes. Indoors or out. A single diamond stud pierced his left ear.

Stevie had followed their careers. She could rattle off their statistics like an auctioneer. Even if they did play for Richmond. Craning her neck, she peered around the men, awaiting Aaron Grayson's arrival. There was no sign of him.

"Stevie, sweetheart, two lattes grande and a bottled water," Romeo called from the back of the line, not wanting to wait his turn. He patted his stomach. "And two turkey and cranberry wraps. I'm starving. Psycho refused to stop for lunch."

Psycho was the leanest of the group with only three percent body fat. He worked out four hours a day and fasted twice a week. Mondays and Thursdays.

Spotting Zen Driscoll, the men joined him at his

table. Handshakes and slaps on the back were followed by deep chuckles and boisterous conversation. The Bat Pack was still high from winning the World Series.

Stevie whipped up the lattes, grabbed a Perrier, then piled a tray with the turkey wraps and several plum-date bars. The bars were Jacy's latest dip into *healthy* decadence. Once delivered, Romeo and Chaser gobbled the sandwiches and bars right down to the crumbs.

On the far side of the table, Psycho caught her about the waist and tugged her close. Her breast flattened against his cheek. Her nipples neither tingled nor tightened as he spoke to her cleavage. "A little trivia, Stevie. A kiss for every question you miss. Who was the first professional baseball team? Name and year."

She touched her finger to her chin as if in deep thought. After thirty seconds, she bent, her mouth within an inch of his own. "Cincinnati Red Legs in 1869."

"Do-over," Psycho quickly called. "What was the first athlete's number ever retired?"

"Lou Gehrig's Yankee number four."

Psycho pulled back, groaned. "So close, yet so far from those lips. I've been waiting two years for that kiss. Anytime you want to fool around . . ." He lifted and lowered his brows suggestively and let the sentence trail off.

Stevie smiled. If she wasn't so intent on marrying Aaron Grayson, she just might stray and play with . . .

her gaze flitted from Psycho to Zen Driscoll. *That man.* The one called Einstein.

Her heart slammed at the thought. Relaxed on his stool, arms folded over his chest, Zen watched her interact with his teammates. Beneath his steady gaze, her nipples once again did the unthinkable. They pointed straight at him.

His eyes widened.

And she wanted to die. Pulling free of Psycho, she covered her chest with the serving tray.

Moments later, Romeo pointed toward the window. "Check out the ride."

Chaser squinted. "Bomber insignia on the door. Looks like Walt Llewellyn's limo."

Stevie recognized the name. Big Walt owned the Tampa Bay Bombers. As wide as he was tall, he was known for his love of community, his players, and his daughter, Natalie. Walt had a big heart and lived lavishly. The limo was one in a fleet of ten.

She stared along with the men as the stretch blocked traffic. A uniformed driver exited the black vehicle, circled the hood, and opened the passenger door. They caught sight of a dark blond head, a dipped shoulder, and then Aaron Grayson stepped onto the sidewalk.

Stevie's breath caught and her knees went weak.

"Looks like Grayson is one of the family now," Chaser grunted. "Anyone with him?"

Psycho craned his neck. "Appears he's alone."

Romeo scratched his chin. "No truth behind the rumor then."

Stevie turned on Romeo. "*What* rumor?"

The Bat Pack closed up like clams. It was Zen who finally answered. "Locker room talk. Nothing more."

Locker room talk cut her out of the loop. Whatever the rumor, it had yet to reach Frostproof.

"Over here, Shutout," Psycho called to Aaron as he pushed through the door. After greeting and shaking hands with several local residents, Aaron crossed to their table.

His gaze immediately lit on Zen and held. An undercurrent of tension ran between the men; this had some deeper origin than the outcome of the World Series. It was personal. Stevie wasn't aware they shared a history outside of baseball, yet the conflict was unmistakable. Strong and private. A core dislike.

Either immune or purposely ignoring the opposing forces, Romeo whistled. "Nice set of wheels."

Aaron glanced toward the limousine, now sliding into traffic. "Loaner for the weekend."

Chaser noted his suit. "Dressing up?"

"Kenneth Cole," Aaron informed him.

He took a round of ribbing for buying designer. As he caught up with the players, Stevie took in everything about him. Five foot ten, lake blue eyes, square jaw. He looked familiar . . . yet different. Gone was the Aaron Grayson of the worn T-shirts, torn jeans, and year-old Nikes. In his place stood a man whose hair was gelled, his male scent masked by Gucci, his clothing torn from the pages of *GQ*.

When he turned the full force of his smile on her, she saw his twice-broken nose had been straightened, his chipped tooth capped. Deep within his gaze, shadows banked his greeting. "Glad to see me, Stevie?"

So very glad. She closed the distance between them and accepted his hug. In his arms, her life rolled back ten years to a time when holding each other held their worlds together. She closed her eyes, pressed her cheek to his chest, heard the steady rhythm of his heart. A heart that had once beat wildly with her nearness. So wildly, he'd struggled for control.

He released her slowly. Yet, too quickly for her liking. In that instant, she wanted to shrink, become so small she could live in his shirt pocket, right over his heart. Forever.

"I'm glad you've come home," she finally managed.

"Yeah, me too." His tone held a hint of reserve.

"Care for coffee?"

He nodded. "If you'll join me. We need to go over the weekend events."

"Take our table," Chaser suggested. "We want to check out the town."

"Have you driven Wall Street?" Aaron asked.

Chaser nodded. "End to end."

"Then you've seen Frostproof."

Stevie heard the derision in Aaron's voice. Apparently the town was too small for the big city boy. "There's a new strip mall off Orange Grove Way," she quickly pointed out. "Bookstore, sports memorabilia, pizza and wings, and the Silver Dollar Saloon."

Psycho snapped his fingers. "Damn, I forgot my cowboy hat and boots."

She narrowed her gaze on him. "No fighting, Psycho." The wild man had been fined and suspended for misbehavior on and off the field more than any player in the league. "If you're not a fan of Alan Jackson and line dancing, don't stop for a beer."

Psycho pushed off his chair and stood toe to toe with her. "Care to ride along? Crack the whip?"

Through the window, she caught a glimpse of his Dodge Ram. Three dirt bikes filled the truck bed. Badass and ready for back road action. "There's not enough room in the cab for a fourth person."

He patted his thigh. "You could sit on my lap."

"Not while you're driving."

"Shame." He swooped in and kissed her cheek. "I promise to leave your town in one piece." He looked to his two friends. "Let's hit the road."

Stevie watched the three hot young players cross to the door. Two tables of women, all over sixty, followed their progress. Widower Abigail Gates leaned toward her tea-sipping companion. *Tight butt* and *auction* rose from their table on a raspy giggle.

Stevie couldn't help smiling. "Those two ladies will be spending their social security checks tonight."

"Anticipation ups the ante," Aaron agreed. He then glanced at his gold watch, a Cartier Panther that shouted money. "I've got less than an hour. Let's get down to business."

Stevie's heart squeezed. When had Aaron started making his exit the moment he entered? Where was the laid-back man who once lingered over coffee and her?

Zen started to rise. "I'll switch tables. Give you two some privacy."

Aaron hesitated as if he hated to ask. "Are you involved in the charity events?"

"Risk added my name to the celebrity golf tournament," Zen informed him. "Do you have a problem with me being here?" His tone turned cool, challenging.

"Your name's as big a draw as Risk's or mine." Aaron motioned him to sit back down and Zen obliged. "Stevie and Jacy can give us a quick rundown on all that's taking place."

"Jacy's in the kitchen with Risk," Stevie stated. "I'll get them."

"On your way back—"

"Coffee, white?" she recalled.

Aaron nodded. "Always liked a little coffee with my cream."

She turned to the shortstop. "Refill, Zen?"

He shook his head. "No thanks. I'm set."

Silence held between the men as Stevie crossed the room. Surely they had something to discuss. There was always the weather. A safe topic, even between strangers.

Pushing through the swinging doors, she spotted Risk and Jacy near the sink. They were so hot for each other, they had yet to notice her arrival. Risk's full-body press pinned Jacy to the wall as he licked caramel glaze from her fingertips. Jacy's cheeks were flushed red from the swirl and sweep of his tongue.

She cleared her throat. "Risk, get Jacy's fingers out of your mouth so she can meet with her cousin. Aaron's out front having coffee."

Jacy jumped and Risk grinned. "We'll be out as soon as she washes her hands," he informed her.

Stevie rolled her eyes. "You've licked them clean."

"My sugar fix. Jacy tastes sweet."

Risk had sampled her fully. His whisker burn reddened Jacy's cheek and chin, her lips were swollen from his kisses.

"Five minutes," Stevie called on her way out.

"Make it ten," Risk shouted back.

She figured it would be at least fifteen before they made an appearance. Back behind the counter, she brewed a fresh pot of coffee. She inhaled the rich Guatemala Antigua blend. Scanning the selection of china, she decided on her favorite French pattern, the cup, saucer, and creamer hand-painted with green pears and dark red cherries.

Jacy had a love for fine china. She'd brought that love into the coffee shop. An assortment of eclectic patterns enhanced the coffee experience.

Returning to the table, Stevie served Aaron, then took a seat next to him. A seat that placed her directly across from Zen. His dark gaze touched her face and drifted to her breasts. She locked her jaw against the tingle that set her nipples to diamond-hard points.

Rubbing her arms, she crossed them over her chest. "Is it cold in here?"

"I was finding it warm." Aaron shrugged off his gray suit jacket, revealing a crisp white shirt and pale blue tie. Dropping the jacket over her shoulders, he asked, "Better?"

So much better. Tailored and expensive, the material held his scent and warmth. Dwarfed by its size, Stevie smiled when she saw that the sleeves hung nearly to the floor.

Aaron glanced down. "Careful, Stevie. Don't get the sleeves dirty. There's not a decent dry cleaner in Frostproof."

Not a decent cleaner? Had Aaron forgotten Parson's Fresh Press? Three generations had seen the town through sixty years of service without complaint.

Besides, the black-tiled floor of the coffee shop had been mopped after the afternoon rush. It was presently clean enough to eat off.

Aaron was on his second cup of coffee by the time Risk and Jacy joined them. Risk slapped Aaron on the back. "I see Frostproof allows even their losers to come home."

Aaron stood, hugged Jacy, then pumped Risk's hand. "You've never hit a cutter in your life. I swear, I thought I had you out."

"You thought wrong."

"Major set of plums to point to the nosebleed seats."

"Couldn't leave Zen hanging on third." He winked at Jacy. "Home run was for Pink."

"Jacy in Heaven's Row," Aaron teased. "Thought Risk could afford box seats for the hometown crowd."

"He offered," Jacy returned. "I preferred to hang with the rowdy Rogues. Fans can party."

Aaron looked at Zen. "How's the hamstring?"

"Sore." Zen stretched out his legs. "I'll be able to golf as long as I don't have to walk the course."

"Carts are available," Aaron assured him, then asked, "Have you met Jacy?"

Zen smiled across the table. "Haven't had the pleasure. But I hear you give good sugar."

"No sugar for you," Risk said to set his friend straight.

Zen cast a glance at Stevie. "I much prefer a good blow."

Aaron blinked and Stevie rushed to explain, "We're talking coffee."

"Let's talk business." Aaron motioned everyone to take a seat.

Chairs scraped and everyone settled in. Stevie's heart quickened when Aaron covered her hand with his own, then squeezed her fingers. "When the event planner caught the flu, I thought this weekend would be cancelled. Thanks for stepping in and pulling it all together."

"She's worked hard," Jacy said in praise of her friend. "You owe her. Big time."

Aaron traced Stevie's fingers. "I've ways to repay."

Repay me *how?* Stevie wondered. A walk down memory lane? A slip between the sheets? A marriage proposal?

Happiness seduced her until Zen's frown brought her down. She couldn't understand his disapproval. Yet it was there, evident in the visible tic in his jaw, the narrowing of his eyes.

"Tell me about the donations. The player auction." Aaron drew her back to the weekend events.

Stevie was proud of the items collected. "Bidding starts with tickets to Disney World and Sea World, a weekend at the Fontainebleau in Miami, deep-sea fishing in the Keys, and a brand new Mustang. The auction ends with the players going on the block."

Aaron brought her palm to his lips and kissed it lightly. "Which players?" he asked.

The moist press of his mouth proved distracting. She tried to stay focused. "You and, uh, Risk, Zen, and the Bat Pack. We're expecting a huge turnout. The auction will take place on the high school football field."

"Whoa, back up a sec." Zen's eyes were now wide. "I'm to be auctioned?"

Risk looked unrepentant. "Sorry, man. Guess I forgot to mention your participation."

"Strike two." Zen held up two fingers. "My kidnapping, now the auction. No more surprises."

"We're tight," Risk assured him.

"You owe me a change of clothes."

"You've got the run of my closet," Risk stated before turning to Jacy. "I'm expecting you to bid on me. Take my checkbook and raise the bid until you take me home."

"What happens *after* the bidding?" Zen asked.

"A grandfather, child, or lovely lady could win you for the evening," Stevie explained. "Drinks, dinner, playing catch, talking baseball, are all entertainment options. The Twilight Drive-In Theater will run a double feature starting at nine. *Sleepless in Seattle* followed by *Die Hard*."

Stevie looked from Risk to Aaron. "Someone needs to remind Romeo if a hottie wins his body, there's no tucking her into bed. Couples part at the door."

"I'll have a word with him," Risk said.

Aaron looked at his cousin. "What are you auctioning, Jacy?"

"Coffee with me every morning for a week might bring in a dollar or two."

"More than a few bucks, babe," Risk drawled. "Frank Stall would sell his orange grove for your morning sugar."

Jacy pointed to Stevie. "Baseball trivia with our own Stevie Cole will be a highlight. One hundred dollars per question."

"Update me on the golf and softball tournaments," Aaron pressed.

"The Shadow Woods Course will host the golf tournament, and the softball game will be played on the high school diamond," Stevie told him. "Major league players versus Frostproof's Finest."

Risk looked at Jacy. "You playing ball?"

"Center field."

He rolled his eyes. "You're not that athletic, babe."

She pinched his arm. "I've been practicing. Hit a ball my way and I'll catch it on the fly."

"The country club dance?" Aaron's last question wrapped up all the details for the weekend.

"We hired Day's Night." Stevie awaited his reaction.

Aaron's expression softened. "One of my favorite groups."

She had banked on his liking the band. That was why she'd booked them. To trigger the good times and draw him back into her life.

"What time should I pick you up tonight?" Aaron

asked her. "Sponsor and chairperson should arrive at the auction together."

"Let's make it six," Stevie suggested. "I just moved into the Blue Heron Condominiums on South Ninth. The condo with the lime green shutters."

"Lime green?" Aaron looked at his cousin. "From Jacy's palette?"

Stevie nodded. "She gave the place a little color."

"I'll find you." Then as an afterthought, he asked, "Do you have something presentable to wear?"

Presentable? She slid her hands down her sides, felt the slight bulge at her waist. Was he embarrassed by her weight? Her size sixes had evolved into tens and twelves over the years, and the occasional fourteen. Though she would have preferred a little black dress, she'd be squeezing into a conservative rose silk suit. With elastic inserts around the waistband of the skirt.

"New outfit," she assured Aaron.

Aaron rose and Stevie returned his suit jacket. "Tonight is very important to me." He instructed, "Everyone be on time."

Jacy scrunched up her nose. "I'm never late."

Aaron disagreed. "You're always late when Risk is in town." He sent Risk a pointed look. "Keep it in your pants."

The ring of his cell phone cut off further conversation. Sliding it from the inside pocket of his jacket, he checked the number, then signaled his departure. "Later." And Aaron was gone.

Jacy stretched, stood. "I need to get back to work. Caramel rolls won't glaze themselves."

"I'll help." Risk rose also. Shooting Zen a look, he promised, "Thirty minutes and we're off." He patted Stevie on the shoulder. "Keep him company, sweetheart?"

"Yeah . . . sure. Why not?" It would be the longest half hour of her life. She knew more glaze would go on Jacy's fingertips and into Risk's mouth than would ever reach the rolls.

Absently, she glanced around the coffee shop, which was nearly empty. Her gaze strayed to Zen who sat silent, looking as if he were still assessing the weekend ahead. "So . . ." She glanced at the clock above the counter. Four-thirty.

"So . . ." He reached for a magazine. "Don't feel you have to entertain me. There's lots here to read."

She'd do her duty by Risk and give Zen five whole minutes. Then split. "You read a lot?"

"Whenever I have time."

"Favorite authors?" No doubt he preferred intense, thought-provoking, and extremely boring books.

"Carl Hiaasen, Randy Wayne White, Dave Barry."

Surprise, surprise. The man liked a little humor in his stories. So did she. She'd never known Aaron to crack the spine of any book that didn't pertain to baseball.

Zen flipped through *Business Week*.

She drummed her fingers on the table and sought the clock a second time. Four thirty-five. Time to fly. She hunched her shoulders and scooted off her stool. . . .

"Want to talk about Aaron?"

She stopped scooting. "Do you?"

"You're not sure if he was really glad to see you."

"He held my hand." *For a very short time.*

He nodded, a hint of sympathy in his gaze, before returning to his magazine.

"Why the pity face?" she demanded, calling him on the look.

He glanced up. "No pity, Stevie."

She kicked him under the table. Not hard, just enough to get his attention.

He jerked on his stool. Bent to rub his leg. "Pulled hamstring, remember?"

"Stop feeling sorry for me."

"I'm feeling sorry for *me*. No more kicks."

She met his gaze squarely. "I saw pity in your eyes."

He blinked twice. "Still there?"

"Don't be cute."

He slipped off his reading glasses, folded them on the table. "There's nothing cute about me."

"Not cute, but maybe . . ." She licked her lips.

"Maybe . . . *what?*"

"Sharp. Intelligent. On a good day."

His gaze pinned her. "I'm also good at reading people. I know for a fact you're incredibly insecure. Nervous to the point of panicking that this weekend will bomb and Aaron will return to Tampa and forget you completely."

The man was friggin' psychic. She hated his insight. "Don't look so smug."

He drew his hands down his face. "Pity, now smug. How about neutral party?"

"Why would you bother?"

"Because you need to talk," he said gently. "I can see it in *your* eyes. Since Jacy can't see beyond Risk, I'm the closest thing to a bartender or shrink you've got at the moment. I won't judge. Only listen."

Her insecurities were alive and at the forefront. She could use an ear. The man looked trustworthy. "Everyone in town knows I've loved Aaron since I was twelve. He noticed me when he turned fourteen. We've been together ever since." She paused, then voiced her worst fear. "This past year has been rough. We've drifted apart. I'm scared of losing him. This weekend is do or die for me."

"Do or die? Aren't you being a bit dramatic?"

She shook her head. So hard she almost twisted her neck. "Sunday could spell the end of our relationship."

Zen looked at her thoughtfully. "Memories can't be denied. Aaron would have to be blind not to see how pretty—"

"Pretty?" She blinked at his compliment. "That's a first."

"I'm a fan of hazel eyes and freckles."

"I have freckles all over my body. You could play connect the dots on my—"

"Breasts?" He looked directly at her chest.

"And belly." She sucked in her stomach only to have her chest expand. Her nipples went on full alert. Points so visible it looked like she was smuggling raisins.

Zen's sexual tug on her libido would be the death of her.

She belonged with Aaron Grayson. Annoyed at

herself, she stood to collect the cups and saucers. Her conversation with this man was at an end.

Or so she thought until he cleared his throat and threw a trivia question her way. "Who flapped his back elbow up and down like a chicken while waiting for a pitch? Who did a backflip during his pregame routine?"

"Questions for a rookie." She smirked. "Joe Morgan flapped like a chicken and Ozzie Smith did the acrobatics."

"Who caught Hank Aaron's 715th home run?" he asked as she wiped down the table.

Who . . . indeed? No immediate answer jumped to mind. Her heart slowed, as did her breathing. A full minute passed, her mind a total blank. She repeated the question. Twice. Searched deeply. Another minute, and the answer finally hit her.

Relief washed over her. She felt weak in the knees. "Tom House, a Braves reliever who was in the bull pen."

"Made you think," he said, a slow grin spreading over his handsome face.

He damn sure had. "Bring lots of money to the auction," she told him. "I'd love to break your bank in baseball trivia."

"What if I stump you?"

"Not a chance, Einstein."

"But if I do, what do I win?"

She stepped away from the table, her back to him now. "What could you possibly want?"

His silence stroked her, sending shivers along her

spine. His words came to her on a heated whisper. "Another blow."

She closed her eyes, as visions beyond coffee struck brightly. Erotic visions of unbuckling his belt, lowering his zipper, revealing . . . boxers or briefs?

Or perhaps the man preferred his freedom.

Fear seized her entire body.

She'd better brush up on her trivia.

She couldn't afford to lose.

CHAPTER 3

Jacy Grayson had lost track of time. She drifted, day-dreaming, surrounded by steam and pulsating water as she washed her hair, watching the lavender hair dye go swirling down the drain. She planned to go orange tonight.

A chill seduced her as the shower door opened, then closed on a soft click. Silence embraced the steam until Risk Kincaid tucked her into his body. His groin pressed her buttocks. Strong hips. Major hard-on. The man was in the mood for pre-auction sex.

She turned to face him. Beneath the spray, his hair was slick, its dark brown color almost black when wet. Water sluiced off his broad shoulders, soaking his hair-roughened chest. Strength emanated from his big body. The very power of his presence drew her to meet his gaze. Spiked lashes outlined green eyes, his sexy mouth was smiling as he said, "I missed you."

"We've been apart less than an hour."

His fingers grazed her bare shoulder. "Longest fifty minutes of my life."

"Where's Zen?"

"At my parents' house." He drew a callused finger up her neck. "They're on an Alaskan cruise. He has the place to himself."

"How will he get to the auction?"

"We'll swing by and pick him up." His thumb played at the corner of her mouth. "I'm driving the old man's Lexus."

"The one you bought him?"

"The one he's had an entire year and keeps locked in the garage." He gently skimmed his knuckles over her cheekbones. "The one with eighteen miles on the odometer."

"Frostproof's not a Lexus town."

He drove his fingers into her hair, pulled her up on tiptoe. "I'll trade it for a Camry."

He kissed her then, angled his mouth right, then left, then turned up the heat. He teased their desire. His hands wandered and her thighs parted to his touch. They were two people who knew what the other liked, making each other crave more.

Her body pinkened, as much from the pounding spray as from Risk's own heat. As his kisses deepened, she gripped his arms, sinking her nails into his water-slick muscles. She rubbed her foot along his calf, hooked her toes behind his knee, tugged, wanting to climb his divine body. All cut and tight and solidly male.

"Condom?" he breathed against her mouth.

She kept them in a traveling soap container on her

shower caddy. Once sheathed, he took her, lifting and penetrating, and infinitely slow in his strokes until she urged him to deliver.

The man had hip action. He moved her to orgasm within several slamming beats of her heart. Breathless, she clung to him as his body tensed, arched, and he poured into her.

Their sighs of release echoed off the shower walls.

His sigh as dark and guttural as a growl.

Her sigh softer, yet equally as satisfied.

His slow grin cast a dimple in his five o'clock shadow. "You give good shower."

Her smile was as shaky as the lasting spasms of her orgasm. "I give better loofah." She then went on to show him how a soft sponge and softer mouth could make him hard once again.

Afterward, she sank against his chest. He held her gently. Each touch was tender as he ran his hands over her shoulders, then down her back to her hips.

As he massaged her lower spine, she nuzzled his neck. "Mmmm. Don't stop."

"Sorry babe, we have to go. It's getting late," he reminded her.

Her arms tightened about his waist. "Ten more minutes."

The slight shift of his weight should have warned her of his intentions. He'd pulled this trick before. Risk knew how to make her move. And move fast. A turn of the shower dial and ice cold water shot down her back. She shrieked so loudly her own ears rang.

He slapped her bare bottom as she scooted from the shower. Risk withstood the cold for sixty seconds before stepping out. He shook his damp hair. "Toss me a towel?"

She tossed him a hot pink towel, a match to the one that was now wrapped around her body. She swallowed her smile as he scratched his chest, frowning. "No brown or navy?"

"I just redid my bathroom," she explained, gesturing toward the arresting pink, purple, and olive green stripes. "The towel's to dry off, not to wear."

"I dry better with a darker color."

"I could blow you dry."

His eyes darkened, narrowed. And his sex twitched. "Don't go low. We're late enough as it is."

"You brought a change of clothes?"

"Pair of jeans and a sport coat," he told her. "As dressed up as I ever get."

Jacy shimmied the towel down her back making her breasts jiggle. Her skin was buffed and glowing. "Did you see the suit on Aaron?"

Risk's gaze fixed on her bouncing breasts. "Man spent some coin."

"For what reason? Who was he trying to impress?"

"Can't rightly say, babe."

Jacy bent to dry her legs. "Maybe Stevie?"

If Jacy Grayson didn't lower her pert little ass, he would take her from behind. Doggie style. He averted his gaze, only to catch her reflection in the mirror. A three-sectioned mirror that flashed three sets of sweetly rounded butt cheeks. Sweat broke out on his brow. His sex started to rise.

She slowly straightened, her hands on naked hips. Curvy hips. Hips that supported a soft abdomen and a triangle of blond curls. She caught the direction of his gaze and lowered her own.

The touch of her eyes stroked him like a hand. Fully erect now, and horny as hell, he drew the towel across his groin, drying his *Bad to the Bone* tattoo. Jacy had been the first to see *Bone*, the first to kiss every single letter.

With a flick of her tongue to her upper lip, Jacy lifted her gaze. "How does Aaron feel about Stevie?" she asked.

Risk shrugged. "Don't know. We haven't talked women in a long time."

"Any league rumors?"

He'd heard a few. But rumors were rumors. He had no hard facts on Aaron. If he told Jacy what he knew, she'd panic and run to Stevie. Female hysteria was a man's worst nightmare. "Nothing worth repeating," he said, downplaying the gossip.

Jacy tossed her towel in the pink wicker hamper and headed for her bedroom. "I hope the weekend goes well for them."

Risk could only hope. If it went badly, he'd be the fall guy for not relaying the rumor. He followed Jacy into a room with a king-size waterbed.

Heated and moderately firm, the mattress rocked and rippled. During sex, his thrusts became as rhythmic as the roll of the bed. Sometimes he thrust so hard, his knees hit the base on the bed frame.

The orgasms they shared went beyond the physical. Each climax embraced the collective oneness of mind and soul. A oneness he felt only with this woman.

Lover to life partner: Could Jacy make the transition?

He came up behind her. She stood in an aqua bra and matching lace panties. He pulled her back against him and rested his chin on her damp hair. He enjoyed the soft press of her spine against his chest. "Don't worry about Aaron and Stevie. If they're meant to be together, they'll reconnect."

"I want Stevie to be happy."

He ran his hands down her arms, laced his fingers with her own and squeezed gently. "Are you happy?"

She cast a glance over her shoulder. "Very happy. You always make me feel great on the rebound."

"Yeah, as long as I remain single."

She stiffened, wide-eyed with surprise. Releasing his hands, she turned to face him, a bit pale and somewhat unnerved. "H-have you met someone? Are you seriously involved?"

He was head-over-heals involved. With her. "There's no one in my life at the moment, babe. But when the right woman comes along, she's mine."

"Yours." She drew in a breath. A breath that hitched in her chest. "I never thought . . ."

"Thought *what*, Jacy?"

Her hand fluttered as she waved off the thought. "Never mind. It isn't important. You're here with me now." She ran the tip of her finger down his bare chest and belly. "I plan to enjoy you."

The tip of his sex stretched up to meet her finger. Exhaling sharply, Risk snatched her hand and nudged her toward the closet. "Enjoy me later. Aaron will kill us both if we're late for the auction."

Dressed long before Jacy, he strolled into her living room. He couldn't help smiling. No one decorated quite like Jacy. He flicked on her black-and-white television, acquired broken from the local flea market. He'd spent hours replacing parts, getting it to work. He now tinkered with the rabbit ears until he got a decent picture. No cable, which limited his viewing to the four major networks. All were now focused on the evening news.

He scooped a handful of Valentine candy from a cranberry dish atop an antique vaudeville trunk turned coffee table. Jacy enjoyed the hearts with the crazy sayings all year round. He popped *Baby, Baby* and *Be Mine* into his mouth and let the sugar dissolve on his tongue.

Sweet as Jacy.

He then focused on the main room. Where to sit? Church pew, red antique barber chair or the leather backseats from a Mercedes Benz? He crossed her navy Oriental carpet to the barber chair. Jacy's central lighting consisted of an old-fashioned streetlight that curved over the chair to reach the middle of the living room. It shed a lot of light when on.

She'd painted again, he noticed. Which she seemed to do every three months. Exhausting to his way of thinking. But Jacy loved change. The room reminded him of a sunburst, the walls ranging from pale yellow to the brightest orange. In a cluster above the church pew, she'd arranged framed copies of Picasso's most abstract art.

Somehow, the room came together. Risk had always felt comfortable at Jacy's place, no matter how small it might be. Over the years, he'd offered to buy her something bigger. He'd even enticed her with a maid. Jacy hadn't even debated. She stood on her own two feet. Paid her own way. She'd told Risk to take his big fat baseball contract and shove it up his butt.

That was what he loved about her. She didn't want a piece of him. Well . . . maybe one piece. The one that satisfied her sexually.

"Why the smile?" Jacy asked as she entered the room.

"Just thinking about how much you like me."

She blinked. "I do?"

"Parts of me."

She laughed then. A sweet, hearty laugh that touched him deeply. "Pull all your parts together and let's hit the road."

He took her in as she came to him. Jacy of the Jungle. Tonight a leopard print crisscrossed her breasts, showing a lot of skin. X marked the spot near her navel where an amethyst belly stud flashed above zebra print loose-legged pants. Pink ballet slippers clad her feet. Multicolor parrot earrings hung to her shoulders. Wide gold bands captured her upper arms, Egyptian style. Tangerine tinted her hair. Amber contacts gave her a jungle cat look.

"I like," he said simply.

She bent over the barber chair, brushed a light kiss over his lips. "You taste like candy."

"Care for a heart?" When she nodded, he slipped *Love You* between her lips. He was crazy for this woman.

She kissed him again. Deeper this time, and with

enough tongue to stir a response. Just as he was about to pull her across his lap, her grin broke against his mouth. "Remember the time I decorated your chest with those little hearts?"

Did he ever. From neck to navel, she'd licked, sucked, nibbled the sweetness from his body. A total turn on during a rainy afternoon. He'd prayed for a week of thunderstorms. He would have built an ark for a month of flooding.

Feeling his body respond to the memory, he bolted from the chair. "The auction. Move, Jacy, *now*."

Damn, she could entice. The sexy sway of her hips as she walked ahead of him nearly had him dragging her back to the barber chair. For more than a shave and a hair cut.

"The town has tripled in size," Jacy noted as the charity committee stood on the makeshift stage in the middle of the football field. The stadium was packed, along with the standing-room-only inner track. It would prove a wild night.

She spotted Stevie, pretty in pink, standing next to Aaron. Her suit fit perfectly, complementing Stevie's auburn hair. Aaron wore a second designer suit, jet black with a chalk stripe, more expensive than the one he'd worn that afternoon. Jacy was surprised and disappointed that her cousin would rub his success in the faces of the local residents.

The Bat Pack arrived, looking casual in their baseball jerseys and jeans. While Romeo and Chaser wore their Rogues baseball caps, Psycho had chosen one imprinted with *Keep Staring and I May Do a*

Trick. Jacy prayed his *trick* wouldn't land him in jail. The man was the embodiment of reckless and crazy. And unpredictable.

She glanced up at Risk and found him checking her out. He winked and her heart went wild. She craved this man. Sometimes with a desperation that scared her.

He'd wanted her to bid on him, to bring him home after the auction. Which she was more than willing to do. Stepping closer, she stuck her hand in the right front pocket of his jeans and felt around. *Found him.*

"Babe, now's not a good time," Risk whispered near her ear.

Jacy blushed. "I was looking for your checkbook."

"Back pocket." He pulled it free and handed it to her.

Moments later, Stevie Cole stepped up to the microphone, requesting that the crowd settle. The auction was about to begin. Jacy decided to wait until her morning coffee winner was announced before hiking up the bleachers, megaphone in hand, to help collect bids. The crowd had raided their cookie jars and mad money—if not their savings accounts—to win either a vacation or a major league player.

Once Stevie welcomed the crowd, an auctioneer stepped forward and brought the spectators to their feet with the first item up for bid: an all-expense-paid week at Disney World for a family of four.

The excitement spread, as uproarious as the bidding, as both locals and out-of-towners built the new recreation center dollar by dollar. When it was Jacy's time to turn on the charm and sell her coffee, people cheered and stomped so loudly, the auctioneer had to stop and catch his breath. Risk was at the heart of the bidding. He jumped each bid by five hundred dollars, forcing any contenders to dig deep into their pockets.

Orange grower Frank Stall dug deeply. His voice was loud, his blood pressure high. When she'd reached five thousand dollars, Jacy nudged Risk. "Let Frank win."

Risk raised a brow, and Jacy explained, "I'm yours for lunch, dinner, and into the night. Frank's a good customer. Allow him breakfast."

Risk begrudgingly agreed. He raised the bid one final time, then allowed Frank Stall to take Jacy for a cool six grand.

"Stump Stevie Cole" came next. The baseball trivia session lasted for thirty minutes. She answered the questions as rapidly as they were fired her way. The woman was amazing.

Jacy saw Stevie's face tighten when Zen Driscoll bid five hundred dollars for the right to the last question. Standing on stage, waiting to be auctioned, he squeezed through to the microphone. He looked handsome, a stand-up guy with a whole lot of brains. Jacy saw him as more professor or philosopher than in-the-dirt player.

Zen now wore a navy button-down shirt and khaki slacks borrowed from Risk's closet. His female fans whistled and whooped their approval. As he stood beside Stevie, Jacy watched her friend's chest rise and fall, caught the slight hitch in her breathing. Only one well acquainted with Stevie would sense her unease.

Zen cleared his throat, then spoke into the mike. "On what two teams were Preacher Roe and Billy Cox teammates?"

Within seconds, the crowd grew silent as Stevie contemplated Zen's question. As the silence stretched on, people grew edgy. No one stumped Frostproof's whiz kid. Yet Zen had her sucking air.

"Pittsburgh Pirates." Stevie spoke slowly into the mike as she named the first team.

The crowd cheered her on. Stevie's supporters were on their feet and clapping so loudly Jacy was surprised her friend could think.

Stevie looked at Zen and stared, as if trying to read his mind. A moment of panic seized Jacy. Had Zen stumped the unstumpable Stevie? Jacy clenched her fists, willing her friend to answer correctly.

That was when she caught Zen's mouth move. The slightest, yet unmistakable twist of his lips, like a ventriloquist speaking for his dummy. No one had caught the movement but her and Stevie. By the look of relief in Stevie's eyes, Jacy knew Zen had fed her the answer. "The Brooklyn Dodgers," Stevie finally managed.

"The lady knows her baseball," Zen shouted into the microphone as he peeled five hundred dollar bills from his money clip, then faded into the background.

The crowd embraced their hometown trivia buff.

The Bat Pack came next, offering themselves as three for the price of one. They strutted to the edge of the stage, hot, sexy, and ready for action. The women pushed and shoved and rushed the stage. Security stepped in, enforcing crowd control. The uniformed men demanded a moderate distance be kept between those being auctioned and those bidding. The women booed, but stepped back.

Grabbing a megaphone, Jacy dove into the crowd and elbowed her way toward the east sector of the stadium. From there, she relayed all bids that rose from the bleachers. She would surely be hoarse by morning.

A collective bid from the Farnsworth Senior Center bought the Bat Pack. The young players would soon be playing bridge, checkers, and dominoes with the elderly supporters of the game. Jacy caught Psycho extending his arm to widow Abigail Gates, a customer from the coffee shop. Her wrinkled face smoothed into a smile. She had six granddaughters. All in their twenties. Jacy would bet the coffee shop old Abigail had each one primed to visit the Senior Center that very evening to meet the young players.

A light tug on Jacy's hand, and she found Ellie Rosen, one of her T-ball players, by her side. "Coach Jacy, I want to bid on that man." The girl with dandelion-blond hair and dark brown eyes pointed to Zen Driscoll, who stood next to be auctioned. She carried a book by Dr. Seuss in one hand and her piggy bank in the other.

Jacy bent down, eye level with the six year old. Ellie's clothes spoke Goodwill, the outfits clean, yet outdated. And often purchased large to cover a growth spurt. "How much do you have in piggy?" she asked.

"I saved my milk money from school. Three quarters and a dime," the girl said proudly. She pointed toward an elderly lady with cloud-white hair in a dark green dress with a crocheted collar who was seated on the first row of the bleachers. "Gram has two dollars in her coin purse if the bidding gets real high. It's her mad money."

Jacy's heart squeezed. "Why do you want to bid on Mr. Driscoll?"

Ellie looked toward the stage. "He looks like he can read." She held up Green Eggs and Ham, then pointed to her "Red Flyer" parked beneath the bleachers; the wagon was piled with books. "I brought all my fairy tales."

The shortstop would be sold for more than milk money—this Jacy knew. She placed a protective arm around the little girl and hugged her close, wanting to shield her from a world of disappointments. She'd suffered enough already. The tragedy of Ellie's parents being killed in a car accident when she was four had paralyzed Frostproof. The court had awarded the grandmother custody of the child.

Legally blind, Naomi Rosen could no longer read to her book-starved granddaughter. There had been numerous days following Bluebell practice when Jacy had sat with Ellie in the dugout and read to her until dark.

"Can we win him, Coach?" Ellie raised her voice to be heard over the crowd.

Jacy ran her hands down her zebra-printed thighs, contemplating how best to let Ellie down. As she nervously patted her hips, Risk's checkbook brushed her palm. The answer to her prayers. Zen Driscoll was one fat check away from reading to Ellie Rosen.

She listened closely to the auctioneer, who egged the crowd on to fifteen thousand dollars. The women were selling their souls to win the shortstop. Jacy understood his desirability. The man had a quiet presence that suggested strength and dignity. And subtle sex appeal.

Her mind made up, Jacy pressed the siren on her megaphone, held it to Ellie Rosen's lips. "Seventeen thousand," she whispered to the little girl. And Ellie repeated the number in her big girl voice.

A wave of silence sucked the air from the crowd, all eyes now focused on Jacy and Ellie. She waved Risk's checkbook and the auctioneer yelled "Sold." Jacy quickly wrote out the check and forged Risk's signature.

People parted like the Red Sea as Ellie Rosen walked proudly to the stage. After delivering the check, she took Zen's hand. A lump formed in Jacy's throat as the little girl led the shortstop from the stage.

Risk's gaze touched her and she held her breath. She prayed he wouldn't be angry over her expenditure. A nod and a slow smile stamped his approval. She went weak with relief. Risk loved kids. Known throughout the league as a fans' player, he arrived early at the ballpark and stayed late, signing autographs for the children who loved him.

Jacy blew him a kiss, promising to show her appreciation after the auction. He could have his way with her.

Risk drove the crowd insane when the auctioneer announced he was next to be auctioned. The noise grew as loud and boisterous as the World Series. Jacy's ears rang.

She stared across the field, taking the man in. He was unsettlingly handsome. He set a woman's heart to beating twice its normal rate. Judging by the wildness of the crowd, hearts were pounding. He might be older than the Bat Pack by six years, but Risk bore the chiseled maturity of a man who'd lived and learned, yet still planned to explore. Crows feet and laugh lines etched his face with character. That made him hotter than any young batter. He set the gold standard for major league baseball.

The auctioneer set the starting bid at ten grand and the bidding soared from there. Jacy let the excitement run through her. Risk's price alone would lay the foundation for the new rec center. He was one hot commodity.

Should she bid or bow out? She still had Risk's checkbook. She'd spent an enormous amount on Zen. Perhaps she should allow someone else to enjoy Risk—

"Twenty-five thousand." A woman's voice blared over a megaphone from the second row of bleachers on the west side of the stadium.

Jacy blinked at the enormity of the bid.

"Sold!" the auctioneer shouted.

Jacy's jaw worked as she watched the sway of the blonde's hips on her way to the stage. The woman looked familiar. . . .

"Sherry Sherman, Risk's high school flame, now living in Atlanta." Stevie jarred Jacy's memory as she joined her on the bleachers. "Rumor has it she's home for the weekend." Her friend scrunched up her nose. "Put on a few pounds, hasn't she?"

About twenty, by Jacy's calculation. Jealousy scratched, drawing out her claws. Time hadn't tarnished Sherry; the woman was still bold as brass and twice as shiny in her gold sequined top and matching capris. Big hair, big smile, and even bigger boobs. Boobs that entered a room five seconds before the rest of her body.

To Jacy's dismay, those breasts now pressed Risk's chest in a welcome-home hug. Risk had the balls to smile. That smile grew even broader when Sherry whispered in his ear. An ear Jacy would be forced to cut off if he continued to listen to Sherry's secrets. With a girlish giggle, Sherry grabbed Risk's hand and pulled him from the stage. The man went willingly. Too willingly for Jacy's liking.

She stared at the spot they'd vacated. Apparently Risk was as anxious as Sherry to turn back the clock to a time when life was centered on hormones, hooters, and hard-ons.

Irritation soon replaced her disappointment. Risk was her ride home. If worse came to worst, she could always call a cab.

The pulse of the crowd kicked wildly when Aaron Grayson stepped front and center. He gave a short speech, praising Stevie Cole for all her hard work, then thanking everyone for coming out and supporting parks and recreation. He then spread his arms as if to embrace the stadium. "What am I worth?"

The townspeople rewarded him with high bids.

Jacy heard Stevie's own voice soar through the megaphone, "Twenty thousand."

If her friend were to win, she'd be raiding her savings to pay for the evening. To Jacy's surprise, the crowd stilled, as if hesitant to raise the bid. Everyone in Frostproof knew Stevie adored Aaron. In the townspeople's eyes, their hometown boy was darn slow to walk her down the aisle.

In unison, the people of Frostproof handed Stevie a gift. No one would outbid her. She had Aaron all to herself. Jacy sent a silent prayer of thanks. The heart of a small town beat for its own.

"Thirty thousand." The bid came from the stage, from directly behind Aaron. The voice was low and deep, almost smoky. Yet utterly feminine. Jacy craned her neck to get a look at the woman. Beneath the floodlights, her hair glistened blue-black, long and shiny. She moved with a fluid grace, her black dress as slinky as her body. She looked rich. Pampered. And very into Aaron Grayson.

Her cousin's expression shifted from startled to ecstatic as he eased the woman close and took her hand. Clearing his throat, he spoke into the mike. "Your attention, please. In honor of this charity event, I'd like to make an announcement. A secret I've been keeping until after the World Series when I could claim a life away from baseball."

Jacy froze alongside Stevie. *Life away from baseball* could only mean—

"I'm engaged." Aaron didn't miss a beat. "Let me introduce Natalie Llewellyn. My fiancée."

The ripple of applause came from the out-of-towners. Anyone living in Frostproof sat rigidly still, unsure how to react. One minute Stevie Cole had appeared to win Aaron's favor, the next, he'd announced a fiancée. The town sat on the edge of the fence, uncertain which way to lean.

Jacy leaned into Stevie and lent Stevie her strength and support as her mind raced. *How had she been caught so unaware?*

However secret, someone had to have known about Aaron's engagement long before tonight. Rumors always circled the major league, some true, some false. Surely the Bat Pack, Zen Driscoll, or Risk Kincaid had heard the gossip. Yet no one had spoken up and saved her friend from learning the truth before God and a packed football stadium.

Had Stevie known Aaron's intent, she could have braced herself against the announcement. She wouldn't be standing there now, gripping the railing, white-knuckled and pale. And totally shocked.

Once the auction was concluded, the crowd dispersed. It had been an evening to remember. Only Jacy, Stevie, and the cleanup crew remained. The women sat high on the bleachers, shoulders pressed together, commiserating, until the lights on the field dimmed and the crew picked up the last paper cup and discarded program.

"Go home, Jacy," Stevie finally said.

"Come home with me," Jacy pleaded. "I've got chocolate. Lots of chocolate. We'll talk some more."

Stevie shook her head, her eyes sad. "All's said and done. There's nothing more to discuss."

They hugged then, two lifelong friends, as close as

sisters. Responsible for writing a check for the use of the football field, Stevie soon left Jacy to seek out the groundskeeper.

After several minutes, Jacy followed. Standing alone, she looked about the parking lot. It was dark and empty, with no sign of Risk Kincaid. He hadn't returned for her. She was minus a ride home.

Ballet slippers and a ten-mile hike didn't quite mesh. She'd wear a hole in the bottom of her footwear. She needed to call a cab. Or search out Stevie.

A horn honked behind her and she was captured in the glow of headlights. "Sweetheart, need a ride?"

Jesse "Romeo" Bellisaro pulled up beside her in a vintage turquoise Thunderbird. Jacy lifted a brow. "Widow Gates's car?"

Romeo's elbow jutted out the window. "Abigail asked me to take it for a spin. It hasn't been driven for years."

Jacy circled the hood and climbed in. She was glad for the ride. "How was the Senior Center?"

"Psycho danced with every lady there, including all six of Abigail's granddaughters. They played records. Old Sinatra. Chaser sampled all the baked goods, then drew promises from three of the ladies to send him care packages during spring training." He shot her a smile. "As for me, I got my ass kicked at checkers."

"You're a good sport, Romeo."

"I'm more than a pretty face." He drove easily, one hand on the steering wheel; the Thunderbird was the only car on the road at that time of night.

Jacy rolled down the window, let the cool night air lift her hair. She was tired, yet wired, still angry Stevie had been caught unaware by Aaron's announcement.

"How long have you known?" she asked Romeo.

He cut her a glance. "Known what, hon?"

"That Aaron was engaged to Natalie Llewellyn."

No flinching. No furrowed brow. His strong profile remained impassive, a slight twist to his lips. "I heard the announcement along with the crowd."

"Any league rumors?" she pressed. "Any locker room talk?"

"I'm not the man to ask," he said as they pulled to a stop in front of her house. To her surprise, Romeo leaned across the seat, his mouth a hairbreadth from her own. His heat played across her lips, as if he was about to make a move on her. "Ask Risk."

"Risk? No can do. He's—"

Romeo straightened. "Coming down your walk. Long strides. Pissed-off expression. The man's on a mission." He patted her thigh. "Out, sweetheart. I don't want to go a round with him."

She slid out and Romeo peeled off.

Risk met her at the curb. The sensual curve of his mouth was tight, his tone sharp. "What were you doing with Romeo?"

"He gave me a ride home."

"I swung by the stadium to pick you up, but Stevie said you'd already left."

"How was your date?"

He jammed his hands in his jeans pockets. "It wasn't a *date*. Sherry bought me when you refused to

77

bid. She flew in from Atlanta for the charity auction. We went for drinks, then I dropped her off at her sister's. End of night."

"Did twenty-five grand entitle her to a kiss?"

Color crept across his cheeks. "We kissed."

"Enjoyably?"

"Sherry stuck her tongue down my throat and tried to hump my thigh. I pulled her off. Not a fun time."

"Stevie had the worst night of her life."

He shifted his stance, looking uneasy. "What happened?"

"Right after you disappeared with Sherry, Aaron announced his engagement to Natalie Llewellyn."

"Holy shit." His tone and the dip of his head were signs he'd heard the rumor, yet hadn't shared it with her.

She jabbed a finger at his chest. "You knew about the engagement and never said a word."

He looked heavenward and blew out a breath. "Aaron's proposal was rumored, but never confirmed. If I'd told you, you would have freaked."

"I'm *freaking* now. Stevie was humiliated."

"I'm sorry, babe."

He looked sorry, but after what Stevie had suffered, not sorry enough. "I'm not in a forgiving mood." She pushed past him but only made it halfway up the sidewalk before he caught her by the arm and spun her around.

His eyes were wild and his confusion and frustration hit her hard. "*Not forgiving? Why the hell not?*"

All words died in her throat. They had never

fought before. She hated confrontation. Especially with a man she loved. "Because when you hurt my friend, you also hurt me."

"Stevie's my friend too. I've known her as long as I've known you."

"Friends share secrets."

"It was never a secret," he growled. "It was unconfirmed gossip."

When she remained silent, he released her. He breathed in deeply. Exhaled slowly. Then narrowed his green gaze on her once again. "What do you want from me, Jacy? How can I make it better?"

In the heat of her hurt and anger, she hit on a drastic measure. Celibacy would get his attention, which she relayed in the baseball lingo he'd understand. "Stevie's temporarily out of the game. Until she's back at bat, you won't be rounding my bases."

She turned then, and left Risk Kincaid and his stunned expression on the cracked sidewalk with his unshared secrets.

CHAPTER 4

Tap. Tap. Tap.

Jarred from her misery, Stevie Cole looked up from the kitchen table—a table littered with two flavors of Ben and Jerry's ice cream, strawberries dipped in chocolate, and enough silver Hershey Kisses wrappers to toss for confetti. A mug of hot cocoa grew cool, the marshmallows long since dissolved. Her high school and college yearbooks lay open, haunting reminders of her past.

Tap. Tap. Louder this time.

Zen Driscoll stood on the back stoop, visible through the almond-colored sheers. If she could see him, he could see her. Even if the only light came from the dim bulb above the stove. She cringed, then blushed. She'd been caught pigging out. Big time.

She debated sliding off her chair and hiding under the table, pretending to be invisible. Or crawling from the room on all fours. Anything to avoid the shortstop.

She sat totally still in the semidarkness and prayed he'd take the hint and take a hike.

Bam! His fist thumped the door.

"I can see you, Stevie," he called. "Five minutes. Open up."

Damn. Defeated, she pushed herself to her feet and plodded across the sage-and-sandstone tiles. She brushed back the almond sheers. "Whatever you're selling, I'm not buying."

His eyes narrowed and his brow creased. "Cut me some slack, woman. It hurts to walk. My leg's damn sore."

She cracked the door and cool night air rushed in, followed by a slower moving Zen. "You've walked a long way?"

"Down your driveway." He eased himself around her. "I took a cab from Ellie Rosen's house."

"How did you get my address?"

"My fingers did the walking."

Next year she'd go unlisted in the phone book. "It's late."

"Planning to turn into a pumpkin?"

She placed her hand over her stomach. She felt like a pumpkin in her gray sweats with the orange baseball stripes. Her belly was now round and protruding. And five pounds heavier than when she'd left the auction.

He looked at her over his wire rims and noted, "You've got chocolate on your chin."

"On my chin." She swiped at the spot. "Also on my sweatshirt." She looked down at the smear of

Chunky Monkey on her left breast. "On my sweat-pants." A dribble of hot chocolate. "On my bedroom slippers." Her gaze dropped to the long-necked, fuzzy pink flamingos. A gift from Jacy, now splotched with Cherry Garcia. She appeared as chocolate-dipped as the strawberries.

"I'm a mess," she confessed. He stood before her, all clean and pressed in his navy blue shirt and khakis, while she needed Shout and a full-cycle wash.

Tilting her head, she looked into his dark brown eyes. "Reason behind your visit?"

He took in her comfort food. "I came to steal your spoon. No more ice cream. Chocolate won't bring Aaron back."

He'd left the stadium before Aaron's announce-ment. "Word sure spread fast."

"Small town. Chatty cab driver."

Her shoulders slumped. Aaron and Natalie were hot news. She felt chilled to the bone.

Zen limped passed her, straight for the kitchen table. After sweeping the Hershey's foil onto his palm, he collected the half-eaten containers of ice cream and dumped them in the trash. That's when he spotted the empty bag of M&M's and the torn box of Junior Mints.

He shook his head, returned the chocolate-covered strawberries to the refrigerator. After pouring out the hot chocolate, he tossed her spoon in the sink. All that remained on the table was a bat-and-ball set of salt and pepper shakers and a ceramic catcher's mitt filled with artificial sweetener.

With one hand on the table to steady himself, Zen

dropped onto a chair, stretched out his leg, and asked, "You holding your own?"

Zen would see through any façade she might put up. There was no point lying. So she openly admitted, "I'm hanging on by my fingertips and slipping fast."

"I'm sorry Aaron hurt you."

"Me too." She ran sudsy water in the sink, swishing the spoon around. "How late did you read to Ellie Rosen?"

He rested his elbows on the table and steepled his fingers. "Until she fell asleep. Around eleven. I promised to return tomorrow and take her to the bookstore. Buy her a set of Junie B. Jones. She's a sweet little girl."

Stevie could picture him reading to Ellie. Zen seated on the couch, the six-year-old snuggled up against him. She would turn the pages, absorbing every word, adoring the man with the dark eyes and deep voice. The man who "looked like he could read." Jacy had shared Ellie's comment. He'd make a good father.

"Spoon's clean," Zen stated, after she'd dipped and swished it a dozen times. He patted the seat on one of the chairs. "Join me."

She hesitated. "I'm not feeling talkative. I was about to heat some warm milk, then head to bed when you arrived."

"No, you weren't," he contradicted. "You were sitting at the table, poring over yearbooks, wishing you could turn back time." He kicked the chair leg with his good foot and slid it back from the table.

"Neither warm milk nor a hot bath will cut it. Sugar combined with shock will have you staring at the ceiling for hours. So sit, Stevie."

She slowly did his bidding. As discreetly as possible she closed her high school yearbook, only to have Zen tug it toward him and flip to the dog-eared page. His expression remained impassive as he took in a photo of her and Aaron, arms wrapped about each other, big smiles, and "Most Likely to Marry" captioned beneath their picture.

He raised one brow. "At eighteen you believed in happily ever after?"

"Still do." She cracked her college yearbook and found a small photo of the two of them at a fraternity dance. She could still hear the music, the laughter, his words of promise. Words now whispered to Natalie Llewellyn.

"Life shifts, sometimes shakes like an earthquake." He spoke as if from experience. "Little remains constant. No matter the heart's involvement."

"I still believe in Aaron," she stated. "Somewhere deep inside him is the memory of how good we were together."

"A good memory, I'm sure," Zen returned. "But a memory nonetheless."

His words made her bleed. "You trying to hurt me?"

"I'd say you were hurt long before I arrived."

She took a deep breath and asked, "Did you know Aaron was engaged?"

Zen turned the page in her high school yearbook. "Heard the rumor."

"No surprise to you then." She rubbed her chest,

feeling vulnerable and bruised. "Unfortunately, I hadn't a clue. Being the last to know sucks."

Returning to her college yearbook, she flipped through several more pages and found Aaron pictured in Sports: an action shot of him on the mound, releasing a pitch. She remembered that game. A major win that had cemented his contract in the minors.

Tears filled her eyes, yet she refused to cry. "Ever been in love, Einstein?"

He rubbed the back of his leg. "I've never loved blindly. I evaluate the strengths and weaknesses in the women I date. Then determine on what levels we best connect."

"Sounds calculated."

He shrugged. "Perhaps. But when boundaries are set in advance, there shouldn't be any kicking, screaming, or tears of regret when two people call it quits."

Stevie couldn't help smiling. "You've had a screamer?"

He grimaced. "She had the lungs of an opera singer."

"I cry. Eat chocolate."

"I'll get Kleenex, but no more sweets."

"Chocolate-covered strawberries are great comfort food."

"Find comfort elsewhere."

"Why all the concern?"

His gaze darkened to jet, dropped to her breasts, then to her belly. "I told you at the coffee shop, I'm a sucker for hazel eyes and freckles."

Her nipples puckered and heat speared low. A heat

she hadn't felt since the last time she and Aaron made love. A heat that left her flustered. And wet.

She blushed and shifted on her chair. Zen did the same. He rolled his shoulders, rested his spine low, stretched his long legs. He looked damn uncomfortable.

A discomfort, she noted, born of a hard-on. There was a tent in his khakis. His sex jutted like her nipples.

Stevie stared, shaken. They'd turned each other on.

Zen was embarrassed when he realized Stevie was staring right at his erection. Desperate to focus on anything but her sexy freckles, he turned to a round of trivia. "Who pitched Yoo-Hoo? Who advertised Mr. Coffee?" he forced out.

Stevie mentally shook herself and focused on her answers. "Yogi Berra and Joe DiMaggio."

"Who modeled Jockey underwear?"

"Pitcher Jim Palmer."

"Viagra?" A product he'd never need around this woman.

"Rafael Palmiero."

"One more," he said as the tightness left his body. "Who endorsed Preparation-H?"

Her smile broke on a soft chuckle. "George Brett."

They both breathed easier, once again comfortable with each other. The sexual tension remained on the fringes of their minds, but was pushed out of play. For the moment. Until Stevie rolled her ankles and her bedroom slippers brushed his leather loafers. One soft, pink flamingo now pressed his bare ankle.

He was once again aware of their closeness. Sharply aware.

"How old were you when you first swung a bat?" she asked.

"Four, during my T-ball days. All good memories. My father coached. He insisted I move beyond the batting tee at five and start hitting actual pitches."

"Jacy coaches a T-ball team. The Bluebells."

"She doesn't look athletic."

"What Jacy lacks in coordination, she makes up for in enthusiasm," Stevie told him. "She's coach and cheerleader rolled into one. The Bluebells adore her."

"You've been friends a long time?"

"Best friends. She always has my back."

Jacy would take Stevie's heartbreak as her own. That same pain would snowball onto Risk Kincaid. Zen wondered how his teammate had weathered the storm. "I know you like sports," he said. "Are you more spectator than participant?"

She grew self-conscious. "I used to jog ten miles a day. Played tennis twice a week. Really pushed myself to stay fit."

"When you and Aaron lost contact, you turned to chocolate." He read her well. "Not quite as satisfying as your man, but it took the edge off. Am I right?"

Her cheeks heated. "Are you always so blunt?"

He nodded. "I believe if something needs to be said, people should say it. Blunt doesn't stab as deep as being cut by a secret."

He caught the flash of sadness in her hazel eyes. Her hands trembled as she ran them down her thighs. "I appreciate your honesty."

"With honesty, what hurts at the moment won't hurt for a lifetime."

She drew in a fortifying breath and asked, "During your time with Tampa Bay, did you ever meet Natalie Llewellyn?"

"Sizing up the competition?"

"I saw her on stage. She's perfect. Compared to her, I'm a blimp."

"Natalie isn't perfect."

"How would you know?"

Because I know Natalie. They'd once dated. For a very short time. In that time, he'd discovered her dark side. Natalie had a lust for public sex. A lust that provoked and taunted, drained a man of his sanity and suckered him into dropping his drawers before God and any passing stranger.

Her fear of getting caught worked like an aphrodisiac. She loved it fast and furious. And utterly dangerous. A tangle of clothes and exposed skin.

Zen had played her game. Twice. Once behind a velvet curtain at the opera during the final aria, and again in an elevator. They'd dropped fifty floors with his pants and boxers around his ankles. Natalie gave a whole new meaning to "going down."

He'd called it quits the day she hinted at marriage. Dating a woman for three months was not a commitment in his book. Natalie, however, felt otherwise. His retreat set her off. She turned ugly. Really, really ugly. She'd slapped, scratched, and screamed at him. Her inch-long nails had left scars on his chest. She'd wanted to tear out his heart.

Within a week he'd been traded to Richmond, all

because her crocodile tears had worn on Walt Llewellyn. Her father caved. Tampa Bay lost their Gold Glove shortstop.

Natalie was not his favorite person. Not by a long shot.

"No one's perfect, Stevie," he finally stated. "Outer beauty attracts, but inner beauty captivates."

She scrunched her nose, shuffled her feet. The movement sent a long-necked flamingo up his pant leg. The soft flamingo felt as if she'd brushed her toes against his calf. A feeling of sexual intimacy closed in around him. Once again.

It was time for him to leave. He pushed to his feet. "No more chocolate tonight."

She rose slowly. "Promise."

"I need to call a cab."

"I'll drive you."

"No reason for you to be out this late," he replied. Locating the phone on the far wall, he dialed the number from memory. After requesting a pickup he hung up, then turned back to her. "Five minutes."

She approached him slowly, a hesitancy in her steps. "I've yet to thank you for"—her cheeks pinkened—"for giving me the answer to the trivia question at the auction. I knew one, but not both of the teams where Preacher Roe and Billy Cox were teammates."

Zen shrugged. "My pleasure."

She looked down on her flamingo slippers and scuffed one toe on the tiles. "You saved me a whole lot of embarrassment."

"I would never purposely embarrass you." He

tipped up her chin with one finger, forced her to meet his gaze. "I'm sorry you suffered from Aaron's announcement. He should have told you privately before going public."

She moistened her lips with the tip of her tongue. A beautiful mouth, soft and cupid-pink. "Thanks, Einstein. I owe you a blow."

A blow. Silence fell between them, an embracing stillness filled with undercurrents of emotion. Tension arced, unrestrained and intensely . . . sexual.

She paled. And he swallowed hard.

Neither moved. The seconds drew out. His instincts told him if he kissed her, she'd respond. A part of him knew that would prove a mistake. She was lonely and vulnerable and still loved Aaron Grayson. Zen didn't do rebounds. Even for one night.

A loud honk and flash of headlights indicated the cab had arrived. He took one final look at the woman with the hazel eyes and freckles. Pretty and wholesome.

"Thanks for coming by," she said softly. "Otherwise, I might have passed out in a container of Chunky Monkey."

"See you on the golf course tomorrow," Zen cast over his shoulder. "I'll be the one in the cart."

"I'll be the one with the chocolate hangover." She closed the door, rubbed her stomach and moaned at its fullness.

"No room service. No spa. This place is a dump," Natalie Llewellyn complained as she slid down the zipper on her black dress and let it shimmy down her body. A body she openly admired in the mirror above the burl walnut chest of drawers. Her high, perky breasts, and tight, round bottom now curved beneath smoky wisps of beaded LaPerla.

At thirty-five, she could pass for twenty-eight. A little nip and tuck next year, and she'd claim thirty on her fortieth birthday. She thanked God for good genes, a personal trainer, and a discreet cosmetic surgeon. All kept her sleek and at the top of her game.

Her game tonight was playing with Aaron Grayson.

Sex play. Raw, urgent, and clawing. Wild and insane. *And public.*

Her heart slammed with the fear of getting caught.

"Pull the drapes, Natalie," Aaron requested as he shrugged off his Armani suit coat. "You're nearly naked."

Not naked enough. She moved to the sliding glass doors and stood framed in the moonlight, visible to anyone walking past. She fingered the edge of the curtain. "Mock velvet."

Aaron loosened his silk tie and unbuttoned his dress shirt. "I thought you'd like Crawford House. The bed and breakfast is considered quaint."

Quaint, if she hadn't been blinded by the tangelo exterior and electric blue shutters. Quaint, if she was into quilts, homemade crafts and antique reproductions. "It's not the Ritz."

Aaron remained quiet. Unusually so. He toed off his dress Oxfords, then unzipped and stepped out of his tailored pants. He faced her in his T-shirt, black

Calvin Klein briefs, and his socks. "I warned you against coming. It's a charity weekend. Over in three days. I would have returned home on Monday."

Monday had seemed a lifetime away. Absently, she flipped a light switch by the glass doors, curious as to what would be illuminated. Beyond the glass, a flower garden came to life. Tiny frosted bulbs lit the ivory roses and gardenia bushes. A short hedge enclosed a rope swing beneath a trellised arbor.

She turned slightly, pressing her back and bottom to the cool glass. The arch of her spine pushed her breasts high. "How would you have spent your free time if I'd stayed away?"

He shed his T-shirt and pulled off his socks. "The weekend's packed with player activities. I don't have a lot of time to socialize."

"Not even with Stevie Cole?" She caught his flinch and pressed him further. "Didn't take you for a chubby chaser."

His jaw tightened fractionally. "Stevie's not fat," he said in defense of his friend. "You know our history. I laid it out clearly when we started dating. The same night you told me about Zen Driscoll."

Zen . . . her heart hadn't healed after all this time. She missed him with a constant ache. Even now she called him on occasion, quickly hanging up, just to hear his voice. She'd chosen Aaron Grayson as her revenge against Zen.

Aaron, the pitcher with the most lucrative contract in major league baseball. Aaron, with the golden boy looks and the naive belief she loved only him.

In a fit of pique at being left alone for the weekend, she'd phoned Frostproof's Chamber of Commerce and inquired as to which players would be attending the weekend events. When she'd discovered Zen Driscoll had been added to the list, she'd called for the company Cessna and flown to the backward town.

Her appearance at the charity auction had forced Aaron to announce their engagement. But her ploy hadn't worked as well as she had hoped. Her timing was off. By about thirty minutes. She'd shocked Stevie Cole, but Zen had already departed with some brat and a bunch of books.

Tomorrow would be soon enough to face the shortstop. To flash her smile and ten-carat engagement ring. She wanted Zen to see her deliriously happy. A happiness she would fake for the weekend.

"Zen Driscoll is my past." Her passion for the man with the intelligent eyes and sexual control was still buried in her soul. "Have you truly put Stevie behind you?"

"You know I have."

Her gaze fixed on his sex beneath his black briefs. It was shriveled and lifeless. "Stevie bid on you tonight."

"*You* won me," he reminded her. "The money will help raise the roof on the recreation center."

"What can you raise for me *now*?"

He yawned. "How about I salute the sun in the morning? It's late. I'm whipped."

She wasn't the least bit tired. "Bet you could get it up for Stevie."

He ran one hand down his face. "Damn, Natalie, don't go there."

"Bet her plump breasts and thighs would entice you."

His sex twitched. "Stop talking about her."

"Afraid you'll ejaculate?"

"Nasty thought, even for you." His expression was pure disgust. "I don't want to fight."

Oh, but they were going to fight. She'd gotten excited thinking about Zen. Aaron would have to appease her need.

She licked her lips. "Would Stevie take you in her mouth? Would she expect you to go down on her?"

There was a shortness in his breath. A definite bulge in his briefs.

"You want Stevie, don't you, Aaron?"

"Stop baiting me." His voice was deep and aggravated.

Natalie was getting to him. "If I wasn't here, you'd be at her place right now, wouldn't you? All naked. Screwing your brains out. For old time's sake."

"Bitch." Aaron crossed to her, fire in his eyes, his sex straight up against his belly. He grabbed her by the shoulders, jerked her close. "I want you."

She tossed back her hair, bared her teeth. "Liar."

Provoked, he brought his mouth down on hers with the force of his anger. Not the savage anger she preferred in most men, but still the taste of his temper parted her lips and lingered on her tongue. She scratched his shoulders, his back, his buttocks. Enjoying the flex of his muscles, the rise of welts from her long red nails.

She slid her fingers beneath the elastic on his Calvin Kleins. Tugged them down. Freeing him.

He jerked backed. "The drapes." His breathing was as tight as the elastic that wrapped his thighs.

"Remain open." She caught the narrowing of his eyes, the uncertainty in his expression. Tonight was a first for Aaron. She'd never taken him *public*. Yet at that moment her desire was strong to take him naked in the moonlight.

She shoved back the glass doors. Cool air rushed in as she stepped out.

Aaron Grayson blinked. "Where the hell are you going?"

"To take a walk in the garden," she cast over her shoulder.

"In your bra and panties?"

"Soon only my skin."

Sweat beaded his brow. "Are you crazy?"

Her nostrils flared. "Not crazy. *Creative*."

His testicles tucked tight against his body. "It's too public."

She crooked one finger. "It's private beneath the trellis."

"Natalie . . . damn!"

He jerked up his briefs, grabbed Natalie's French blue chenille robe, and followed her to the arbor trellis. The moonlight illuminated her face and body, casting her in white light. The innocent fragrance of climbing, intertwining roses mixed with the sin of her musky scent. He tossed her the robe. "Put this on."

She slapped the robe aside, then snagged his Calvin Kleins. "Take these off."

A police siren wailed in the distance. The thought of getting arrested in his hometown for indecent exposure had him sweating and swearing, "Damn it, Natalie, have you no decency?"

"I prefer naughty." She ducked deeper beneath the trellis. He heard her inhale, caught the rise and fall of her naked breasts. When had she slipped off her bra? "Roses smell divine." Her voice sounded sultry and seductive. "The petals are as soft as my inner thighs."

Aaron dove for her and she squirmed away, her silky laughter sliding over him like a flicking tongue.

They circled the trellis once, twice. He stepped on her discarded panties. When he finally caught her, she was completely naked. Her body welcomed his with heat and suggestion, her arms wrapping his neck, her thighs cradling his sex.

His heart kicked, his body alive with wanting this woman. "Natalie . . . not here." He could barely breathe.

"Right here." She stole the breath from his lungs with her first kiss. Her second kiss stopped any thought of protest.

Aaron allowed Natalie to have her way with him. Tucked beneath the trellis, she plied him with hot kisses, erotically stroking hands, and whispered words that made him blush.

His Calvin's soon wrapped his ankles.

When she nudged him toward the old swing that hung beneath the arbor, he hesitated, uncertain whether it would hold his weight. He soon discovered it held not only his, but Natalie's as well.

He sat on the wooden seat.

She straddled him. Took him inside her . . . the little there was of him. He was having a hard time holding an erection.

The rope squeezed his hips as splinters stabbed his ass. He faced rope burn and an hour of tweezing his butt.

"Push the swing," she breathed against his neck.

She had to be kidding!

"Motion, I need motion." Her voice was harsher, more demanding.

He dug one foot into the grass and set the swing in motion. The swing squeaked and the trellis groaned under their weight. Moonbeams bounced off their bodies with each to-and-fro. Rose petals fluttered onto his shoulders and down Natalie's spine.

"Higher!" She ground her groin against his.

He swung his legs back. Wild rose thorns stabbed his ass. Gliding forward, his feet hit the hedge.

"Close, so close." The night air captured her rising orgasm. An orgasm that went from low moan to mighty scream. When he covered her mouth with his hand, she bit him. Not a love bite, but a full set of teeth marks in his palm.

He hoped their room had a first aid kit.

He was current on his tetanus shot.

Aaron lay in bed, unable to sleep. He tossed and turned and counted sheep. Yet the scene in the garden played over and over in his mind like pornography. He'd been so dazed by Natalie's naked display, his heart had yet to slow down. Any guest at the bed and breakfast could have looked out the window and caught them *swinging*.

Had he not muffled her scream, she would have wakened the entire population of Frostproof. He'd been so nervous, he'd barely remained hard. Natalie had been the only one to climax. Tonight he'd seen a side of her that scared him soft. He might never have another erection.

She'd relished his fear and laughed in his face. Teasing and taunting and taking charge. Always dominant, she preferred to be on top. Even in bed, she rode him until his hips hurt and he was totally drained.

In the early months of their relationship, he'd enjoyed the sense of power, the respectability of dating the team owner's daughter. Walt Llewellyn treated him like a son. For a small-town boy, the big-city lady held major appeal.

Until tonight.

Tonight she'd *gone public*. Natalie's need to be close to nature made him very, very nervous. He had scratches on his back from both her nails and the thorns on the roses. And rope burns on both hips. Their garden tryst had destroyed Mrs. Crawford's prized roses. He doubted there was a decent bloom left.

At first light he needed to locate his Calvin Kleins. He'd searched on hands and knees, but there had been no sign of the black briefs. Thank God Natalie had found her bra and panties.

She lay on the far side of the bed now, so near the edge, she could easily fall off. The green comforter was tucked beneath her chin. Sated, her desire to touch and be touched had faded with her climax.

She'd made it quite clear she wanted nothing more to do with him that night. Nothing at all.

Aaron had known from the beginning she wasn't a cuddler. She demanded her own space. She'd already suggested separate bedrooms after they married, which was still under debate. Oftentimes heatedly.

He rolled onto his side the exact moment she cut loose like a buzz saw. Damn, the woman could snore. He'd forgotten to pack his earplugs. Earplugs that had cost him six dozen coral roses and an engagement ring when she discovered he used them to block out her snores. She'd given him the cold shoulder until he'd produced the diamond. A diamond of her choice.

He'd paid a high price to keep Natalie happy. In the process, he'd broken Stevie Cole's heart. His announcement had crushed her. He'd watched her bleed.

Jacy had shot him a look that sent him straight to hell.

He was in hell now. Scared shitless by Natalie's exhibition. The wild, yet satisfied look in her eyes told him she'd enjoyed the experience and expected more of the same.

Public sex put pressure on his performance.

He wasn't sure he could rise to the occasion.

Ever again.

Desperately seeking sleep, he eventually dreamed. A restless, frightening dream in which he stood bare-assed before fans, other ball players, and Mother Nature on the first tee of Shadow Woods Golf Course. Natalie, his very nude caddy, gripped *his* putter and balls.

CHAPTER 5

Risk Kincaid laced up his golf shoes and slipped on his golf glove. He and Zen Driscoll had arrived at Shadow Woods before the rooster crowed. Both men wanted time to warm up before the charity tournament.

To the east, the sun rose and grew stronger. The golden rays flickered through the cypress branches, patterning the grass.

"Putt or drive?" Zen asked.

"I'm going to hit a bucket of balls," Risk said. "You?"

"I'm going to practice my short game."

Risk shrugged Zen's golf bag off his right shoulder near the putting green. With the cart barn yet to open, he'd offered to carry both bags, not wanting Zen to strain his hamstring further.

"I'll be on the driving range." He shifted his own golf bag from his left to right shoulder as he circled the table-top green where Zen would practice his putting.

After purchasing a bucket of balls, he poured them out, then withdrew his driver from his golf bag. He rolled his shoulders and shook out his arms and proceeded to stretch his muscles in a practice swing.

Feeling fluid, he placed a pockmarked white golf ball on a two-inch wooden tee. Then drew back the club and slashed through the air to meet the ball with a resounding whack. The ball launched, long and straight. A solid three hundred yards.

"You hit the sweet spot," Jacy Grayson said from behind him. He slowly turned to face her.

"I've been known to find the sweet spot in golf, baseball, and women." He caught her blush, the sweep of heat along her neck and into her cheeks. The hot flushing of her skin aroused him. He angled back to the driving range and teed up a second ball. "Still mad at me, babe?"

"Mad enough to keep this conversation short."

He'd have to see how long he could drag it out. "What brings you to the driving range?"

"I'm killing time." She pointed toward the putting green. "Last night Zen saved Stevie from death by chocolate. She wanted to speak to him privately, so I wandered over here."

He looked over her shoulder. "Romeo and Psycho have arrived. A crowd's building around the players. There is no more privacy. You're free to return."

"I'll leave when I'm good and ready."

A smile tugged at the corner of Risk's mouth. *Stubborn Jacy?* This was a side of her he'd yet to see. During the short times they'd shared together, she had always been sweet and loving. He liked knowing she had backbone. Not many people stood up to him.

Perhaps he had screwed up by not sharing the speculation over Aaron and Natalie's engagement. There would be neither rest nor romance until he once again gained Jacy's good side.

She looked damn good today. Her hair, light and streaked a dozen shades of blonde, was swept off her face and tucked behind her ears, exposing her smooth forehead and sharp cheekbones. Almond-brown contacts darkened her eyes.

Her flamboyance flashed in the amethyst-and-crystal broach pinned to her tangerine-and-peach Madras top. Floral print Bermudas showcased her legs. He admired the long-stemmed red rose that climbed her thigh; the yellow daisy tucked next to her zipper.

It might be a long time before she let him unzip her again. The thought depressed him greatly. Slamming the club against his palm, he said, "I made a mistake by not mentioning the rumor to you. Aaron's announcement's been made. It's now old news." He looked her straight in the eye. "I'm only home for a month, Jacy. I'd like to spend time with you. Tell me how I can make it better."

"I'll think of something." She turned then, and without a backward glance, walked away.

Risk watched her go, noting the straightness of her shoulders, the slight sway of her hips. The way her black-and-white saddle shoes left imprints on the dewy grass. Lolita Lampeka caught on the breeze, the warm vanilla scent a crooked finger, enticing him to follow.

He swallowed hard and held back. He'd get through the charity tournament, then charm Jacy out of her shorts.

The power of his swing sent the remaining golf balls beyond his original mark. He worked through a second bucket before heading toward the putting green. His gaze narrowed on Romeo, who now stood and spoke to Jacy. Whispered to her really, the man's lips brushing her ear. When Jacy giggled, Risk saw red.

"Morning, pops." Psycho grinned at Risk when he stepped onto the putting green. "Think you can walk all eighteen holes or should I call for a cart?"

Risk glanced at the young power hitter. Prior to the tournament, it had been decided the Richmond players would wear their team colors: a red golf shirt and navy slacks. Psycho had not conformed. Besides that, he'd breached golf course etiquette. Big time.

He stood before Risk in a gray T-shirt imprinted with a Dalmatian resembling a pirate: The sea dog wore a peg leg, single gold earring, and a black bandana decorated with skull and cross bones. Between his teeth, the Dalmatian clutched a skimpy bikini top. The words *Free Those Puppies* was scripted in red. Psycho's worn black jeans looked older than dirt.

Risk shook his head. Psycho's jabs at Risk's age had begun the day Psycho rose to the majors. Psycho reminded Risk of himself, when he was in his midtwenties. Wild, edgy, believing life was a thrill ride.

From extreme sports to wild women, Psycho lived on the edge. At times dangled over.

"Zen is the only one driving a cart," Risk replied. "I've decided to walk the course. Same as you."

"I'm in your foursome."

Could the day get any better? "Behave yourself," Risk warned.

"I promised Stevie I wouldn't go off."

Risk knew that Psycho's promise could be twisted by situation and interpretation. Trouble embraced him like an old friend.

Selecting his putter from his bag of clubs, Risk practiced his short game along with six other players. He was just about to putt when he heard Jacy giggle. Again. Risk looked up in time to catch Romeo graze his fingers over her shoulder, then grin. A grin he flashed when flirting.

Risk was about to wipe that grin right off his face. Moving to a practice hole nearer the twosome, he gauged the distance from the green to Romeo's groin. He had no plans to take Romeo out of the tournament, he just wanted the third baseman's attention.

A nice easy stroke with just enough power . . .

"What the hell?" Romeo jumped back, clutching his right thigh. "Who—"

"Me," Risk said softly, just loud enough for Romeo to hear. He dropped a second ball on the green and pulled back his putter. Romeo quickly covered his groin with both hands.

"Didn't know golf was a contact sport." Psycho nudged up next to Risk. "Romeo's not wearing a cup."

"All the better." Risk's next ball bounced an inch off the man's zipper.

Hands in the air, Romeo took one giant step backward. "Message received."

"Take it to heart."

"Total retention," Romeo assured him.

Jacy Grayson's jaw dropped. *A jealous Risk Kincaid?* Surely not. Yet the possessive sharpness of his stare was as potent as his touch. Her body responded, tingling as if stroked. She was so drawn into his eyes, she nearly jumped out of her skin when Stevie Cole bumped her shoulder.

"What's going on?" Stevie asked.

"One minute Romeo was teasing me, the next Risk was hitting golf balls off his groin."

"I saw him swing. Three balls aimed to scare, but not to slay."

Jacy nodded toward Romeo, now surrounded by golf groupies gushing sweet sympathy. "Romeo will survive."

"The man does bounce back fast," her friend agreed. She glanced down at the clipboard she held against her chest. "Risk, Zen, Aaron, and Romeo tee off at nine. I plan to tag along with the gallery. Care to join me?"

"Unless you're short a volunteer, I'd love to watch Risk golf," Jacy said.

"Presently, I have more volunteers than assignments," Stevie assured her. "Signs have been hammered into place and the concession stand's set up. Tournament marshals have stretched guard rope along the fairways and holes to separate the fans from the players. The only thing left is for the golfers to draw for their caddies."

The caddies would be selected from a group of teenage boys whose names had been placed in a glass bowl; they would be randomly drawn by the players. There were thirty-two golfers and two hundred boys vying to caddy. For those whose names weren't drawn, Stevie had arranged a barbecue following the tournament so the teenagers could rub shoulders with their heroes. No one would feel left out.

Within minutes, the country club president was gathering the golfers together at the first tee. Teenage boys stood three deep around the green, all hoping to walk the course with their favorite baseball player.

"Hey, Jacy." Tommy Mitchell wedged himself between Jacy and Stevie. "Have they drawn the names yet?"

Jacy smiled at Tommy, a lanky boy with sandy hair. "Is your name in the bowl?" she asked.

He shook his head. Disappointment was evident in his gray eyes. "I'm three days shy of turning thirteen."

Rules dictated that the caddies had to be teenagers. The golf bags were heavy. Stevie hadn't felt anyone younger than thirteen could endure the entire course.

Jacy stepped around Tommy and came up on the far side of Stevie. They exchanged whispers. Once given Stevie's approval, Jacy pressed through the crowd toward the first tee. Standing behind the roped-off area, she motioned to one of the marshals. "I need to speak with Risk Kincaid," she informed him.

"Now?" The marshal looked over his shoulder.

Risk had stepped before the country club president, ready to reach into the glass bowl and select the name of his caddy. A charged current of expectation circled the green.

"*Please* get his attention," Jacy pressed.

The marshal moved swiftly. Waving his arms over his head, he distracted Risk from the drawing long enough to point him in Jacy's direction.

Jacy crooked her finger.

Risk cocked his brow.

Her gaze pleaded with him to cross to her.

His eyes narrowed, dark and assessing.

"Give me a sec," Risk said to the club president. "I'm being paged. Zen can draw ahead of me. I'll be right back."

Risk crossed the green, ducked under the guard rope. Snagging Jacy's hand, he drew her through the crowd. Locating a dirt pathway that divided a tall hedge encircling the golf course, he pulled her behind the bougainvillea. They stood alone on a narrow sidewalk. The sun was hot on her face.

Releasing her hand, Risk jammed his hands in his pants pockets and said, "Talk fast, Jacy. The tournament's about to start."

Shielding her eyes with her hand against the sun, she looked up at him. "I have a way for you to set things right between us."

He glanced at his watch. "Thirty seconds, babe."

She drew in a deep breath, then quickly delivered her request.

Risk took it all in. "I'm back in your bed if I grant your request?"

She nodded. "You'll be hitting home runs off me the entire month of November."

His smile was slow and sexy. A total turn-on. "Love to round your bases."

On the sidewalk amid the rising heat of early morning, he took her hand and tugged her close. His arms encircled her waist; his palms flattened on her bottom. He rested his forehead against hers, so close, barely a flutter of an eyelash separated them. Then he claimed her mouth with a quick kiss.

A rustle of branches, and Psycho appeared on the narrow dirt path. He motioned to Risk. "Delay of game, old man. Move it or lose it."

Risk cast Psycho a dark look.

Jacy patted his chest. "Your public calls."

He released her. "If I don't get back on the green, Psycho will bat out of order. He's itching to tee off first."

Once back on the green, Risk made an announcement. "To honor his thirteenth birthday, Tommy Mitchell will caddy for me today."

Tommy hugged Jacy so hard, he stole her breath. He then jumped the protective rope that separated the gallery from the golfers, and strode toward Risk. The two shook hands, and in that instant, Jacy watched the excitement build in Tommy until she was sure he'd pop with pride and purpose.

Within minutes, the remaining caddies had been drawn and the golfers readied themselves for play. The crowd had grown expectantly silent.

"Cut the music," Jacy heard Risk pointedly say to Psycho, who was playing his driver like an air guitar.

Psycho strummed wildly, as if wrapping up a concert, then bowed to the fans, who applauded his actions.

Jacy shook her head. "Psycho's out to rattle Risk."

"Risk doesn't rattle," Stevie stated. "Once he gets into his rhythm, naked women could streak the course and he'd play around them."

Play was ready to start. Risk was ready to drive. Addressing the ball, he swung. Swung so powerfully Jacy was certain the wooden tee and grass would catch fire. The whistling whoosh, followed by the fans' appreciative *aah* gave evidence that the shot had gone long and in the middle of the fairway.

Zen and Aaron followed Risk, sending their golf balls within feet of Risk's own drive. Psycho came last. His preshot routine was a serious chat with the golf ball.

Jacy listened along with the crowd as Psycho held the white pockmarked ball at eye level and directed, "Don't go flying toward someone you recognize in the crowd. No rolling into divots or footprints. Stay out of the sand. No drinks of water at the lake. No hiding in tall grass. We're playing golf, not hide-and-seek.

"In case this is your first tournament," he continued, "you need to know holes begin at tees and end at greens, where the holes begin again. I want to get on a few of those greens today. Rush toward the metal cups identified by staffs and flags, and you'll get to play another day."

Stevie groaned. "Talking to a golf ball? The man's certifiable."

Jacy agreed. "He's trying to throw off everyone's rhythm."

"Aaron looks ticked," Stevie observed.

Jacy caught her cousin's narrowed-eyed, tight-lipped expression. "Care to place a bet as to which player wraps a golf club around Psycho's neck first?"

"My money's on Psycho getting buried in a sand trap."

When Psycho finally hit the ball, he did so without finesse. He whacked the living daylights out of it, as if he was swinging a baseball bat—not a golf club—and aiming for the stands. "Smasharoo," Psycho shouted.

Jacy's jaw dropped. "Total whiff. The divot traveled further than his ball."

Not the least bit embarrassed, Psycho called, "Do-over."

"One Mulligan," Risk said from behind Psycho. "You're not turning the tournament into a round of do-overs. We want to finish play without a flashlight."

Psycho hit his next ball hard, with no sense of direction. "*Fore!*" he yelled, warning fans his drive had gone wild. He squinted down the fairway. "Damn, I caught a palm. No rebound off coconut."

Positioning themselves on the leading edge of the gallery, Jacy and Stevie walked quickly to where the golfers would take their next shot. A par three, Risk, Aaron, and Zen managed to get on the green in two. Psycho, however, was all over the course.

From the base of the palm, his next shot landed on the cart path. "I'm entitled to a free drop," Psycho quoted the rule book.

"A *drop*, not a throw," Risk reminded him.

Jacy admired Risk's control. His temper remained

in check, his concentration honed on the course. The man was an all-around athlete. His swing remained fluid, effortless, perfectly timed. Even when Psycho used the grinding ball washer just as Risk was about to putt, Risk ignored the noise. He continued with his ritual of stooping, squatting, and circling the green of closely clipped grass, silently reading the break and evaluating the slopes and depressions.

When Risk was ready, caddy Tommy Mitchell lifted the metal stick with the fluttering yellow flag from the metal cup. Risk then hit the ball, his tap sure, smooth, successful. The ball landed with a *clink* in the cup.

Zen and Aaron also sank their putts without much effort. Psycho, unfortunately, ringed the cup four times before the ball finally went in. He then stabbed his putter in the air like a sword, as psyched as if he'd made a hole in one.

"Don't get creative on the score card," Jacy heard Risk say to Psycho. "It took you eight strokes, not three."

Psycho looked offended. "I'd never cheat."

Risk's raised brow had the younger power hitter retracting his words. "Yeah, well, maybe once. No more than twice."

Outside the protective ropes, throngs of fans trudged along with their favorite golfers. Risk's powerful drive, pin-point putting, and personality drew the largest crowd. The fans' excitement was infectious. Jacy found herself raised on tiptoe to get a better look at each shot Risk made.

"Zen's holding his own," Stevie noted as the short-

stop knocked his shot onto the green at the thirteenth hole. "Aaron, I'm afraid, has fallen to Psycho's needling."

Fallen hard, Jacy noted. Once under Aaron's skin,
Psycho rode the pitcher's last nerve, just for the hell
of it. He distracted Aaron's putting with the slow rip
of the Velcro on his golf glove, then hopped around
and shook out his pant leg as if invaded by ants. At
the fourteenth hole, he deliberately checked his
watch a dozen times, all the while yawning, forcing
Aaron to play faster. Faster meant less accurate.

It took Aaron six strokes to sink his putt. Psycho
shook his head in mock sympathy. "Left your ego on
that green."

Moments later, Aaron hooked the ball left off the
fairway on fifteen. The crowd moaned as it shot over
a hibiscus hedge and directly toward a condominium
complex.

"High fly to left field," Psycho called out.

Several bounces and the ball came to rest on the
indoor-outdoor carpeting at the foot of a sunbather.
Startled, the Swedish blonde sat up so quickly her
bikini top slipped, exposing tanned flesh to her nipples.

"I've a sudden taste for melons," Psycho muttered
loud enough for Jacy to hear him, which meant the
majority of the fans also heard him.

Several women blushed while the men grinned in
agreement.

Risk Kincaid read Psycho's mind. "Don't you dare
hit your next ball in that direction," he warned.

Psycho waggled his brows like Groucho Marx.
"I'm good at carpet putting."

Psycho wasn't, however, good at getting his ball out of the sand trap on seventeen. Risk shook his head as Psycho once again talked to the ball. "Get along, little doggie," he said, herding it clear of the lip.

The eighteenth and final hole showcased a table-top green in the middle of a lake, where fountains blasted. The manmade island could be reached only by a narrow bridge surrounded by spectator mounds. The placement of the pin was near the slope on the southern tip. A difficult putt at best.

With a strong drive and decent bounce on the fairway, Risk's golf ball landed near the bridge. There, he debated which club would take him over the water hazard.

"Three wood," his caddy, Tommy Mitchell, suggested.

Risk squinted against the sun. "You sure?"

"As sure as you were when you hit the home run in the World Series."

Risk took the young man's advice. He quickly became the only golfer to hit the green with one stroke. Among Zen, Aaron, and Psycho, more balls went into the lake than on the island green. Psycho threatened to put water wings on his next golf ball.

The lake diver who retrieved golf balls would make a fortune later that day.

While waiting for them to succeed, Risk surveyed the crowd, seeking Jacy Grayson. He knew she stood near. He could *feel* her presence. He found her less than a hundred feet away, pressed between Stevie and a queen palm on one of the spectator mounds. One hand shielded her eyes; the spray from the fountains misted her face. Their eyes locked for several heartbeats. The contact warmed him, driving a mating heat straight to his groin. His *Bad to the Bone* tattoo felt on fire. When she lifted her hand, her fingers were crossed. He knew she wished him luck.

He would sink the putt in two. Easily. He'd win the tournament for her. Tonight he'd give her both the trophy and his body. The trophy would go in her curio cabinet. His body in her bed.

The weekend had turned around nicely.

It took thirty minutes for the foursome to wrap up their round of golf. When Aaron sank the final putt, the crowd cheered as loudly as when the golfers had first started the day. As they crossed the bridge, the gallery broke through the protective ropes and mobbed the men. Under the direction of the marshals, the crowd was moved off the fairway so the next foursome could play through.

So much for getting to Jacy quickly, Risk thought as she faded into the crowd. For the next hour he shook hands, smiled, and signed autographs. He wrote his name on the bill of golf caps, on magazine photographs, and on baseball jerseys. When one young woman requested he write his name across her crocheted breast, he pointed her in Psycho's direction. Psycho obliged, printing both his name and team number in permanent marker.

"We need to get the players to the barbecue," Risk heard Stevie Cole call to one of the marshals. He took the initiative. Easing through the crowd, he motioned to Zen. Zen nodded and crossed to his golf cart.

"I'm riding back with Einstein," Psycho announced as he dove behind the wheel.

"Maybe you ought to let Zen drive," Risk called after him.

"Maybe you ought to start walking back to the clubhouse now, old man, so you arrive before dark," Psycho shot back.

Risk took a step forward, and Psycho hit the accelerator before Zen was completely settled on the seat of the cart. Zen banged his knee against the dash and Risk saw the shortstop wince. Psycho was a royal pain in the ass.

Releasing a breath, he watched the cart cut across the course instead of staying on the golf path. It barreled over the hillside. Fans scattered and the group of golfers still on the fairway looked ready to run for their lives.

"After eighteen holes with Psycho, you deserve a medal."

Lolita Lampeka seduced his senses. The warm vanilla scent was pure Jacy. He turned and watched her approach. Damn, she was beautiful. He took her hand and gave it a squeeze. She squeezed back. "I'll let you reward me tonight."

"You won't be disappointed."

As one, they dipped beneath the protective ropes that once again divided golfers from the gallery. It felt good to have Jacy by his side, Risk realized. It felt right. When a fan approached, she stopped when he stopped. She took one step back, allowing Risk to give his undivided attention to the person requesting an autograph. From his earliest Little League days, Risk had understood the importance of fans. In the majors, fans paid high prices to fill the seats at the ballpark. Without them, he had no game.

He appreciated Jacy's patience. Even when a group of cropped-topped, short-shorted brunettes surrounded him, she gave ground. Jacy looked more curious than jealous. Almost amused by the attention given him.

"Such a stud," she said when the groupies cleared and they could again proceed along the path.

"Think so?"

"Your fans see you as one."

"How do you see me, babe?"

"Haven't you had enough ego stroking for today?"

"Not by you."

"I'll stroke you tonight."

Tonight was good. They would come together for the burn. If commitment slipped between the sheets, Risk would propose. It was all in the timing. . . .

"Look, there's Stevie near the clubhouse entrance," Jacy noted. Stevie motioned them to join her.

"Slip in and take a breather before the barbecue," Stevie suggested. "We're waiting for the remaining golfers to gather."

The Shadow Woods clubhouse sprawled in shades of forest and olive green, offset by mauve; the decor was highlighted with black-and-white photographs of Frostproof in its infancy. A wall of glass captured the view of the golf course and the massive redwood deck where preparations were underway for the barbecue. Risk spotted Zen and Psycho seated within a cluster of brown leather chairs. Aaron and his fiancée, Natalie Llewellyn, stood off to the side. Neither looked overly sociable.

By the time Risk hit the bar and returned with two tonics and lime, the second group of golfers had appeared. Romeo and Chaser were among them.

"Jacy, sweetheart." Romeo draped an arm about her shoulders and planted a kiss on her cheek. "Am I safe from golf balls to the groin in the clubhouse?"

Jacy looked at Risk. Risk darted a dark look in Romeo's direction. "Eventually you'll have to step outside," he warned.

Romeo released Jacy. He then reached into the side pocket of his navy slacks and slipped out a money clip. He peeled off a fifty and dropped it on the glass coffee table next to a crystal vase arranged with red and yellow freesia. "Ante up, gentlemen. It's time to tally."

Time to tally meant adding up the phone numbers, pictures, and panties the golf groupies had slipped in the players' pockets during the tournament.

Psycho and Chaser added their money to the pile. As did two other Richmond players. Zen shook his head. Risk refused to play.

"Bet the old man's pockets are empty," Psycho said, openly challenging Risk.

Chaser grinned from behind dark aviator glasses. "Maybe one pity number from a woman over fifty."

Risk didn't take the bait.

Jamming his hands in the front pockets of his navy slacks, Romeo unfolded pieces of paper and business cards. He spread them out and quickly added them up. "Anyone collect more than thirty-six phone numbers?" he asked.

The count was on. Emptying his pockets, Chaser discovered twenty-five numbers and a purple thong. "Thong has to be worth ten numbers," he proclaimed.

"Rules state only five, unless it's red. Then you get ten," Psycho informed him as he turned his own pockets inside out. "Damn, only thirty-four. Thought I had you beat, Romeo."

The remaining Rogues players also fell short of Romeo's tally.

The third baseman's gaze shifted to Jacy. "I'm the man," he said.

"I need all you men outside," Stevie announced, coming up behind them. "It's time for the trophy presentation."

The Bat Pack strutted off, leaving Jacy, Risk, and Zen momentarily alone. Giving in to female curiosity, Jacy surveyed Risk's pockets. Until that moment, she hadn't realized how much they bulged. The man had a pocketful of phone numbers. "Time to tally, old man."

He shook his head. "I don't play those games anymore."

"Just a peek," she persisted.

"There's nothing worth seeing. Let it go, babe."

She wasn't about to "let it go."

He took a deep breath as she delved into his pockets and her fingers brushed more than paper. "Not so deep." He flattened his hand over her own, controlling her search.

"A phone book of numbers," she said as she laid

out her findings. "As well as a *red* thong and six condoms inscribed with *Batter Up* in candy-apple red lipstick. There's a small photograph clipped to the foil packets. A blonde with lots of cleavage." She flipped over the picture. "She's Mandy from Miami. She loves the beach and having sex on the sand. She cooks naked in the kitchen. Reads erotica. She's listed her cell and home numbers along with her e-mail address: playsball@inanypark.com."

Zen peered over Jacy's shoulder. "Major tally. Old man's got game."

"As do you, Einstein," Risk returned. "How many panties?"

Zen patted his pocket. "A pair or two."

Jacy sighed inwardly. She knew the Bat Pack played the field. The young power hitters scored nightly. She wondered how often Risk indulged in the softer sex. Judging by the phone numbers, he had his choice of women. Women who stuffed their panties in his pockets and carried condoms. Groupies like Mandy and her double D's.

She didn't feel insecure. Just more aware of how accessible women were to Risk. Day or night. At least she had him for the month of November. She planned to make the most of the days ahead.

"The caddies are gathered on the deck," Stevie called to them from across the room. "The president of Shadow Woods will present the trophies; then we eat."

"What about the phone numbers and photograph?" Jacy hesitantly asked Risk. "The condoms?"

Risk handed them to Zen. "Give them to Romeo."

As they walked toward the door, Risk nudge Jacy and teased, "Why didn't you slip your thong in my pocket?"

"I'm not wearing panties."

That stopped him in his tracks. Once outside, he took Jacy's hand and drew her through the crowd as he searched out Psycho. He found the young power hitter perched on the railing of the redwood deck, scarfing down a hot dog. Risk frowned. "It's not time to eat."

"It is if you're hungry." Psycho stuffed the remainder of the bun in his mouth.

"How many have you eaten?"

Psycho chewed and swallowed. "Three."

"Show some manners. Hold off on the fourth." Risk's tone brooked no argument.

Psycho wiped his mouth with the back of his hand. "Yes, mother."

Jacy stood quietly as Risk asked the most important question of the tournament. "Did you turn in our scorecard?"

"Damn." He slapped his thigh with his palm. "Thought Aaron had that covered."

"You kept score. It was your responsibility—"

"Gotcha." Psycho grinned. Incorrigible as ever. "One of the marshals found me, actually. He took the card for the final tally."

"The card, correct or creative?"

Psycho didn't miss a beat. "Correct for you, Zen, and Aaron. Creative for me."

Risk's gaze held Psycho's. "You shot an eighty-seven."

Psycho scratched his head. "You sure? Thought it was a seventy-eight."

Even with Psycho hedging his score, Risk took home the trophy. Jacy stood back, deep within the crowd and watched as he accepted the honor. Risk thanked Tommy Mitchell for his caddie expertise on the course. Risk's appreciation raised Tommy's status at the country club. The young man would be in demand by all the local golfers. Big tips were in his future.

As the presentation continued, Zen was awarded second place, Chaser third, and Romeo and Psycho tied for fourth. Only one trophy was awarded for fourth. Psycho snatched it from Romeo, then held the trophy over his head and did a victory dance. The caddies jumped back, out of his way.

"The man's insane," Risk muttered once he'd returned to Jacy's side.

"He walks a fine line," Jacy agreed. "Beyond the craziness, I think he's a little lost."

"Lost?" Risk spiked a brow.

"The entire Bat Pack has gotten too much too fast," she said slowly. "They're rich and get bored easily. Fans and fame are a dangerous mix. Psycho will take a hard fall before he picks himself up and sees life beyond the women and the thrills."

"As long as he doesn't take that fall during baseball season." Risk cast a glance at Psycho, who was circling the brick barbecue pit, once again eyeing the hot dogs and hamburgers. "He doesn't give a damn about much beyond baseball. He's a hell of a right fielder. The team needs him."

Their conversation was cut short as the country club president continued his speech, thanking the local volunteers and businesses for their support of the golf tournament. Since nearly every business in Frostproof stood behind the charity event, the list was long. Applause followed each name read, and time seemed to stand still.

Her mind wandering, Jacy scanned the crowd. Off to her left, she caught Natalie Llewellyn in a fashionable blue pantsuit staring openly, almost *hungrily*, at Zen Driscoll. Which seemed highly inappropriate with Aaron by her side. The twosome didn't at all appear the happy, newly engaged couple.

They seemed stiff together. Totally ill at ease.

Throughout the speech, Natalie's eyes returned to Zen. Aaron's own gaze didn't miss her interest in the shortstop. His expression tightened, his frown cutting the corners of his mouth.

Then there was Stevie, casting glances at Aaron. Long, meaningful glances that laid her heart bare. To complete the circle, Zen eyed Stevie with utmost concern and something . . . deeper. The crowd shifted, blocking her view of Zen before Jacy could determine his feelings.

Jacy blinked. So many looks! Some disguised. Others open. All penetrating. When she caught sight of Risk's high school sweetheart sneaking onto the redwood deck, Jacy's stomach knotted as Sherry Sherman of the big smile and bigger breasts squeezed through the crowd. Obviously, she was seeking out Risk.

The look in Sherry's eyes indicated her willingness and availability, her desire to catch up on old times. She wanted a hot, juicy foot long.

Not necessarily a hot dog.

CHAPTER 6

The two hot dogs Jacy Grayson had forced down at the barbecue did not agree with her. Her stomach hurt, as did her heart. Standing beneath a white-hot sun in center field, she adjusted her scarlet straw hat with the white satin band and big red rose. Stylish, yet more appropriate for Kentucky Derby fashion than a softball game, she'd chosen the hat for its broad brim. It kept the sun out of her eyes.

Shifting her stance, she slapped her baseball glove against her thigh. She wished she could forget what had happened at the barbecue.

Uninvited, yet undaunted, Sherry Sherman had cornered Risk on the redwood deck and discussed the auction. She'd paid big bucks for the man and wanted a second night on the town.

The moment had been awkward. Risk had turned to Jacy, then informed Sherry he had other plans. Sherry grew insistent. Her voice had sharpened, risen, and her features had twisted, her color high.

Risk had tried to pacify her with brunch on Sunday. Sherry wanted Saturday night.

Jacy only wanted to get away from the woman.

The louder Sherry raised her voice, the more people looked their way. Bowing out gracefully, Jacy faded into the crowd. She kept right on walking, even when Risk called her back. She'd woven through the caddies until she'd bumped into Romeo. Risk's gaze had burned a hole in her back when she'd stopped to chat with the third baseman. When Romeo covered his zipper with his hand, Jacy knew he was protecting his boys from Risk's cutting stare.

After shared hot dogs and raspberry lemonade, Romeo had offered her a ride to the high school diamond. She'd accepted. Stevie had assumed Jacy would leave with Risk, and had departed with Zen Driscoll. Risk, however, remained with Sherry. He'd stood Jacy up at the stadium the previous night. She wouldn't be left behind again today.

Risk had arrived at the ball field on the bumper of Psycho's Dodge Ram. Risk's expression was tight, his eyes narrowed, as Romeo clutched her waist and lifted her from the cab.

Risk had approached her then, his lip curled. "Bat Packing?" he'd asked.

She saw no reason for him to be riled. "A ride is a ride."

"Did you sit on Romeo's lap?"

"That was an option. However, I sardine-squeezed between him and Chaser."

"You should have waited for me."

Jacy glanced at his Lotus. Sherry Sherman was easing from the low-slung car. "Definitely room for three," she said sarcastically.

"Wait for me after the game," he insisted.

"Doubt there will be any more room going than there was coming." She'd headed toward the dugout then, joining the hometown team, slipped her baseball jersey over her top and laced on a pair of metallic-silver high-tops with tangerine laces.

"Play ball!" The umpire now shouted to start the softball game. Jacy jumped and once again focused on the ballpark. On the cheers and applause of the fans. On Risk Kincaid headed to bat. On Sherry Sherman, who stood behind the fence of the players' dugout and shook her pom-poms for old time's sake. All very juvenile to Jacy's way of thinking.

She fanned her face with her glove, then proceeded to unbutton the top two buttons on her baseball jersey, white with a gold stripe, and the inscription *Frostproof's Finest* across the back. It was damn hot in the outfield. No breeze, just beating sunshine. She wiped her brow with the back of her hand.

As the crowd looked on, Stevie pitched the first ball. Risk didn't hesitate. He started the tournament the exact same way he'd ended the World Series. With a ball flying long and strong in Jacy's direction. The ball soared over her head and beyond the outfield fence. She watched it fly. So high, it could have knocked a bird out of the sky.

Fortunately for her, a group of boys chased after the softball. She wasn't about to retrieve it from the dense bushes that bordered the fence. She didn't need the scratches or the off chance of a snake. Let the boys have their souvenir.

Moving like an action hero, Risk jogged around the bases. Smooth and fluid. Incredibly handsome. Magnificently fit. Utterly irresistible. He had the crowd on its feet, clapping and stomping the bleachers. Sherry Sherman crossed to home plate and rewarded Risk's power hit with a kiss, full on the lips. The resounding smack could be heard all the way in the outfield.

Jacy clenched her jaw. Jealousy was beneath her. She refused to get caught up in Sherry and Risk and their high school reunion.

Play continued until Stevie called, "Third out, we're up to bat." Jacy trotted toward the dugout.

She passed Risk as he headed to center field. He wore his Richmond Rogues jersey, red with a blue stripe, and a pair of worn jeans. He snagged her upper arm and brought her to a halt.

Beneath the bill of his baseball cap, his gaze bored into her. "You're reading more into the Sherry Sherman situation than is warranted."

She scrunched up her nose. "What's warranted?"

"Sherry is coming on strong. She's flirting—"

"And kissing you."

"—and it means nothing to me."

"You're telling me this because . . . ?"

"I felt you needed to know. I don't want you upset."

"To be upset, I'd have to be jealous. And I'm not," she lied through her teeth. "At least she's not humping your thigh."

"Not funny, Jacy."

"I'll laugh if I want."

She would have too, had Romeo not called to her. "Jacy, sweetheart, you're holding up the game. It's your turn at bat."

She forced a smile, waved, and signaled she'd heard him. "Be right there."

Risk ground his teeth. "Stop flirting with Romeo."

"A wave is not flirting."

"The way you wave, it's an invitation for sex."

Jacy stood her ground. "I find him nice and fun and—"

"He'll break your heart."

"Maybe he'll fall in love."

Risk shook his head, released her arm and jogged toward center field.

Jacy scuffed her feet all the way to the dugout. The only person capable of hurting her was Risk Kincaid. She'd foolishly alienated him with her smart mouth.

"Let me help you select a bat." Romeo left third base to assist her.

"You're on the opposing team," Jacy reminded him.

Romeo shrugged and selected a bat. "Should be light enough."

He snugged up behind her, positioning her hands on the bat, giving her a quick lesson in swinging. His body was warm against hers, sending heat along her spine; a warmth that contrasted greatly with Risk Kincaid's own heat. Risk turned her on. Romeo smothered her. She wiggled free and approached home plate. She turned to face the pitcher.

Aaron Grayson stood on the mound, his gaze dark, his jaw taut. Jacy sensed his anger; an anger that had nothing to do with the softball game, but everything to do with Natalie's interest in Zen Driscoll. His fiancée openly tracked the shortstop. Zen wasn't fazed. His gaze continually cut to Stevie Cole as she organized her team and rattled off the rules.

Facing Aaron now, Jacy released a breath. She wasn't athletic and didn't stand much chance of hitting the ball. She had no chance whatsoever of making it to first base if she did.

"Hit the ball, Jacy!" Stevie called from the dugout. "Knock it out of the park." Stevie had more faith in her ability than Jacy herself.

Jacy took a practice swing, glanced over her shoulder at Chaser, the catcher for the Rogues. She licked her lips and asked, "How's my swing?"

"Like you work in a coffee shop."

Great. She swung wildly at the first pitch. "*Strike one!*" The umpire yelled so loudly, Jacy jumped a foot.

Romeo left third and jogged toward her. "Aaron's pitching high. Swing at boob level," he whispered in her ear before returning to his base.

Boob level. Jacy took his advice and popped a fly ball to third. Romeo feigned sun in his eyes and miscalculated his catch. Jacy took off for first. She ran so fast she kicked up dust. The crowd cheered her on.

"Throw the friggin' ball," the first baseman shouted to Romeo.

Romeo collected himself. Tossed the ball underhand toward first, allowing Jacy enough time to touch the base. She jumped up and down on the bag. In her excitement, she blew Romeo a kiss.

The kiss was witnessed by the entire park. Including Risk Kincaid. He had a sudden need to pound Romeo into the ground.

He was such a fool. He'd allowed Sherry Sherman to step on Jacy's toes. Sherry now assumed their past could be recaptured in an afternoon. She was dead wrong. The only woman Risk wanted in his life was Jacy Grayson. He needed to make amends before Romeo succeeded in charming her any further.

Two local ringers followed Jacy: the high school baseball coach and his assistant. They both got on base. Jacy now stood on third. Where Romeo crowded her.

Risk swore Romeo rubbed himself against her. Sniffed her hair.

Stevie batted next. She slammed the ball past Zen Driscoll. Risk was certain that if Zen had stretched an extra inch, Stevie would have been out. The second the ball passed Zen, Jacy took off for home. She looked damn fine in her baseball jersey, Bermudas, and straw hat. Her blond hair was wild about her face. Her bright tangerine shoelaces flapped, untied. She'd be tripping over herself if she wasn't careful. Risk didn't want her to fall.

Jacy scored the first run for Frostproof's Finest. Two additional runs followed before the inning came to an end.

This time when Risk passed Jacy in the outfield, he pointed toward her high-tops. "Tie them," he told her.

She tied the laces in double bows.

The innings passed quickly. By the ninth, Frost-proof's Finest and the major leaguers had a tie score. Risk found himself at bat at the bottom of the ninth, with two outs. The exact position he'd faced in the World Series. Yet with a lot less pressure.

"Home run, Kincaid!" the crowd chanted.

Dozens of young boys lined the fence, waiting for their chance to snag the winning ball. He looked at Jacy Grayson. His woman was not an athlete. Sunburned, shoulders slumped, she'd wilted in the heat. She'd never forgive him if he slammed a home run over her head.

Stevie's first pitch was high. Her second low. A little too low for Risk's liking, yet he swung. He knew the second he connected, he'd pulled the ball. Instead of flying right, the moon shot popped straight for center field.

Straight toward Jacy.

Risk took off for first, slowing as he rounded the base, watching as Jacy caught her second wind. The flash of her shoelaces flying out behind her gave him pause. She'd retied those laces every inning, yet the bows continually loosened.

He hit second just as she tripped. She was suddenly as airborne as the softball. She seemed to fall in slow motion. She went down with her arms outstretched, her gaze never leaving the fly ball. Miracle of all miracles, his moon shot dropped into her mitt.

Risk was out.

The explosion of applause echoed for miles. The hometown sweetheart had taken down the major leaguer. Risk's stomach clenched as Jacy lay sprawled, face down on the grass. Her straw hat was crushed beneath her hip. Not a muscle moved.

Damn shoelaces!

He cut across the field at an all-out run. Romeo, Psycho, and Aaron were on his heels, with Stevie coming up fast behind them.

"Jacy?" He dropped down on one knee, gently touched her shoulder. Her eyes were closed, her breathing shallow. Blood trickled from a cut on her cheek.

"Careful turning her over," Stevie warned.

"I've got her legs." Aaron assisted Risk in getting Jacy onto her side.

Risk brushed back her hair. The cut on her cheekbone proved minor, more grass burn than scrape. "Jacy, open your eyes, babe."

She blinked, spat grass and gasped for air. "You're out."

Risk exhaled, then drew her close.

Jacy winced. "My ribs. My ankle."

Aaron studied Jacy's ankle, already blue and swollen to twice its size. "Could be broken."

"Do we need an ambulance?" Stevie asked, pulling her cell phone out.

Jacy shook her head. "Just an emergency room."

With utmost care, Risk lifted Jacy against his chest, then stood. He carried her across the baseball diamond to his Lotus. He settled her as comfortably as possible on the leather seat, but a soft moan escaped as her head dropped onto her chest. Her left wrist hung limply. Her right arm was wrapped over her rib cage, holding in the pain. Jacy was in a lot more pain than she let on.

"Risk, how will I get home?" Sherry Sherman's whine cut through the crowd that had gathered around his Lotus. Concern for Jacy was evident in all eyes.

Risk didn't have the time or inclination to deal with Sherry. Spotting Psycho amid the group, Risk hesitated, then motioned him forward. "See that Sherry has a ride."

Psycho took a visual tour of the woman's body, taking in jutting breasts and hips straining beneath a too-short sundress. A slow grin split his face. "Sure, pops."

Risk didn't need to hear more. Sherry liked edgy men, and Psycho always walked the edge. The power hitter would thrill and excite her, make Sherry feel eighteen once again.

Fifteen minutes later, Risk pulled into the Emergency Loop. He'd phoned ahead to request that Jacy be met at the entrance. Two nurses assisted her into a wheelchair and rolled her away to be x-rayed. The doctor's evaluation would follow.

Time ticked slowly. Too damn slowly. He sat patiently in the waiting room for twenty long minutes, counting every fish in the fifty-gallon aquarium. Flipping through several magazines. Catching headline news on CNN.

He could sit still no longer. On his feet, he pushed through the swinging doors. The smells of the antiseptic and illness assailed him. A hospital volunteer seated near the admitting desk requested he return to the waiting room. No way in hell.

"Richard Kincaid, this is a restricted area."

Frostproof was a small town. The use of given name was a clear-cut sign the person blocking his path had known him since he was in diapers. And she had. "Mrs. Decker," he acknowledged the RN with the gray hair, stern expression, and a metal bedpan in her hand. "I'm looking for Jacy Grayson."

"Family only beyond this point."

His jaw tightened. "Her parents live in Savannah. I'm as close as family."

"I can't allow you—"

Risk was beyond pleasantries. He was worried about Jacy. Needed to see her. Now. "Let me go in, Mrs. Decker. Even for a minute. Please."

"She's getting x-rays," The nurse explained. Drawing back a curtain, she pointed toward an empty cubicle. "There's a chair against the wall. Sit and be still."

He was too antsy to sit. So he paced the white tile floor. Paced until the transporter returned Jacy to her cubicle. She lay on a padded table in her hospital gown, a sheet covering her legs. She looked pale and in pain.

She forced a smile. "You here to play doctor?"

He crossed to her, took her hand, ran his thumb over her wrist. He could feel the slight kick in her pulse. He still affected her, even while she was laid low. "I'm here to apologize for hitting a fly ball to center field. I caused your fall."

"I tripped over my shoelaces."

"I'm stripping your high-tops of those damn laces."

She squeezed his hand. "I'm not very coordinated. If not the shoelaces, I would have tripped over a blade of grass."

"You're the MVP, babe, for catching the ball."

"No talent involved. The softball found my mitt." She sucked in a breath, her expression grim. "Hurts to talk. My ribs feel like broken toothpicks."

"Cracked ribs and a broken ankle," the doctor said as he entered her cubicle, a stethoscope around his neck and several x-rays in hand. "Not much I can do for your ribs. Once the pain goes away, they'll heal on their own." He tapped her bare foot with his finger. "We'll put a cast on your ankle."

Jacy swallowed hard. "My coffee shop. My T-ball team. My—"

The doctor shook his head. "Bed rest." He looked to Risk. "You'll keep an eye on her."

Risk nodded. "She'll follow your orders. To the letter."

He caught Jacy's scowl, which said he was a traitor. *Bed rest*. How lucky could a man get? He would have her alone, in bed, where he could wait on her hand and foot. Show her how much she meant to him.

If all turned out well, he might even frame her shoelaces.

While Jacy had her ankle set, Risk stood close by. He signed autographs for the nurses and technicians. Even the doctor requested his signature across a prescription pad for his son.

When Nurse Decker tried to shoo him out so Jacy could dress, he ignored her and stuck by Jacy's side. He'd helped her out of her clothes dozens of times.

Seen her deliciously naked. Today he'd help her put them on.

It was slow going. She leaned on him, her soft body now stiff and sore from the cracked ribs. Bending and twisting was out of the question, so he pocketed her bra and panties. Which left her in the loose-fitting baseball jersey and floral Bermudas. Her plaster walking cast was hot pink.

Nurse Decker returned with a wheelchair and instructions for Jacy's medication. "Stay off your feet. Elevate your foot. Take the Lortab as prescribed. Early next week, call the doctor's office for a follow-up appointment in about six weeks."

"Will do," Risk answered for Jacy. Before they left the hospital, he insisted she take one of her pills to ease the pain.

The pill took effect quickly. Jacy grew exceptionally quiet on the ride to her house. She dozed off, only to waken with a start, gasping and clutching her ribs. Risk hurt for her. He'd broken his ribs as a kid. He was familiar with the acute ache that stole her breath.

Once home, he lifted her from the Lotus and carried her inside. "Put me down, I'm fine," Jacy said, her cheek pressed to his chest.

Fine, his ass. She was limp and tired and couldn't stand on her own two feet. He crossed the living room and entered her bedroom. He blinked against the colorful raspberry and turquoise walls decorated with tropical paintings. The waterbed was sheeted in raspberry satin.

"Taking me to bed, Kincaid?" Jacy's lips curved

slightly as he propped her near the headboard. She swayed a bit, but kept her balance.

"Not taking, but tucking you into bed," he stated as he turned to her dresser and opened the top drawer. A wide, deep drawer displaying her collection of underwear, color-coordinated to match a sixty-four-count box of crayons.

Toward the back, a lump curved beneath a champagne satin tanga. Curious, he lifted the lacy edge. His knuckles brushed his World Series baseball. He ran his fingertips over the grass-streaked, slightly dented ball. Lucky baseball, he thought, as he covered it with lace. The ball would be far happier in her panty drawer than encased in glass on his trophy shelf.

He found an oversized man's T-shirt folded neatly beside a magenta bra. One of his Rogues shirts, so worn and faded his number eight looked more like a three.

"I need to get you out of your clothes," he said, coming up behind her.

Jacy's sigh was as much pleasure as pain. "Naked is good."

The pill had definitely relaxed her. Standing before her now, Risk slowly unbuttoned her baseball jersey. Her eyelids fluttered, and without conscious thought, her body leaned into his hands. His knuckles grazed her nipples as his thumbs curved between her breasts. Her skin flushed and her body heated.

Warmth slipped beneath his skin. His fingertips now felt hot and itchy with the need to touch her. *Christ, Kincaid, get a grip*, he mentally chided himself. *Jacy has cracked ribs and a broken ankle, and you're wanting to jump her bones.*

Teeth clenched, he slipped off her jersey, then went for the zipper on her Bermudas. She pressed her pelvis against his palm. Sexual heat radiated through her shorts. His sex pressed painfully tight against his button fly. He was going to hell for lusting after a hurt and helpless woman.

"Stand still, Jacy." His words came out low and husky as he unzipped and tugged down her shorts.

Her flat stomach, curvy hips, and sweet length of leg were now bare to him. Her body was toned, but not athletically tight. He loved her softness, her femininity.

She shifted, lifted her cast to kick aside her shorts, and nearly took a header onto the waterbed. Risk grabbed her hip and she giggled. He looked up, found her watching him. So sexy and silly, he couldn't help smiling. Her eyes were slightly dilated, a *very* happy expression on her face.

The pain pills were definitely working. Needing to get her into bed, he gently pulled the T-shirt over her head. The shirt hung on her shoulders and reached nearly to her knees. At least she was covered.

Once she was on the waterbed, he propped two pillows behind her head and one under her walking cast. The motion of the bed had her closing her eyes with a soft sigh. Sleep was what she needed most. He covered her with a bright orange comforter, then straightened and stretched.

The scent of sunshine and sweat and a trace of

Jacy's Lolita Lampeka lingered on his skin. He needed a shower. Afterward, he'd make a few phone calls. Stevie being first on his list. Stevie would be disappointed that neither he nor Jacy would be able to attend the country club dance that evening. But she'd understand. Risk's responsibilities lay with his woman. Holding her while she slept.

One step toward the door, and Jacy's hoarse whisper called him back. "Don't leave me."

The shower and calls could wait. Stripping off his baseball jersey and jeans, he climbed onto the waterbed, dipped beneath the satin cover. The silken slide of the sheets was slippery against his skin. "I'm here, babe."

She snuggled as close to him as she could get. Her head rested on his shoulder, her left hand splayed on his thigh. "Thanks for taking such good care of me."

He'd take care of her for the rest of his life if she'd let him. Yet, he kept things light. "Friends take care of each other."

She yawned, her words slightly slurred. "Friendship and sex. Always there when I need you."

He stroked her cheek. "I need you too, babe."

"I need you more."

Don't bet on it. He needed her as badly as the air he breathed. He kissed her brow, the scratch on her cheek. "Go to sleep, Jacy."

She tilted her chin, met his lips in a soft kiss. "Not before I tell you . . . important." She yawned again, deeper this time, and her body went totally lax.

She was dead to the world. Leaving him hanging

on her words or confession or whatever the hell she'd been about to tell him. He tugged the comforter to her chin and kissed her brow a second time. Held her as closely as he dared. He was filled with a deep need to make her all better.

CHAPTER 7

A dateless Stevie Cole stood at the edge of the dance floor, sipping champagne. A wallflower in an ice-blue cocktail dress. It was tea length and a little snug. She'd forfeited all formfitting undergarments in favor of breathing. She sucked in her stomach, attempting to look a size smaller, and failed miserably.

Purchased to make her calves look trim and tight, her matching heels pinched her toes and rubbed a blister on her heel. She was a tennis shoe person at heart. She knew she should have stuck with flats.

All around her the room was filled with soft lighting and light rock. Songs that reflected her love for Aaron. Sadness settled in her soul. When she'd booked the band, she'd pictured herself and Aaron laughing, reminiscing, and dancing to each tune. It wasn't going to happen. The man was engaged.

She hugged the far wall and maintained her smile as a steady stream of congratulations flowed her way. The charity weekend was proving a tremendous success. Close to a half million dollars had been raised.

In a private donation, Risk Kincaid had written a check for a hundred grand. She understood his support of parks and recreation. He valued his roots. Zen Driscoll's additional fifty thousand had both surprised and mystified her. His generosity could not be chalked up to hometown spirit. He needed to be thanked.

She looked across the room, caught a glimpse of Aaron and Natalie as they mingled with local residents and out-of-state fans. Aaron appeared to be enjoying himself. Lots of smiles and handshakes. Pats on the back. Natalie, however, looked bored to tears. If she yawned one more time, she'd put herself to sleep.

A light touch on her elbow signaled Zen's arrival. "Great party." His gaze skimmed her body, then cut away when her nipples tightened in greeting. "Nice dress."

Stevie silently groaned. Her body welcomed this man, yet her heart beat for Aaron. She slowly took Zen in, from his navy suit and crisp white shirt, to his plum-and-blue striped tie. His hair was brushed off his face. No glasses tonight. His brown eyes were incredible. Warm and dark and studying her closely. "You clean up nicely," she finally managed.

"One of Risk's suits," he confessed. "The suit he would have worn had he made an appearance."

"Jacy needs him more."

"They're quite a pair." He grew thoughtful. "I knew Risk flew to Frostproof on occasion, but never realized the reason behind his visits. After meeting Jacy, I understand his frequent flyer miles."

"They're amazing together." Soft strains of "Endless Love" sifted through the crowd. It was a slow-dance song that had couples whispering in each other's ears, brushing discreet kisses to parted lips. Stevie's heart squeezed. The words echoed Aaron's pledge of love. He'd sworn he couldn't live without her. The man had lied.

Zen cut her a glance. "Thinking of Aaron?"

She sighed. "The music draws a lot of memories."

"You need new memories to replace the old," he said with conviction. "Pretend you're having a good time, and maybe you will. Dance with me, Stevie?" It was more statement than question.

She hesitated. "What about your hamstring?"

"It's pulled, not paralyzed. I can shuffle around the floor."

They set their empty champagne glasses on the corner of the bar, after which Zen laced his fingers with hers and drew her onto the dance floor. Surrounded by a crowd of other dancers, he pulled her close. Not uncomfortably close, but close enough for her to feel the man beneath the suit.

It had been years since she'd been held by a man other than Aaron. Yet, Stevie felt Zen's pull. The contact felt good. Maybe even a little too pleasurable.

As his arms tightened about her, her body sought a natural fit against his. Her cheek pressed his shoulder. Her nipples poked his dress shirt. Pretend or not, she had no control over her body where this man was concerned. He unnerved her to the point that she teetered on her heels, one heel catching the leather instep on his dress shoe.

Zen winced and set her away from him. "Take them off."

Stevie blinked. "Dance in my stocking feet?"

"As a precautionary measure."

She gripped his arm, bent, and slipped off her shoes. Zen took them from her, and stuffed them in his suit coat. The heels bulged out his pockets.

Once she was in his arms again, they swayed to the music. The man had some nice moves. She followed him easily. A turn. A dip. An exchange of smiles. Without her heels, Stevie rested her cheek against his chest. She could hear his heartbeat. Rhythmic. Strong. She tried to relax, tried to think beyond Aaron Grayson.

Zen made it easy for her. "Who was nicknamed the Mustache Gang?" his voice murmured near her ear, warm and deep and a bit husky.

This she could handle. "Oakland A's. Owner Charles Finley paid his players to grow mustaches during the 1970s."

He brushed his chin against her temple and nodded approvingly. His male heat sifted into her, momentarily soothing her wounded pride. Aaron's image blurred with his next question, "Who was called the Big Train?"

She tilted her head and met his gaze. His expression was so warm and encouraging she couldn't look away. "William—no, Walter Johnson," she quickly corrected. She'd been focusing on Zen's mouth and not on her answer.

The man had sexy lips. Strong and masculine with a hint of softness. A mouth no more than a hairbreadth from her own. "Who hit sixty-one homers in '61?"

Stevie couldn't think straight. She nearly jumped out of her skin when he touched his mouth to hers for a single heartbeat to whisper, "Roger Maris."

However brief, his kiss jarred her. His breath was warm. His taste rich with champagne. Her interest spiked, along with her desire. In that instant, she saw beyond the intelligent, smartly dressed man; felt the intimate pull of his male animal.

A maleness so tangible, it touched her deeply.

Her stomach fluttered and her skin flushed, rosy and hot. Zen sparked an appeal she couldn't deny.

It was utterly terrifying.

Stevie's sexual shiver struck Zen Driscoll like a lit match. He'd felt their connection. The twist of attraction that sparked her nipples to hot little darts left him too stiff to dance.

When the slow song ended, he set her from him, relieved that the band announced a short break. "Did you reach your goal for the recreation center?" he asked, making conversation.

"We hit our mark," she responded. "Your private donation was very much appreciated."

"My absolute pleasure."

"*Pleasure?* One of my favorite words," announced Natalie Llewellyn as she entered Zen's space. She stood so close that the pointed toe of her stilettos jabbed his black dress shoes. Sheathed in strapless black satin, her hair in a tight French twist, she breathed money and confidence.

Aaron, Zen noted, appeared grim. Eyes narrowed, he stood stiffly behind her, visibly ill at ease.

"Not physical pleasure," Zen informed Natalie. "Financial satisfaction. Donating to a worthy cause."

Natalie rolled her eyes. "We're still focused on the kiddie playground?"

Stevie took the slam with grace. "It's more than a playground," she explained. "Construction will include a brand new recreation center, swimming pool, and tennis courts."

"The ceiling was falling in on the old building," Aaron added. "The swimming pool had started leaking like a sieve."

Natalie turned to Aaron. "You pulled off this charity event. Pat yourself on the back."

Aaron shook his head. "It was never just me. The weekend would have bombed without Stevie. She took up the reins, organized, did the leg work."

Natalie finally acknowledged Stevie. Zen watched her look Stevie over with a critical eye. Natalie's smile didn't reach her eyes. Barely tipped her lips. "I'm Natalie. You must be Stevie, one of Aaron's old friends."

Zen sensed Stevie's insecurities. She was feeling fat and outclassed as she shook Natalie's hand. A long-fingered, lily-white hand that Zen knew felt as soft as hand cream compared to Stevie's own athletically callused palm.

"Aaron and I have a history," Stevie finally managed.

Natalie sniffed. "A short history, from what I understand. Though he may appreciate your setting the stage, the major league players supplied the weekend draw." She shot Aaron a warning look. "Don't involve yourself further."

"Aaron grew up in Frostproof," Zen said, entering the conversation. "From what I understand, local sports fans gather at the VFW to watch the Tampa Bay games each spring. The town backs its hometown boy."

Stevie drew in a breath. "I'd hoped Aaron would return to cut the ribbon on the new recreation facility."

Natalie waved off Stevie's suggestion. "Let Risk Kincaid do the honor. He's kept his small-town mentality."

Zen looked at Aaron. He felt sorry for the man who had ditched his past to fit into this woman's future. If Aaron didn't know it now, he'd soon learn that Natalie Llewellyn was an utter and complete bitch.

A light tug on the sleeve on his sport jacket gained his attention. "I want to dance," Natalie said as the band came back on stage.

Zen held back. "I was about to dance with Stevie."

Inserting herself between Zen and Stevie, Natalie insisted, "Surely she won't mind if I steal you for a minute or two. For old time's sake." She nudged Stevie closer to Aaron. "Feel free to talk high school."

Natalie would cause a scene if Zen didn't oblige. "Aaron?" Zen looked at the man for permission to dance with his fiancée.

"As if I have a say," Aaron returned, his voice sharp, his expression granite hard.

Once on the dance floor, Natalie pressed herself

against Zen's body, suggestively close. She ran a finger down his cheek before tucking her left hand behind his neck. There, she stroked beneath his shirt collar. Ran her thumb over his Adam's apple.

"Nice strong neck," she whispered, her breath hot against his throat. "Sexy ears." A flash of white teeth, and she bit his lobe. Hard.

Zen jerked back. "Do that again, and I'll walk off the dance floor."

Natalie tugged on his tie. "I've missed you, Zen."

He looked down his nose at her. "So much so, you got engaged to Aaron."

She pouted. "You dumped me. I wanted to hurt you."

"No broken heart here."

She poked him in the chest. "We had good times."

"That's a matter of opinion."

She tilted her head. "What about Saint Kitts?"

He remembered the strip of Caribbean beach where swimsuits were optional. Natalie had shed her bikini, then stolen Zen's towel and swim trunks from his gym bag. Miles from nowhere, she'd hidden the car keys, forcing him to choose between lying on the sand in his T-shirt and jeans or floating on a double-sized air mattress offshore. He'd chosen to ride the waves. Naked.

"Not a fun day," he returned. "I got sunburned, then peeled in places never meant to see the sun."

"How about Lucerne?" One corner of her mouth curved slightly.

She'd tried to mount him on a ski lift in Switzerland. The lift had rocked, and he'd seen his life flash before his eyes. "We could have been killed."

"I thought you more adventurous," she softly complained.

"I like my sex private. Not a spectator sport."

"I've yet to be caught."

"Someday you will."

She placed a hand over his heart, sighed. "I don't want to argue."

"Then stop talking."

There were no further words, only the touch of her hands as they moved freely over his body. Hands he couldn't contain. He caught the stares of other dancers as she slowly humped his leg. Somehow, Zen managed to keep his cool—until Natalie rubbed her belly against his, leaned back, and licked her lips. "You're hard for me."

Hard, his ass. Natalie didn't have the power to turn him on. "That's Stevie's shoe," he said as he slipped one from his suit pocket. "The *heel*," he emphasized, "poked your stomach."

Natalie looked none too pleased.

From the corner of his eye, Zen caught Aaron and Stevie in conversation. Stevie looked at Aaron as if he'd set the moon and the stars. Even though Aaron kept one eye on Natalie, his expression was animated. He nodded, smiled, openly enjoying Stevie as much as she enjoyed him. Something he said made Stevie laugh. The sound drifted to Zen. A heartfelt laugh. Happy and carefree.

Apparently the spark he'd felt with her had been

lit by her loneliness, and had now been doused by Aaron's undivided attention.

Clipped by disappointment, Zen felt his throat go dry. He'd grown fond of Stevie. Fond of her smiles, her curves, her sense of loyalty to Aaron, however misplaced. She deserved better—someone kind and considerate and appreciative of her good heart.

He blew out a breath and wondered: If Natalie was removed from the equation, would Stevie's chances with Aaron improve?

Zen could give Stevie such a chance . . . if that's what she truly wanted.

When the song ended, Zen returned an aroused Natalie to Aaron. "We've had our dance."

Natalie stood flushed, her eyes dilated, while Aaron appeared ready to kill. Disgust darkened his features as Aaron took in the rapid rise and fall of her chest, her sidelong glances at Zen. Aaron shot Zen a dark look before taking Natalie by the elbow and steering her across the room.

Stevie watched them walk away. "So much for old time's sake."

"Old times aren't all they're cracked up to be."

"Aaron mentioned that you and Natalie were once involved."

"That's behind me now."

"Her dirty dancing says different."

"I wasn't the one humping."

"She humped for two. She wants you bad."

"Natalie wants until she gets. Then she loses interest."

Stevie looked at him thoughtfully. "She never got you, did she? You were the one who got away."

"Natalie is fickle. She'd have lost interest eventually."

"Think she might lose interest in Aaron?"

Zen shrugged. "I can't foresee the future."

What he could see, made him cringe. Across the room near the black velvet curtain that divided the ballroom from the buffet, Aaron and Natalie were engaged in a heated exchange. They were drawing a lot of public speculation. Aaron's jaw was locked; Natalie's features twisted, her color high. Zen knew that look. She was turned on, taunting Aaron, pushing the man toward public sex.

He felt a pang of sympathy for Aaron. He wondered how often the Tampa Bay pitcher had been caught in a public place with his pants down. A man could go from hard to soft in a heartbeat. How fast was Aaron's heart beating now?

Aaron Grayson was furious. "How did it feel humping another man's thigh?" he growled low in his throat.

"I wasn't humping," Natalie shot back sharply.

He disagreed. "Stop denying what everyone in the room witnessed. You were trying to get off on Zen's pant leg."

She tossed back her head and bared her teeth, looking almost feral. "What if I was? Wouldn't be the first time. If the song hadn't ended, I would have come."

"You're my fiancée," he bit out. "Stay away from Zen."

"Satisfy me, and I won't go near the man."

"We had sex before the dance."

"*Boring* sex," she tossed back, a little too loudly. "Missionary position is for preachers and small pricks."

Aaron heard several people clear their throats, several more chuckle. Then came the whispers. "Sixty seconds, and the entire town will know I fail you as a lover."

"You do."

He snapped, so angry his blood flowed hot. Grabbing her by the arm, he jerked Natalie behind the black velvet curtain, away from those taking in their every word. The room it curtained off was empty except for the buffet table, which stretched its full length. Arranged with sliced fruit and raw vegetables, dips and salsa, and other late-night delicacies, the table was set, ready to serve the hungry dancers.

Releasing Natalie, Aaron glanced at his watch. Twenty minutes and the curtain would be drawn. He needed to wrap up their discussion. Quickly. "What do you want from me?" he asked, desperation leaving him less a man.

She came to him, flushed and aroused, her hands dipping beneath the waistband of his slacks and tugging him closer still. He sucked air as she pulled down the zipper on his dress pants, reached into his boxers, and freed him. One stroke of her nail, and all the blood in his body drew south.

GET UP TO 4 FREE BOOKS!

You can have the best romance delivered to your door for less than what you'd pay in a bookstore or online. Sign up for one of our book clubs today, and we'll send you **FREE* BOOKS** just for trying it out…**with no obligation to buy, ever!**

HISTORICAL ROMANCE BOOK CLUB

Travel from the Scottish Highlands to the American West, the decadent ballrooms of Regency England to Viking ships. Your shipments will include authors such as CONNIE MASON, SANDRA HILL, CASSIE EDWARDS, JENNIFER ASHLEY, LEIGH GREENWOOD, and many, many more.

LOVE SPELL BOOK CLUB

Bring a little magic into your life with the romances of Love Spell—fun contemporaries, paranormals, time-travels, futuristics, and more. Your shipments will include authors such as LYNSAY SANDS, CJ BARRY, COLLEEN THOMPSON, NINA BANGS, MARJORIE LIU and more.

As a book club member you also receive the following special benefits:

- **30% OFF** all orders through our website & telecenter!
- **Exclusive access** to special discounts!
- **Convenient** home delivery and **10 day examination period** to return any books you don't want to keep.

There is no minimum number of books to buy, and you may cancel membership at any time. See back to sign up!

*Please include $2.00 for shipping and handling.

"I want sex on the buffet table," she told him, leading him across the room. And not by the hand.

Aaron's gaze swept the room, darting and apprehensive. "A server could come to check on the food."

"Then you'd better eat fast."

She shoved a sterling platter of raw vegetables against a glass bowl of fruit salad making enough room to settle herself onto the table. She shifted, hiked her dress up to her hips, and spread her legs slightly. She wore no panties.

Aaron hit the floor on both knees. Natalie made him crazy. She forced him into situations that stole his sanity. Scared him beyond reason.

They could be discovered at any moment.

He did everything he could to make her climax. She clutched his head, her nails scoring his scalp as she panted and moaned, yet she did not come. Time ticked in his head. Ten minutes and the curtain would be thrown back. The townspeople would find Natalie perched on the edge of the table, her legs over his shoulders, his face buried in her crotch.

Maybe what his tongue and lips lacked in talent, he could make up for with his hips. Rising shakily, he unbuckled his belt, then undid the button on his pants. His zipper was already down.

Knowing Natalie's penchant for anytime, anywhere sex, he'd packed a pocketful of condoms. He sheathed himself. Cupping her bottom, he entered her with the force of his fear. Of being caught. Of going soft. Of being humiliated.

He pumped, and her body pulsed.

She wiggled on the starched white table cloth, causing it to scrunch and wrinkle.

Her right hand knocked over the salsa dip. Her left a three-bean salad. Her gyrating hips sent a chafing dish filled with hot wings to the floor.

Water flew from a crystal vase of yellow roses.

A dolphin ice sculpture tilted precariously.

Thank God the sterno hadn't been lit, or Natalie would have set the buffet on fire.

He tried to contain her. Unsuccessfully.

She bit his ear. His neck. Tore at his tie.

He gritted his teeth. Picked up his rhythm.

Her release came from deep inside, an elemental trembling that broke on one hell of a loud scream.

His mouth covered hers, taking her scream deep into his lungs. A scream that echoed down his throat. It could have shattered glass.

Aaron finally pulled back. His breathing remained rapid, his gaze now wide at the picture he and Natalie made should someone walk in on them.

Her dress had worked upward until the hem hung over one exposed breast. Salsa was smeared on her right thigh. A sweet potato slice had been flattened at the small of her back. Perspiration glazed her flushed skin; her expression was pure screwed-on-the-buffet.

He appeared in worse shape. His pants were pooled around his ankles, wrinkled beyond wear. Sweat dampened the front of his shirt, and the top two buttons were now missing. His red silk tie was askew. Reflected in a metal chafing dish, his hair stood on end, as much from fright as from Natalie pulling at it in passion.

Noise behind the kitchen door had him scrambling for his pants. Panic made him clumsy. It took two tries to button his dress slacks. Three tries to fit his belt through the loops. "Pull down your dress," he hissed at Natalie. "Get off the table."

She did a slow snaky slide off the buffet, then snagged a linen napkin and wiped at the salsa stain on her thigh. She smoothed her hands down her dress until it hung properly. She was patting down her hair when the first server entered the room.

The young man's eyes went wide at the sight before him. Aaron saw what he saw: two people mussed from buffet sex, food overturned and squished on the floor. "I was told to light the sterno," he said.

"By all means do," Natalie said. "Get someone to clean up this mess. While checking out the buffet, I accidentally bumped the table and knocked over several dishes."

Natalie's excuse was lame. The server looked at Aaron. Aaron knew if he didn't act quickly, word of their sexual escapade would be all over the country club. Slipping two fifties from his money clip, he slapped them on the young man's palm. "Your discretion would be appreciated."

The server nodded. "I will give you a few minutes before I return." He hesitated, then added, "You, sir, are either bleeding or have salsa on your neck. The lady has pasta salad on her left calf."

Aaron nodded, his facial muscles tight, as disgusted with himself as he was with Natalie. "This can't happen again," he stated flatly after the server had left. "We nearly got caught in the act."

Natalie patted his cheek. "Nearly, but not quite." She looked him dead in the eye. "The day you can't rise on request is the day we part ways. Understood?"

Aaron hated her ultimatum. Yet he knew she meant every word. He knew of her past with Zen Driscoll. Knew how Zen had chosen sanity over public sex.

Natalie Llewellyn caught the conflicting emotion in Aaron's eyes. He was as dazed as he was sated, and at that moment, he hated her as much as he loved her.

Apprehension made him frown. He was obviously a mass of nerves. Natalie feared he was not daring enough to suit her. She needed inventive and stimulating sex to reach her orgasm.

While on the dance floor, she'd checked out the stage. The keyboard looked inviting. Perhaps she and Aaron could sneak in a quickie before the band packed up. The very thought made her wet.

A rustling of the black velvet curtain caught her eye. Those on the other side would soon be bursting through to the buffet. One such person was Stevie Cole. Natalie caught a glimpse of Stevie's auburn curls and blue cocktail dress as she peeked into the room. Zen Driscoll was by her side.

"Are you all set up?" Stevie called to the server, who had just returned and was on his hands and knees, blotting salsa from the beige carpet.

"Fifteen minutes, ma'am," the man on all fours requested.

Stevie stepped farther into the room, took it all in. Natalie watched Stevie's gaze widen, the hurt slicing deep. Amid the room spiced with the aromas of barbecue ribs, honey-glazed ham, and sterno, the scent of sweat and sex was subtle, yet noticeable.

Stevie stood as frozen in time as the ice sculpture. Zen, on the other hand, shook his head in disgust. They both stared at Aaron as he straightened his suit jacket and flattened his tie over the missing buttons on his shirt.

"Your zipper's down." Natalie drew attention to his fly.

Aaron jerked the metal tab and winced, catching more than fabric in the metal teeth. Then he headed for the men's room.

Stevie finally moved. She backed up a step and bumped into Zen. Zen rested a protective hand on her shoulder. Natalie hated the fact that he touched Stevie. Zen's hands belonged on her, not the woman squeezed into an unfashionably tight dress.

"This wasn't the time or the place," Zen stated flatly.

"I'd have preferred an elevator, had there been one on the premises." Natalie returned Zen to a time when she'd taken him in her mouth for fifty floors.

Zen exhaled sharply. "Draw a line, Natalie, and don't cross it."

Natalie tossed her head. "I'm not one for rules or restrictions."

"A little restraint might have served you well," Zen returned. "Three hundred people are waiting to dine."

One corner of her mouth curved. "Aaron ate first."

Her meaning was not lost on either Stevie or Zen. "I'll pass on the buffet," Stevie said tonelessly.

"I'll take you home," Zen offered.

Natalie watched them leave. A jealousy such as she'd never known rose and hissed like a beast inside her. How could Zen Driscoll be attracted to a fat, freckle-faced nobody? A nobody who looked middle-class and shopped markdowns. Who so seldom wore high heels, she'd had to remove her shoes on the dance floor.

Stevie Cole had no class. Zen deserved better. Natalie considered herself prime. Monied, attractive, well connected, she could offer Zen far more than small-town Stevie. That *more* included mind-blowing sex, so public and explosive, they'd never return to the bedroom again.

She'd dump Aaron for a second chance with Zen. Zen need only crook his finger.

CHAPTER 8

Sunday morning dawned with overcast skies. Jacy Grayson woke slowly. And painfully. Every inch of her body ached. Curled on her side, she found it difficult to straighten her limbs. She released her breath on a short pant.

"Looking pretty fetal, babe," Risk said as he rose on one elbow. "Don't struggle. Let me help you sit up."

He tossed back the orange comforter and rolled slowly away from her. Kicking his legs over the mahogany frame, he braced himself against the waves on the waterbed. Once standing, his *Bad to the Bone* tattoo and fine morning erection drew a moan from her. The man was magnificent.

Risk looked down on her and asked, "Pain pill?"

"I can live with the pain, pull on your pants."

One corner of his mouth cut into a smile. "I want you too."

"I'd let you have me, if I could contain my screams."

"Screams of pain are a real turnoff. I'll have you

once you've healed." He walked naked to her dresser and pulled out a drawer she'd reserved for him. He snagged a pair of worn cutoffs and slipped them on.

Jacy admired his body. From boyhood sinew to mature male muscle, he was now cut and tight and fit well in his skin. "Love the tear beneath your left cheek."

"Too ripped to wear?"

"Wish it was bigger."

"I'd be pretty exposed."

"My sugar fix. Pure eye candy."

She tracked his swagger as he crossed to her side of the bed, all sleep-tousled hair, broad, hairy chest, and faded cutoffs. The man made morning look damn fine.

"Let's get you off your side, lay you out flat," he said.

He wrapped one hand over her left shoulder while the other curved her hip. Then with infinite care, he turned her onto her back. "Can you straighten your arms? Legs?"

Jacy tried, grimaced. Her muscles were too tight to comply.

Risk didn't allow her to struggle. He began a slow, deep massage, starting at her shoulders and working down her arms until her flexibility returned. He then started on her hips. Throughout their years together, Risk's touch had always been a total turn on. Yet, at that very moment, he healed with those big, strong hands. He massaged her thighs and calves, hitting pressure points that had her sighing with relief.

"You have incredible hands," Jacy murmured, her eyelids half closed, her body liquid.

"Hungry, babe?"

"I could go for breakfast, after . . ."

"After what?"

"Nature calls."

"Got it covered." Risk bent over the waterbed and scooped her into his arms, adjusting his hold for her utmost comfort.

Naked beneath the oversized T-shirt she wore, Jacy held her breath as his left forearm brushed her bare bottom, his right hand curving just beneath her breast. His thumb pressed near her nipple.

He carried her into the bathroom and stood her by the shell-shaped sink. "Can you manage alone?"

"I'm fine. Give me fifteen minutes."

Fifteen minutes took their toll on her strength. During that time, Jacy washed her face and hands and spritzed Lolita Lampeka at her pulse points. Vanilla warmed on her skin, scenting her T-shirt as well. She brushed her hair and teeth. Each stretch of her arm pulled on her ribs. Her ankle cast weighed like a cement block. She was pale and winded when Risk returned for her.

"Damn, I never should have left you alone," he muttered, lifting her against his chest, then returning her to the waterbed.

Once she was propped against a pile of pillows, her ankle elevated, he said, "A quick shower and I'll whip up breakfast."

Guilt surfaced. "You don't have to wait on me," she said, ignoring the pain in her ribs. "Don't you have places to go, people to see?"

He narrowed his eyes and set his stubbled jaw. "I

hit the softball. You fell. I feel responsible for your nosedive."

Responsibility, not love, kept him at her bedside. Definitely disappointing. She forced a smile. "I'm letting you off the hook."

"I'm here for the duration. Get used to it."

"What about Sherry Sherman? Zen? The Bat Pack?" she pressed.

"Romeo and Chaser can fend for themselves. Zen has a key to my parents' house. He's welcome to stay as long as he likes." He paused, scratched his belly. "I handed off Sherry to Psycho at the ballpark."

"To *Psycho?*" Jacy had no memory of the event.

"Figured he'd provide her with the thrills she's seeking."

"Psycho's a thrill a minute," she agreed. "He might prove more than she can handle."

"Sherry likes 'to handle.' "

"Speaking from experience?"

"Psycho's memories now."

Her stomach growled. "I'm hungry."

"Hold that thought. I'll be in and out of the shower in a flash."

He turned, and Jacy admired his backside. Wide shoulders, tight butt, strong legs. Her heart clenched with unrequited love. For years she'd wanted to tell him how she felt. Fear that he might walk out of her life held the words in check.

He was with her now. Taking care of her. Treating her as if she was vulnerable and fragile, and . . . special. She tucked the *special* close to her heart, wanting to savor their time together.

Risk Kincaid showered, shaved, and retrieved his cutoffs. His gaze caught Jacy's own as he zipped the worn denim. The sound of the snap was loud in the silence. They stared at each other for a solid minute. Damn, she was beautiful. He liked her blond. Her natural color softened her features. Without her colored contacts, her eyes were a sky blue. Soft breasts and curvy hips. Sweetly contoured thighs. Dainty toes, each toenail painted separately and distinctly from a palette of pinks.

She shifted slightly on the raspberry-colored sheets. The hem of her T-shirt slid up, delivering him a flash of all that was female.

His gut pulled as tight as his sex. Jacy might be nearly naked, but she was also sore and bruised. Jumping her fractured ribs was not an option. At least for a month, possibly two. Once she'd regained her strength, there were ways to pleasure her that would not involve pressing her into the mattress. His fingers had never failed him. His tongue loved her taste.

"Cheese and tomato omelet, rye toast?" he asked.

"With a baked potato. Butter and sour cream."

He shook his head, turned toward the kitchen. "You've weird cravings, babe."

Standing before the stove, he wondered what she'd crave when she was pregnant. The image of a pregnant Jacy drew his smile. His protective instinct reared up. He wanted her carrying his baby. No one else's. But convincing her he'd moved beyond fooling around and had fallen in love would take some persuasion.

Sweet talk and gifts might work. Should that fail, he'd enlist the town's help. Jacy couldn't resist her coffee shop crowd. He'd buy a round of lattes and caramel rolls for all those who nudged her to accept his proposal. Nodding, he decided he'd put the plan in motion as soon as possible.

Within thirty minutes, Risk was serving her breakfast in bed. His woman had an appetite. "Chew, Jacy, your stomach doesn't have teeth," he said between bites of toast.

She didn't take a breath until her plate was cleaned.

"Pain pill?" he asked, when she flopped back against her pillows.

"I hate to sleep the day away."

"The more you rest, the faster you'll heal."

"You'll stick around?"

"I gave you my word." He reached across the bed, removed her breakfast tray. "I'd like to check my e-mail, attend to some business. Mind if I use your computer?"

"Go in on my screen name."

"Password?"

Her cheeks heated. "Help me up and I'll get you started."

He wasn't about to let her out of bed. "All I need is your password, babe."

She rubbed her forehead. "Memory loss from the fall."

"You fractured ribs and broke your ankle. There was no brain damage."

Still, she hesitated. One minute ran into two.

164

"Jacy, it's only a password."

"I've been meaning to change it."

"Change it tomorrow."

"You need the computer today."

Their conversation was going in circles. "I'll have Zen drop off my laptop this afternoon."

"Would you also call Stevie and ask her to visit?"

Risk nodded, then left the bedroom. For whatever reason, Jacy didn't want him to know her password. Curiosity pricked him. He wouldn't press her now, but later, he'd play around, see if he could crack the code.

After putting the dishes in the sink to soak, he brought her a pain pill and a glass of water. She downed both.

He eased onto the mahogany bed and took her hand in his, stroking between her fingers. "Last night you started to tell me something, but fell asleep before you finished."

She dipped her head, plucking at the comforter. "What did I say?"

He shrugged. "Nothing much. Just that you had something important to relay."

"I've . . . forgotten."

"Selective memory, babe? First your password, now words of consequence."

She closed her eyes. "Feeling sleepy."

He squeezed her hand. "No secrets, Jacy. I want nothing between us but skin."

"I'll share . . ." Her jaw went lax as sleep overtook her.

Risk slowly released her hand, reached for the comforter, and tucked her in. She'd be out for several hours. In the meanwhile, he had phone calls to make. Then, he'd kick back and read the Sunday paper. Or, perhaps, he'd watch Jacy sleep. He took great pleasure in the latter.

"How long have you been watching me sleep?" Jacy demanded, blinking herself awake. She yawned.

"A while, babe," Risk replied from an armchair pulled flush against her waterbed. His feet were propped on the wooden frame, his body curved deeply into the chair. He appeared relaxed and at home. And very masculine against the rose-colored leather.

"It's so quiet, aren't you bored?" she asked.

"Never bored. You talk in your sleep."

She cut him a sharp look. "Talk, about what?"

"This . . . and that."

She curled her fingers around the corner of her pillow. "How much *that*?"

"Enough to hold my attention."

She brushed back her bangs. "I must have been dreaming."

"A sex dream if your moan and the roll of your hips was anything to go by."

"Hmm," she mulled it over. "A dream lover."

Risk uncurled his spine and straightened. "Did you see his face?"

"Face, what face?" she teased. "I was far more interested in his lean hips and stamina."

His gaze held hers as he slowly folded the newspaper and tossed it aside. "Stamina, you say?"

"Mmmm, he was good. Better than a three-speed, battery operated—"

He rose in one fluid motion, startling her. Thoughts of vibrators gave way to the man now settling on her bed. He leaned so close they shared breath. His gaze pinned her to the satin-covered pillows. "That good, huh?"

She curled her fingers into the comforter. "Very, very good."

"I'm better." He nuzzled her neck, flicked his tongue over her pulse point. As if in slow motion and with ultimate tenderness, he dusted soft kisses across her cheeks and chin, then kissed her eyelids closed. Time fell away to yearning when his mouth sought hers. He took his sweet time drawing her out of herself and into him. Her heartbeat quickened, her lips parted. She wanted more of him.

He gave her his tongue.

She teased him with her own.

He nipped her bottom lip. The bite speared to her nipples, then shot to her loins. Hot and arousing.

She rolled her hips.

Her ribs fought the movement. Pain replaced pleasure, and a soft cry escaped her.

Risk jerked back, horrified that he'd hurt her. "I'm so sorry, Jacy."

She blew out a breath, forced a smile. "No need to apologize for—"

"Turning you on?" He stood, his back to her, and adjusted himself. "Stevie will be arriving shortly and I'm so jacked I can't cross the room to answer the door."

Jacy looked down at her bare legs. "Can you get me a pair of sweats?"

He nodded. "That I can manage. Panties?"

She shook her head. "Too much effort."

Risk's expression remained tight, his steps controlled, as he walked to her dresser and found a pair of red sweats in the bottom drawer. His teeth clenched, he knelt on the bed, worked the sweats over her ankle cast and up her legs. "Lift your hips, babe."

Jacy sucked in a slow, hot breath. Their positioning grew increasingly intimate. Far more intimate than the kisses they'd shared. Her T-shirt had hiked up to beneath her breasts. His face was now mere inches from her bare belly. His hands were tucked beneath her thighs, ready to tug up the sweats. His breath blew warm on her navel.

Steeling herself against the pain in her ribs, she raised her hips, one inch, then two, giving him room to slide the sweats over her abdomen and under her butt.

The warmth of his palms pressed her sides, his fingers pushing the T-shirt higher still, exposing her breasts. He stared at her. Openly, and with desire. So much desire . . .

The doorbell rang, and they both jerked. Leaning closer, he softly kissed each nipple, then flicked his tongue at her belly. The scruff of his stubbled jaw sent shivers up her spine. Lowering her T-shirt, he shifted off the waterbed.

"Must be Stevie," he said over his shoulder as he snagged a blue button-down from the drawer and shot his arms through the sleeves. The shirttail covered the tear in his cutoffs, as well as his erection. He walked stiffly to the door.

Jacy's spirits lifted when both Stevie and Zen entered her bedroom. Pretty in yellow capris and a tropical print blouse, Stevie set a bouquet of apricot daisies in a jelly glass on her bedside table. From *Cosmo* to *Marie Claire*, Zen laid out a dozen women's magazines for her reading pleasure, then handed Risk his laptop.

Zen pushed the sleeves of his white pullover up his forearms and said, "We came by to check your pulse, Jacy. How are you feeling?"

Jacy laid her arm protectively over her ribs and admitted, "I'm sore and bruised, but breathing."

Zen shot Risk a keep-her-in-bed look, which Jacy intercepted. "I'm flat on my back for as long as it takes," she told him.

"Flat on your back? Right where every man wants his woman." Psycho stepped into her bedroom with Romeo and Chaser on his heels.

Risk looked utterly pained. "Breaking and entering, boys?"

"The door was unlocked, pops," Psycho informed him. "We came to check on our Jacy."

Risk spiked a brow. "*Our* Jacy?"

"No ring on her finger." Psycho crossed to the waterbed. "She's as much *ours* as anyone else's."

Psycho stood by her bed in a black T-shirt with *Dangerous When Bored* printed in white across his chest, dark jeans, and athletic shoes. Turned backward, his Rogues baseball cap tamed black hair still damp from a recent shower.

Jacy cringed as Psycho poked the waterbed with

his finger. Poked it again and again. He seemed fascinated by the ripples, ripples that speared pain across her chest.

Catching Psycho by the back of the neck, Risk nudged him aside. "Don't make waves."

Psycho held up his hands. "Go easy on me, old man. I'm here to cheer her up, not make her feel worse."

"Then take one giant step away from the bed," Risk instructed.

Psycho jammed his hands in the back pockets of his black jeans, took a giant step away from Risk instead of the bed.

Romeo removed his baseball cap, his blond hair longer now than during baseball season. His light brown eyes lit with mischief as he leaned in to kiss her on the cheek. "Can I get you anything, sweetheart? I've got a great bedside manner."

"*Sweetheart* has everything she needs." The muscle in Risk's jaw flexed hard.

Romeo pressed a second kiss to her cheek and straightened. "I'll be in town another week if you need me."

Risk did not looked pleased over the Bat Pack's prolonged visit.

"Zen's staying a few extra days as well," Stevie said.

"As long as I can invade Risk's closet, I'm set on clothes," Zen added.

"Mind if I borrow as well?" Psycho asked Risk.

"Hell, yes, I mind. You never return what you take."

"Hey, if you're referring to the tool set—"

"Which you've had for over a year," Risk said, cutting Psycho off. "How long does it take to change the oil in your truck? And how about my lawn mower, patio furniture, and Christmas lights?"

"I bought a big-ass house and haven't decorated it yet," Psycho replied defensively. "Patio furniture looks good in my living room. I don't have a lamp. The red and green Christmas lights work just fine."

"The lights *blink*."

"So do I."

"Hire a decorator and return my stuff."

Psycho grunted. "You don't share or play well with others."

"This isn't the first grade."

Jacy shook her head. A brat at heart, Psycho broke as many rules as he could. Without Risk shoving him in the right direction, Psycho would go off the deep end.

"Frostproof's a small town," she reminded the Bat Pack. "There's not a lot to do."

"There's Sherry Sherman to do." Psycho lifted and lowered his brows suggestively.

Romeo cut Psycho a look. "Boy didn't come home last night."

More than Jacy needed to know. "Where are you staying?" she asked.

"No-Tell Motel," Chaser grunted. "Cars came and went last night on the hour. The walls are thin, the moaning loud."

Stevie gaped. "You had reservations at The Powers. A large central room with three adjoining suites. I reserved the rooms myself. I told Psycho—"

"Who never told us." Chaser glared at his friend.

Psycho held up his hands. "Cut me some slack. Sherry wanted room to spread out, have a little fun."

Stevie punched him in the arm. "It took *four* rooms?"

"Five, if you count the balcony." Psycho rubbed his arm. "She stole my Rogues jersey and a pair of beat up Nikes."

"Buy them back on eBay," Romeo suggested, knowing where the merchandise would land. "Someone's always selling something that belongs to me. I had to bid on a pair of my own boxers last week. The week before that, a friggin' jock."

Jacy recalled that Risk had once mentioned how fans snagged his half-empty drinks in a bar, stole his fork while dining out, then sold the bar glasses and utensils for ten times their usual value online. It was the price of fame.

Jacy pushed herself up on one elbow, doctor's orders foremost on her mind. "I have a favor to ask. Since Risk's enforcing my bed rest for the next few days, I need help at the coffee shop. The pay isn't great, but the coffee's good." She paused. "I also need someone to coach my Bluebells."

Zen nodded slowly. "I can pour coffee."

"I'm a master with the blender," Chaser stated. "I'm good for mocha frappuccinos and fruit smoothies."

"I can bake," Stevie added. "Lemon or pistachio macaroons. Chocolate and vanilla yo-yo cookies."

"I'll bus tables and wash dishes," Romeo offered.

"I'll be the manager," Psycho concluded.

"Management?" Risk scoffed. "I wouldn't leave you in charge of the television remote." He looked down at Jacy. Winked. "I'll coach your Bluebells."

Her T-ball players would be in good hands. Relief settled in her soul. She snuggled back against the pillows, caught Zen looking at his watch. "Leaving so soon?" she asked.

"It's time to pick up Ellie Rosen," Zen informed her.

Psycho cocked a brow. "That little blond girl from the auction?"

"Ellie likes to read," Zen said. "We're headed to the Book Nook for the children's reading hour."

"Zen's going to buy Ellie a boxed set of Junie B. Jones," Stevie said.

Romeo surprised everyone by saying, "Junie B. Jones and Jingle Bells, Batman Smells is a cool read."

"I'm fond of the Clifford series. Love the big red dog," Chaser said.

"I can quote pages of Captain Underpants," Psycho confessed.

Jacy stared at the Bat Pack. "How do you guys know so much about children's books?"

"Team management requires us to put in a certain number of community hours each month," Romeo explained. "Players often read to cancer patients."

Chaser crossed his arms over his chest and widened his stance. "We're more than bat-swinging, ball-catching, crotch-scratching jocks."

"Risk's putting together a camp for the terminally ill," Psycho added. "Swimming, hiking, arts and crafts under a physician's care."

All eyes turned to Risk. "It's just in the planning

stages," he said, brushing off Psycho's announcement. Glaring at the younger player, he asked, "Who told you?"

"Found a set of blueprints in your locker at the ball park."

"You have no business going through my stuff."

"You left your locker open."

"Because someone stole my lock."

"We both now share the same combination."

Risk shot Psycho a warning look. "Don't leak anything about the camp to the press."

"I won't say a word if you'll let me invest."

Risk shook his head. "We can barely share an outfield during season. What makes you think we could work together?"

"Dedication to a project I hold close to my heart."

Risk didn't look convinced.

Psycho ran one hand down his face, blew out a breath. "I lost a cousin to cancer."

Jacy caught Risk's eye. "A silent partner might work."

"*If* Psycho could keep his mouth shut."

"Can't promise silence," Psycho said. "But I've a shitload of cash to invest."

Risk was not a man to be pressured. "We'll talk later."

"Dialogue's good," Psycho agreed.

With that settled, Jacy turned to Stevie. "Did you meet your goal for the recreation center?"

Stevie nodded. "Actually, we surpassed it."

"How was the country club dance?"

Jacy's question was met by silence. A long, uncomfortable silence that ticked a full sixty seconds.

Risk scanned the group, as curious as Jacy.

All the while, Stevie studied the floor.

Zen took off his wire rims, cleaned them on a handkerchief.

Chaser grew inordinately fascinated by a colorful matted abstract hanging above the headboard.

Psycho poked the waterbed when Risk wasn't looking.

A second minute passed before Romeo slapped his palms on his thighs, the first to take his leave. "Time to let the ladies chat. Alone." He bent toward Jacy's cheek. "I'm off, sweetheart. A kiss for the road—"

Risk snagged him by the collar, warning, "I let two kisses slide, but not a third."

"We're talking cheek, not lips," Romeo complained.

"Pretty territorial, pops," Psycho said from the doorway.

Risk glared him into the next room.

Zen, Romeo, and Chaser followed in Psycho's path.

"I'll see them out." Risk departed as well.

Once the men were beyond earshot, Jacy pressed Stevie, "Why the hush-hush? What went down?"

"Aaron on Natalie is what went down," Stevie said stiffly. "They had sex on the buffet table."

Jacy's eyes widened. "No way!"

"I caught the aftermath," Stevie said on a sigh. "It was my job to check on the buffet, announce dinner. When I looked behind the curtain, there was spilled food, salsa stains on the carpet, a wrinkled table cloth, along with a smirking Natalie and a disheveled Aaron, his shirttail sticking out his zipper."

Jacy's heart hurt for her friend. "Aaron's always been conservative. Sex in public is so . . . so—"

"Dangerous?" Stevie supplied. "According to Zen, who once dated Natalie, the prospect of getting caught heightens her pleasure."

Jacy grimaced. "If you'd peeked around the curtain any earlier—"

"I'd have caught them in the act."

"I'm embarrassed for them both," Jacy said. "The focus of the dance was to raise money for parks and recreation, not buffet sex."

"No one knows but Zen, the Bat Pack, and me," Stevie said.

"Who told the Bat Pack?"

"Psycho noted pasta ground into the carpet, and a server confided its origin. Romeo and Chaser overheard."

"They'll keep their mouths shut?"

"Zen's foot will be on their necks if they tell."

"He sounds protective of you."

"I like him looking out for my interests."

"I like the man period," Jacy told her friend.

"Zen's the complete opposite of Aaron."

"Perhaps in good ways, if you give Zen a chance."

"He'd make a good friend," Stevie agreed.

"A friend you'd like to see naked?"

Stevie ran her hands over her hips. "I'm overweight. I'd be embarrassed for Zen to see me without my clothes."

"Do it in the dark. Or burn a single candle."

"Major fumbling."

"Fumbling's half the fun."

"It's been a long time, Jacy," Stevie confessed.

"Soft, first kisses excite."

"Second kisses add tongue." Risk grinned from the doorway. "And tongues like to taste."

Jacy nailed him with a look. "How much did you hear?"

"Enough to know Zen will wake up happy."

Stevie blushed bright red.

"Enjoy Zen." Risk pushed off the doorjamb. "He's a good man. Your secret's safe with me."

"I'll see you tomorrow," Stevie said as she left the bedroom.

"I may stop by the coffee shop—"

"Or you may not," Risk cut Jacy off.

"Follow doctor's orders." Stevie let herself out.

Once the door closed, Jacy scowled at Risk. "You sure are bossy."

"You need someone in control when you're spinning out."

"My body's sore. I wouldn't do anything stupid."

"Stupid doesn't include pushing Stevie on Zen?"

"I made a suggestion. It's up to her to act on it."

"First times . . ." Risk eased onto the bed, inches from where she lay. He leaned in, one hand braced on the frame, the other on the headboard. "Remember the backseat of my black Cougar?"

She certainly did. Prom night. A tight squeeze. His arms around her. Wedged on their sides. A touch of lips, a slip of his tongue, and the car had rocked. "Great rebound sex."

"We're damn good together.

Damn good. Jacy went still, staring into Risk's face. He had such masculine features, sharp and defined. His green gaze darkened as he dipped his head, caught her mouth with his own.

Their hands remained still as their lips made love. Nipping, sucking, laving, and a whole lot of tongue tag. Her heart raced. The rapid rise and fall of her chest was distressing. She moaned softly.

Risk's chest heaved as he pulled back. He ran his hand through his hair, got his pulse under control. "We need to find an activity that doesn't hurt you or leave me rock hard."

"I want to discuss Aaron and Stevie."

He nodded. "Talking's good. Zen filled me in at the door. Appears Aaron's gotten adventurous."

Jacy's hands curled tightly in the comforter. "I'm angry he hurt Stevie. Again."

"For better or worse, for private or public sex, Aaron's with Natalie now," Risk stated. "He's let Stevie go. She needs to do the same."

"Could you let me go?" Her heart nearly stopped. *Had she spoken her question out loud?* Apparently so, given Risk's thoughtful expression and the sudden tightness in his shoulders.

His words came slowly. "We're friends, babe. Friendship lasts forever."

"We're also lovers."

"That only enhances our friendship." He pressed a kiss to her forehead. "I care for you, Jacy. Always have, always will."

She turned her head into her pillow, fought a yawn. "I care back."

"Tired?" Risk asked.

"A little. But I'm not ready to nap just yet."

"What would you like to do? Watch television, listen to music, read a magazine?"

She didn't miss a beat. "I'd like you to paint my toenails."

Risk looked at her cute little toes. "They're already painted."

"I change the color every day."

"You're kidding me, right?"

"Color makes me feel alive," she explained. "My toes are in the mood for Sugar Frosted Angel and Wild Blueberry polish."

"Alternate the colors on your toes?"

"You catch on fast, Kincaid."

"I've never painted a woman's toenails."

"Virgin pedicurist. Let me be your first."

He gave his head a small shake and muttered, "What a man does for his woman."

His woman? Surely a slip of the tongue. "Nail polish remover, cotton balls, clipper, and file are in the medicine cabinet, along with the two new colors."

He returned with the supplies and eased onto the bed. He drew one of her feet onto his lap. She wiggled her toes, and his sex twitched.

"Hold still," he gritted out, then went to work on her toes.

Jacy watched Risk through half-closed lids. Dedicated to the task, he removed the day-old polish,

179

then pressed cotton balls between her toes. Clipped and filed. Then painted.

"The polish goes on my nail," she reminded him, feeling a drip on her toe.

He grunted, reached for the polish remover, and started over. He clenched his jaw in concentration. "Your toenails are so tiny."

His hands were *so* big. The brush on the polish vanished between his fingers as he painted Wild Blueberry on alternate toes. He then held up a second polish. "How about Spank Me Red instead of Sugar Frosted Angel?"

"Red's a turn-on." She wiggled her toes a second time.

His sex shot north. "Not now, Jacy."

Wiggle. Wiggle. *Wiggle.*

He grabbed her ankle. "Babe."

"I want to play."

"I thought you wanted your nails painted."

"I want you more."

"You can't have me until your ribs heal." He finished painting the toes peeking from her cast, then set both feet away from him and stretched. "You rest, I'll be at my laptop."

Her eyelids drooped. "Stay close."

"I won't leave you. Promise."

His promise eased her into a deep, restful sleep.

CHAPTER 9

Stevie Cole stood partly hidden behind one of The Book Nook's overstuffed reading chairs that formed a crescent around a low coffee table. A maternal longing filled her as she watched Zen Driscoll read to Ellie Rosen. Sunday story hour had ended, yet the little girl and the big baseball player lingered. They now sat on a polished wooden bench near the back wall in the children's section. Ellie's shoulders were bent, her forefinger tracing each word as Zen read softly to her.

Several other children hovered nearby, straining to hear *Junie B. Jones Loves Handsome Warren*. Ellie noticed their presence from the corner of her eye, and instead of keeping Zen all to herself, motioned for the others to share the story. Zen was soon surrounded by round-eyed, book-absorbed kids. Each one remained silent until Zen finished the story, then hands and books were raised, each child wanting his favorite book read.

Zen took his time. He tucked Ellie against his side,

keeping her close, protecting her when a bigger boy or pushy girl wanted his attention. He never took his eyes off the six-year-old even when a flirty sales clerk offered him a cup of coffee.

Ellie couldn't contain her smile. She grinned so much her little cheeks puffed.

Admiration for Zen swelled in Stevie's chest. On a Sunday afternoon he could be watching football, hanging out with the guys, yet he chose to spend time with a little girl desperately in need of a father figure. Ellie would remember this day forever.

Rounding the chair, Stevie curled up on the forest green, leaf-patterned seat. She watched and listened as Zen read for the next hour. When he eventually glanced up and caught her gaze on him, a slow grin spread over his face. Nodding in her direction, he pushed to his feet. The kids were not happy. They bemoaned his leaving so loudly, the store manager came to check on the noise.

Laden with books, Ellie crossed to Stevie. The little girl held so many books, Stevie could barely see the top of her pale blond head. Behind Ellie, Zen shrugged helplessly. "I offered to help carry, but she wanted to hold her treasures."

Excitement bursting, Ellie shifted the books, caught her breath and said, "Zen bought sets of Junie B. Jones and all the Disney Classics."

"Lucky you," Stevie said with a smile.

"We're also going shopping," Ellie said, more shyly this time as she looked down at her worn T-shirt and jeans. Her secondhand sneakers.

"New school clothes," Zen said easily. "Christmas in November."

Stevie winked at Ellie. "Girls can never have enough clothes."

Ellie giggled. The sound was rusty, as if laughter was new to her life.

"Shop with us," Ellie said, handing off a set of books to Zen, then capturing Stevie's right hand.

"Great idea." Zen took Stevie's left, holding her hand loosely so she could pull free at any time.

Holding hands with this man seemed surprisingly natural. His warmth produced a tingle along her arm, jutting straight to her breasts. Her nipples puckered beneath her tropical-print top. Zen noticed, but his gaze didn't linger. Instead he checked the time on his wristwatch.

"We have an hour before Purple Moon closes," he announced. "The store's close by. We can drop the books in my car, then walk across the street."

Ellie walked ahead of them, a slight skip to her step. Zen held fast to Stevie's hand. The press of his calluses against her own was oddly reassuring. Although clean-cut and intellectual, Zen earned his living on a baseball diamond. She liked the physical side of the man. The strong shoulders, lean hips, long legs, his quiet air of confidence and consideration. It was a potent combination in her eyes.

They caught up with Ellie, who stood before Purple Moon, her nose pressed to the lavender-tinted glass door. Her features twisted, uncertainty in her eyes.

Zen hunkered down. "What's up, Ellie?"

She scuffed the toe of her sneaker. "Clothes cost money here. Gram says Goodwill fits just fine."

"You'd look pretty in whatever you wore," Zen assured her. "You decide. If you want a new outfit, I'll buy."

Ellie contemplated for a long time. Longer than any child should have to debate about buying new clothes. "Will you buy something for Stevie too?" she finally asked.

Zen didn't miss a beat. "Once you make your selections, we'll find a women's store and shop for Stevie."

Ellie nodded in satisfaction. "You'll buy for both your girls," she said, pushing open the door.

Zen's girls. Stevie's heart skipped several beats as she followed Ellie into the store with Zen close behind her. So close, she could feel his heat.

"Wow." Ellie's mouth formed an O as she looked about the store. A store of plum-painted walls and blond hardwood floors, with an enormous purple moon hanging from the ceiling.

Stevie inched sideways between racks jammed with brand-name clothing. Twirling stands sparkled with youthful jewelry. Every style of foot gear, from colorful flip-flops to Sunday school shoes, was displayed on tiered shelves along both walls.

A pretty brunette with perky breasts and showcase legs zeroed in on Zen. Recognition came quickly. She flicked her tongue against her upper lip. "I'm Paula. How may I assist you, Einstein?"

Her offer of "assistance" touched on seduction. Baseball players appealed to most women. Zen scored on both body and brains.

Sighing, Stevie turned away. She couldn't compete with the younger woman's face and figure. Wouldn't even try.

Zen's words drew her back around. Straightforward, yet kind, he put an immediate halt to the clerk's come-on. "Assist Ellie Rosen in picking out a new wardrobe, and my appreciation will show in your commission."

Stevie caught the disappointment in Paula's eyes before dollar signs flashed. Placing a hand on Ellie's shoulder, the clerk steered the little girl toward a stack of jeans and T-shirts. "What's your favorite color?" Paula asked.

The selection was enormous. And a bit overwhelming. A flustered Ellie looked at the floor and shrugged. Zen and Stevie immediately crossed to her. Zen's expression was as protective as Stevie's motherly instincts. In that instant, she realized they both wanted the little girl's shopping trip to be a positive experience.

"Pastels would go well with your white-blonde hair and blue eyes," Stevie suggested as she flipped through a stack of T-shirts until she found one in powder blue with a design of hot pink hearts. She then located a pair of matching blue jeans with pink hearts on each pocket. "What do you think?" she asked Ellie.

Ellie ran her hand over the outfit but withdrew it. "It's going to cost you plenty, Zen."

Stevie looked at Zen. She needed his help in convincing Ellie he could afford the outfit. "We can't pass it up," Zen reassured the six-year-old. "It has your name on it."

"My name? Where?" Ellie checked out the inside collar on the top as well as the waistband on the jeans. "I only see Purple Moon Designs on the label."

"Figure of speech, sweetie," Zen explained. "If an outfit looks good on you, then it's yours."

Ellie absorbed the information. Tentatively, she moved along the stacks of clothing. She lifted a denim jumper with a red waffle shirt from a revolving rack. "My name's on these too," she said to Zen.

"Definitely," Zen agreed, smiling. "Keep shopping."

Stevie edged closer to the tall man in the white pullover and khaki Dockers. She looked up at him and admired the sharp cut of his features, the sexy curve of his mouth. "Thank you," was all she could manage.

Zen turned slightly and met her gaze. "Life isn't always easy or fair."

She studied him closely. "Speaking from experience?"

"I've had my share of hard knocks," he admitted. "I learned to push forward instead of clinging to the past."

"I'm a clinger," she had to admit.

A corner of his mouth curved. "You'll eventually let go."

"Think so?"

"Know so."

He sounded so sure. So amazingly positive. She found comfort in his words. She suddenly wanted to know more about this man. What made him tick. What type of woman drew and held his interest. No doubt someone thin and poised. Brainy. She sucked in her stomach and searched for something smart to say but drew a blank.

Ellie saved Stevie from herself, from trying to be someone she wasn't. The little girl approached Zen with a pair of bubble gum pink high tops with sparkly silver laces. She clutched them to her chest as if afraid they'd slip away with her dreams and wishes. "I'll put the clothes back if I can have these."

Zen saved the little girl from making choices. "These shoes wouldn't look right with any other jeans but those with the pink hearts on the pockets. I can afford both."

Ellie's eyes rounded. "Are you made of money?"

"Not made of money," Zen chuckled. "But I've enough cash in my pocket to fill your closet with new clothes."

"We can't forget Stevie," Ellie reminded him in a very adult voice. "Maybe if there's any money left over we could buy Gram some carnations. She can't see so good, but her nose still works."

"Forget about me," Stevie said once Ellie had returned to her shopping. "Flowers for her grandmother are a must."

Zen Driscoll stuck his hands in the pockets of his khakis, rolled his shoulders, and picked his words carefully. "Surely you'd accept a gift from an admirer."

"An admirer?" She fidgeted with the hangers on the revolving rack before her.

He sensed her nervousness, the rise of her insecurities. Her need to be told she was beautiful, which hadn't been said for a long, long time. "I'm admiring." He stroked a finger beneath her chin, tipped her gaze up to meet his. "Remember, I'm a fan of freckles."

She blushed. "I don't need clothes or flowers."

He brushed his thumb against her lips. Slowly. Tentatively. "How about dinner?"

He caught the jolt in her pulse at the base of her throat. "Are you asking me out?"

"Could you date a man other than Aaron?"

Her lips pursed. Her apprehension was almost tangible. "I feel like an injured player returning to a new season."

"Spring training will ease you back into the game."

"I could go an inning or two."

A daring statement for Stevie Cole, Zen realized. They'd become friends, and if all shook out in his favor, they'd progress to lovers. All in due time.

"Do you have a favorite restaurant?" he asked.

"I'd rather cook for you."

"I don't want you to go to any trouble."

"It won't be anything fancy," she quickly assured him. "We'll eat at the kitchen table on my great-aunt's chipped china with mismatched silverware."

Sounded relaxing. Homey. Women of his acquaintance preferred dining out, savoring expensive entrees, having someone wait on them. He hadn't had a home-cooked meal in a very long time. "You set the menu, and I'll buy the groceries."

"Sounds fair," she agreed. "I was thinking coconut beer-battered shrimp on rice. Sautéed zucchini, onions, and broccoli."

"Carrots instead of broccoli?"

Stevie grinned. "If you like."

He damn sure liked her smile. The way her eyes lit up, the pink flush of her skin. "Dessert?"

"You don't eat sweets."

"We'll get something for you."

She looked down at her body, then shot him a self-deprecating look. "Do I look like I need cake or pie?"

He admired her full curves and said simply, "I like the way you look."

Flushing again, Stevie turned away. "I'll check on Ellie."

Zen crossed his arms over his chest, stood back and watched Stevie fuss over Ellie. A remarkable woman and a delightful little girl. He decided at that moment he'd return to Frostproof often. He liked shopping with *his girls*.

Shortly thereafter, Stevie approached him with an armload of clothes. T-shirts, jeans, denim jumpers, tennis shoes, and a Sunday School dress. "Have we overdone it?" she whispered.

Zen shook his head. "One of everything in her size is fine by me."

Cradling the clothes over one arm, she rose on tip-toe to kiss his cheek. Zen turned his head, just enough to have the corner of her mouth graze his. Hangers jabbed his ribs as he angled even more toward her and took her lips in a light kiss.

And she kissed him back.

For all of a heartbeat.

Heat sparked between them. Tangible and recognizable. Pulling back, she pressed two fingers to her lips.

She stared at him, fear and feeling darkening her eyes. "I was going for a thank-you kiss, not . . . not—"

"A mouth-to-mouth," he filled in for her.

Her lips parted and closed just as quickly. "You surprised me."

"A good or bad surprise?" he asked.

She blushed. "It all happened so fast."

"We'll slow it down tonight."

"Slow *what* down?"

"The kisses."

"What makes you think we'll kiss again?"

"Curiosity and desire on both our parts."

Ellie entered his space before Stevie could reply. The little girl had gotten into the swing of shopping; her voice was now high-pitched with excitement. "Can I get a sweater?"

Florida had its cooler winter days and Zen wanted Ellie warm. "What color?"

"Like a rainbow!" She breathlessly claimed.

"A sweater and a jacket," Zen insisted.

The sales clerk eased between the racks of clothing. "How about this adorable leather jacket?" She led Ellie to a triple mirror and helped her into the dark brown leather. "Soft as butter."

The little girl turned right, then left. She shook her head. "I'd rather have the blue jean jacket."

"Are you sure?" Paula pressed, attempting to jack up her commission. "Leather makes a fashion statement."

For one so young, Ellie proved very wise. "My name's not on this label," she said softly. "Patti Harris's and Heather Gibson's names are. Girls in my class who leave the price tags on all their clothes."

"I'll get the denim jacket while you ring up the sale," Stevie told the sales clerk. She then handed off all Ellie's selections to Zen. He made the winding trek to the cash register.

Beneath the glass counter, rhinestone barrettes and beaded ponytail scrunchies invited a little girl's hair to glimmer. "I'll take six blue butterfly barrettes and two pink scrunchies," he told Paula.

The sales clerk quickly added the total. Her smile turned flirty once Zen paid the bill. "What are your plans for the off-season?" she asked.

"I'll be in Frostproof for a week or two, then eventually return to Richmond," he told her.

"I have a brother living in Virginia Beach." Paula looked hopeful. "I visit him on holidays."

She was seeking an invitation, hinting to see him. The only woman from Frostproof Zen wanted knocking on his door was Stevie Cole. He wondered how much persuasion it would take to get her there. Gathering up the clear plastic shopping bags designed with a purple moon, he smiled at Paula and said, "Thanksgiving is coming up fast. Enjoy your visit."

Ellie came charging across the store and snagged as many shopping bags as she could carry. "I want to help," she said.

"Watch out for the door," Zen called to her as she trotted ahead, her vision blocked by the bags.

Zen turned and waited for Stevie—a Stevie he

caught checking out his butt. Female interest flickered in her gaze until she looked up. . . .

Busted, she nearly ran into a rack of clothes. Blushing profusely, she dipped her head and brushed past him.

Zen followed at a slower pace. Since they'd met, Stevie had called him clean-cut and smart. And a sharp dresser. He liked the fact she'd looked at him as a man. He smiled to himself. Eyeballing his ass was a very good sign.

They stopped at Wynn's Market and picked up the needed ingredients for dinner. The family-owned grocery sold bouquets of flowers at the back of the store. Ellie debated between pink carnations and white roses. The little girl squealed with delight when Zen combined the two and bought both.

After dropping Ellie off at her grandmother's, he drove to the Blue Heron Condominiums. "Bright shutters," he commented, catching the lime green by daylight.

"Jacy's paint job. She likes color," Stevie said as he pulled into her driveway.

They entered the condo through the side door. Once the groceries had been set on the counter, Zen asked, "What can I do?"

"Small space, there's not enough room for two cooks," she told him. "Have a seat at the kitchen table."

Whether by accident or subconscious intent, Zen brushed against her as he went to sit down. He heard her intake of breath. They had a whole lot of sizzle between them.

She moved to the refrigerator and swung open the door. "Coors, Chardonnay, or Cherry Coke?" she asked.

"Coors works."

She poured the beer into an iced mug. "You pour just right," he commented admiring the merest hint of froth.

Stevie grinned from the counter. "Risk taught me it's all in the angle of the mug and the twist of the wrist."

"Risk has a multitude of talents both on and off the field."

She turned back to the counter, began chopping vegetables. "Just out of college, Risk was the Bat Pack all rolled into one. He ran as wild as Psycho, had the charisma of Romeo, and packed his jeans better than Chaser. Over the years, Jacy rubbed away his rough edges. He's an amazing man."

Zen sipped his beer. "I've only known Risk for a year. In that time, I've admired his character and fairness as team captain. He's straightforward. A man of few surprises."

She tucked an auburn curl behind her ear, then returned to the shrimp. "Surprises can be devastating."

He knew her thoughts had drifted to Aaron. And his engagement to Natalie Llewellyn. He waited for her to pull herself back to the present.

She had by the time he'd finished his beer. "Another Coors?" she asked.

"I'll get it," he offered, standing. He rubbed the back of his leg. No immediate pain. His hamstring was healing nicely.

She was already at the refrigerator when he came up behind her. Startled, she turned. Slammed into him. The top of her head hit his shoulder. Her elbow jabbed his ribs. Her bottom bumped his groin.

They both went still as stone. Awareness blossomed between them, warm and tingly. His breath blew across Stevie's cheek, his five o'clock shadow rough against her temple. The beat of his heart thumped against her back, rapid and strong. His sex felt hard against the small of her back.

The man had a hard-on. For her. Her control slipped, as did the stick of butter in her hand. Tightly cornered between the cool blast of refrigerator air and his male heat, she turned slowly, found her gaze level with his collarbone. Her nipples poked his chest; his penis pressed her belly. She couldn't meet his eyes, was as embarrassed as she was turned on.

"Beep, beep, backing up." Zen held out his hands, took two steps away from her. "I'll let you bring me that beer."

She bent to recover the foil-wrapped stick of butter. Then went for his beer. Her hand shook as she poured the Coors. Two inches of foam crested the top of the mug this time.

"Sorry," she stammered as she set the beer before him.

He snagged her wrist. Rubbed his thumb over the pulse point at her wrist. "Why so nervous?"

Why? Did attraction count? The man made her heart skip and her hands shake. She forced a smile. Lied. "I-I'm calm."

"Your pulse says otherwise."

He was way too observant. She pulled her hand free, dared to meet his gaze and finally admitted. "It's the company."

A smile of pure male pleasure spread across his face. "I'm getting to you?"

"Mm-hmm."

"Because I have a great butt?"

A damn fine ass. One she'd openly admired at Purple Moon until he'd caught her stare. "You do Dockers proud."

His smile slipped. Just a little. He was suddenly serious. "There's a great deal to like about you as well."

"Name one thing."

"Fishing for compliments?"

"Maybe." A little flattery never hurt. It had been a long time since a man charmed her.

He studied her closely. "You are your own worst critic. When you look in the mirror you see a woman Aaron dumped. Not the woman with an incredible gift for baseball trivia, amazing freckles, and a sexy mouth that gives good blow."

Good blow . . . She turned toward the deep fat fryer, added oil, and plugged it in. His gaze followed her preparations as she blended the ingredients for the batter. Her hands shook ever so slightly.

The scrape of his chair soon brought her around. She caught him rubbing the back of his leg. "How's the hamstring?" she asked.

"Tightens up a bit when I sit too long."

"Want to set the table?"

He stood up. "Tell me what we need."

"You'll find the plates and glasses in the cupboard left of the stove. You can add three cups of rice to the boiling water while you're there. Stir."

She rolled the shrimp in the coconut beer batter while Zen prepared the rice. She then placed the shrimp in a basket and lowered them into the fryer.

"What's that?" Zen asked, coming up behind her.

"Dipping sauce." She blended orange marmalade, mustard, and horseradish in a mixing bowl, then scooped out a spoonful and offered him a taste.

Zen's large hand encircled her wrist as he brought the spoon to his lips. She noted his strength as well as his gentleness.

"Lady, you can cook," he complimented, going for a second sample. Releasing her hand, he returned to stir the rice. Shortly thereafter, he went about setting the table while she sautéed the vegetables.

She liked having Zen in her kitchen, Stevie realized. He wasn't intrusive. Whenever she'd had Aaron over for a meal, he'd worn a path between the kitchen and living room, checking on her progress only during television commercials. He'd never once offered to help.

Zen, on the other hand, made cooking a joint effort. He timed the rice, then transferred it into a bowl. Returning to the table, he dropped onto a chair.

Stevie placed the coconut shrimp and sautéed vegetables before him, then took a seat beside him. A man of manners, Zen served her before filling his own plate.

"The shrimp tastes as good as it looks," he praised.

"Aaron enjoyed home-cooked meals."

"Most men do."

"You look like the wine-and-dine type, Einstein," she said between bites.

He sipped his beer. "The team dines out during the season, but one restaurant soon blends into another. Five-star dining eventually tastes like any hamburger joint. It's nice to fly under the radar on occasion. Take a meal with one special person and not a group of jocks and the ever-present groupies."

Special person? She smiled to herself, enjoying the fact that he liked her company. Conversation flowed easily from that point. They joked and teased as if they'd known each other forever. Even flirted a little. She couldn't resist challenging him with a little baseball trivia.

"Nicknames, Einstein," she tested. "Which major league player was called Twinkletoes?"

"New York Yankees outfielder George Selkirk, because he ran on the front of his feet."

"Who was called The Human Rain Delay?"

Zen tapped his fork and took a few seconds to answer. "Baltimore Orioles Mike Hargrove, because he took an exceptionally long time to step into the batter's box before each pitch."

"How about The Junkman?"

"Yankee pitcher Ed Lopar. The man had an ugly assortment of pitches."

"You're good," Stevie had to admit.

"I know."

They wrapped up the meal, feeling full and satisfied. And talked out. Expectancy edged the silence as they cleared the table and washed the dishes.

"Sorry," Zen said, after lightly bumping her shoulder for the third time.

Their bodies continued to meet. "The kitchen's small." Stevie brushed passed him, her hip connecting with his thigh.

Moments later, her arm grazed his chest.

Shortly thereafter, she backed into his groin. She felt him stir with interest.

When he stepped left, she went right. They walked directly into one other. Awareness spiked, sizzled like a sparkler.

She caught his arm for balance.

He grabbed her shoulders. Squeezed.

Her entire body pulsed.

Time seemed suspended. And neither moved. Sexuality took over where sense left off. Stevie knew in that instant she wanted this man. Wanted him to erase Aaron from her heart.

Zen had it all. She embraced his honesty, his intellect . . . his great butt. The fact he cared for her without strings or attachments.

"Your call, Stevie," he said in a low voice. "Where do we go from here?"

They'd hit a turning point, a point where friendship opened the door to intimacy. She swung the door wide and welcomed Zen Driscoll to her bed. "I want you," she said.

He held back, his gaze dark, assessing. "Be sure, Stevie. I don't want Aaron in bed with us."

She made a little cross with a fingernail on her left breast. "There will only be the two of us. Promise."

She led him down the hallway, past a guest room and into the room where she slept. She covered his hand when he searched the wall for the light switch. "Darkness, please."

"How about a candle?"

She shook her head.

"A night-light?"

"I'd, uh, prefer—"

"I don't see you naked."

He'd read her mind. "I don't have a great body."

"My performance is limited by a pulled hamstring."

He kicked the bedroom door closed with his foot, shutting out the hallway light. The room stood pitch dark. "Let me feel you." His voice reached her, as did his hands.

He held her in silence, his arms banding her close.

She leaned on his strength, embraced his warmth.

Under her cheek, his chest was solid. Muscles honed by action rippled beneath his shirt.

His hand smoothed her hair.

She stroked the sharp curve of his jaw. Stubble rasped her fingertips.

The air pulsed with expectancy.

His mouth grazed her ear and his hot breath gusted across her cheek. He gently kissed her forehead. Her cheekbone. The tip of her nose. Her heart missed a beat when his mouth met hers. Whisper soft, yet persuasive.

Desire fluttered in her stomach. Need skittered over her nerve endings. She initiated a deeper kiss. An open-mouthed kiss. The twirl and tangle of their tongues was stimulating and soul stirring. Deep felt. Unforgettable.

He took her beyond herself, stripping away her inhibitions, along with all thoughts of Aaron Grayson.

Attraction bound them.

The scent of their arousal was heavy in the air.

The man must have amazing night vision, she thought, for his touch was slow, sure, as he learned her body. There was no mussing of her hair. No poking her in the eye. No clipping her on the chin.

She, on the other hand, could see nothing in the darkness. Each stroke of Zen's hand was a sensual surprise.

The man was full of surprises.

His fingers grazed her shoulder, traced down her chest, then unbuttoned her blouse. He found the front hook on her sports bra, released her breasts. Swollen and heavy, they spilled over his palm. She was more than a handful. He toyed with the jutting peaks.

"You're pointing at me again." There was amusement in his voice.

Pointing and craving his touch.

He curled his tongue around one nipple, his teeth grazing the sensitive skin as he suckled. Pleasure speared through her, curling her toes.

Urgency incited her to touch him in turn. She tugged his shirt from the waistband of his Dockers, yanked at the buttons. She heard one pop and hit the tile floor. It bounced twice, then rolled across the room.

She turned his shirt over his shoulders, tossed it on the floor, then nestled against him as if she belonged there. The roughness of his chest hair grazed her breasts. Her nipples distended. She fought with the buckle on his belt until Zen relieved her of the duty. He unsnapped his slacks. Slid down his zipper. The swish of fabric sliding down his legs was arousingly distinct in the darkness. His white boxers stood out in the dark.

Her hand deflected off his hip as she reached for him. Her fingers clutched silk. Her thumb poked his sex. A long stretch of hard flesh, totally primed. The man was large.

"Whoa . . ." Zen gently swept her hand aside.

"Wow . . ." His erection impressed the hell out of her. She hadn't had sex for a very long time. Zen was about to break her dry spell. She was already wet.

She went up on tiptoe, sought his mouth. Her body fit against his in all the right places. Her full breasts flattened against his chest. Her thighs molded his erection. Missing his mouth, she kissed his ear instead. He moaned as she blew moist heat against it, then flicked the tip of her tongue inside. His moan darkened into a growl. She took advantage of his weakness. Thrust her tongue again and again until a shudder ripped through him and his legs shook. Until his heart pumped harder and his hips jerked, along with his sex.

Darkness held Zen Driscoll in its grip. A lustful grip that squeezed his testicles and swelled his sex.

Desire burned deep in his groin, so hot and intense he swore he'd ignite. He drew a deep, slow breath. Reason had no hope around Stevie Cole. His dick called the shots.

Releasing the drawstring at her waist, he drew down her slacks, then rolled her white cotton panties over her hips. He slid them down her legs until they wrapped her ankles. She kicked them aside. He could feel her naked heat through his boxers. Boxers that disappeared with one sweep of her hand.

He slanted his mouth over hers once again, firm and possessive this time. Taking as much as giving, she met his kiss with a demand of her own. She wanted him.

He thrust his tongue. Then his hips.

She threw back her head, arced into his body.

He kissed her exposed throat. Sucked the sensitive skin.

She bit his shoulder.

He bruised her neck with a love bite.

She scraped her nails down his back, dug the tips into his buttocks. Clutched him closer.

He palmed her breast, plucked at her nipple. Slipping one hand between her thighs, he lightly skimmed her moist opening with his knuckles. Her thighs parted and his fingers tested her wetness. She pressed upward against his touch. Heated, damp, and swollen, she was ready for him. He fingered her. Penetrating with two fingers while his mouth tugged at her nipple.

His rhythmic stroking drew her to climax.

He sensed the rise, the ache, the helpless tightening deep inside her.

Her breath punctuated the darkness, blew against his chest. Deep irregular sounds. Rapid pants followed by a sharp gasp as she clenched around his fingers.

After several pulsating seconds, she sagged against him. Boneless, barely able to speak. "Nice feel, Einstein."

He'd put his mark on her memories so she'd never forget him. Withdrawing his fingers, he caressed her spine. Long, slow, comforting strokes. Then he cupped her bottom, her rounded, womanly bottom. He liked her curves, the ripe fullness of her body.

When she'd caught her breath, she took his mouth. Kissed the very soul from his body. His sex stood upright against her belly, poking her for attention.

She gave him her undivided attention. Dropping to her knees, she took him in hand. She kissed the blade of his hip, the curving hollow. Hot need blazed over his skin where her breath burned, and it burned the full length of his erection.

His breath solidified in his throat when her tongue flicked the tip, then glided downward in a slow wet spiral. Tentative at first, then bolder. He moaned. He balled his fists and his hips thrust forward. He fought the urge to plunge his hands into her hair and demand an act that should only be a gift.

She gifted him willingly. The hot pull of her mouth drew the tip of his sex between her lips, drew him in farther with her cheeks, then suckled him deeply. He pulsed inside her mouth. She coaxed his desire until he was mindless and his body knew only sensation.

"I want to be inside you." Nerves strung out, he labored for breath. He curled his fingers over her shoulders, drew her up to face him.

Chest to breast, he backed up until his calves bumped the bed. They tumbled onto the mattress. "Condom?" His voice was as tight as his body.

"Second drawer on the nightstand."

He fumbled in the darkness, nearly knocking over a lamp. "New box?" he asked as he broke the seal, slit one foil packet, and sheathed himself.

"Recent purchase," she admitted.

"*How* recent?" He needed to know.

"After the charity auction."

"*After* you knew Aaron was engaged?"

"Mm-hmm." Her lips moved against his shoulder.

Her confession stroked his ego. "Purchased for me?"

"Maybe . . ."

"Your first blow on my coffee turned me on."

"My nipples picked you out of the crowd."

He attended each budded point before easing over her body. With arms braced on either side of her head, he placed his legs between hers, then pushed her thighs farther apart with his knee.

Slick and warm, she welcomed him into her body. But he'd penetrated no more than an inch when a sudden tightness in his hamstring brought him up short. Pain seared like a red-hot poker. He grabbed the back of his leg, groaned darkly, then rolled onto his side.

"Zen?" Stevie turned to him in the darkness. She touched his shoulder, felt his spasm of pain.

He caught his breath. "Hamstring."

"What can I do?"

"Be on top."

"I . . . I'd squish you."

"I'm stiff as a spike."

"I . . . can't."

"Then I'll take you on your side. Face me."

He pulled her up beside him, ran his hand over her bottom, along her outer leg. Then up her inner thigh.

Stevie responded. She wrapped one leg over his hip, opening herself to him. He slid inside her. Made love to her slowly.

Restlessly, she clutched and kneaded his back, increasing their rhythm. He thrust more solidly. She arced, strained, her body begging for release. Zen's chest heaved, and he struggled for breath.

They shattered in a melding of flesh and bone. In gasps and groans and sighs of surrender. His body shook as he ground himself against her one final time. Her final spasms drained him.

Afterward, he held her in silence. Her body eventually went slack, and he knew she now slept. The deep sleep of the sated.

He stared into the darkness for a long, long time, enjoying the soft warmth of Stevie Cole cuddled against his side. Knowing something had changed between them. Wondering if she'd recognize the rise of emotion he'd felt as they made love. Hoping beyond hope, her dreams included him and not Aaron.

He wanted this woman in his life.

CHAPTER 10

"Jacy?"

He was greeted by silence.

Where the hell had she gone? Risk wondered as he stormed through her house. He'd left specific instructions for her to sit tight, not to move a muscle until he returned from the convenience store. Jacy had awakened with a craving for Hostess Snowballs. He'd tugged on a white T-shirt and gray athletic shorts and hauled ass for the coconut cake treat.

His round-trip had taken less than thirty minutes. He'd spent ten of those minutes pumping gas into a near-empty tank. When the red light flashed, the Lotus began running on fumes.

Risk had noticed Jacy's red Mazda Miata in the driveway. But there was no one in the house. Jacy must have sweet-talked a ride. The woman had no business being out of bed. She needed to rest to heal.

The sexy vanilla scent of Lolita Lampeka drew him to the kitchen. There, he found a yellow Post-it stuck to a clay pot with sprigs of fresh mint. *Breakfast with Frank Stall*. Risk wadded up the note and tossed it in the trash can. His temper spiked.

She'd chosen to honor her auction breakfast.

She'd force a grin and bear the pain.

Damn stubborn woman.

Risk showered and shaved, then shoved his arms into a pale blue long-sleeved shirt and stepped into comfortable jeans. He tied the laces on a pair of Nikes—a brand he endorsed.

He purposely drove the speed limit to Jacy's Java. He parked his Lotus in the back alley, out of sight from the coffee shop windows. He didn't want Jacy to see him coming.

Taking several deep breaths, he tamped down his temper, not wanting to accuse or alienate her for ignoring doctor's orders.

He wanted to be calm when he found her.

His calm lasted all of ten minutes.

Jacy sat with Frank Stall at a cherrywood table with high-back chairs. She'd dressed quickly in a hot pink blouse covered by a purple-and-red paisley vest. A pair of tangerine leggings and one yellow flip-flop completed her outfit. Her pink cast bore a dozen signatures in black magic marker.

Sunshine patterned the walls in a kaleidoscope design. All the color in the world couldn't hide her pale profile. Her lips were tightly set in a small smile as she sipped her coffee from a delicate china cup painted with white and yellow daisies.

Frank, on the other hand, wore a brown Sunday

suit with a bottle green tie and pocket handkerchief. The older man chatted away, animated and utterly charmed by her presence.

Risk glanced at his watch. He'd give them five minutes before escorting Jacy home.

The coffee shop was packed. Word had spread that an out-of-commission Jacy had hired several ball players to run her business while she recuperated. The athletes had drawn customers in droves.

The scent of Romeo's burnt chocolate chip cookies permeated the air. The edges were black and crunchy, the centers doughy. Blended by Chaser, the less-than-icy frappuccinos were topped with too much whipped cream. And not enough chocolate shavings.

No one seemed to care.

Risk edged around a tall brunette wearing a cream-colored suit with a red blouse. A professional woman growing impatient over the long line for coffee. Their eyes connected briefly and she took him in. All of him. "Take me out to the ball game?" Her husky voice hinted at play beyond the park.

He shook his head. "Sorry. I'm in the middle of a game."

The game of his life. Innings passed with the speed of light. He had to find the proper time and place to propose to Jacy Grayson.

As if by sixth sense, Jacy turned slightly and sought him out. Their gazes locked across the crowded coffee shop.

He glared and her smile faltered.

She swallowed hard and swiveled back toward Frank.

He stalked through the crowd, seeking out a familiar face. He found Zen Driscoll at a mosaic-tiled table at the back of the shop, near the kitchen door. He looked relaxed and casual in a black pullover and chinos. "You're looking mighty happy," he noted as he dropped onto a cherry red retro pub stool.

Zen lowered his newspaper. "You're looking ready to kill."

"Jacy's out of bed."

"She arrived with the orange grower and caused quite a commotion," Zen confided. "Stevie and the Bat Pack read her the riot act. She promised a short stay."

A second glance at his watch. "Her stay is almost over."

"Coffee, Risk? Refill, Zen?" Stevie stopped by their table, as smiley as the shortstop. The collar on her blue polo was turned up. The hint of a red mark was visible against her neck.

"Cappuccino and a blow," Zen returned.

Color curved Stevie's cheekbones.

"Black coffee to go," Risk added to the order.

"Be right back." Stevie turned toward the counter.

"You're a little old to be giving hickeys."

"She tasted good," was Zen's only comment.

Risk understood. He loved Jacy's taste. All soft skin and womanly essence. More than once he'd marked his woman. He couldn't fault Zen for doing the same.

"Any sign of Aaron?" Risk asked. "I'd hoped to see him before he left town."

"Last time I saw him was at the midnight buffet. No sign of him since." Zen rubbed his forehead. "Natalie Llewellyn wasn't taken by Frostproof. I doubt they'll stay long."

Risk eyed his friend. "Seems like Frostproof is rubbing off on you though."

"Rubbing off real nicely," Zen agreed.

Risk looked around the coffee shop. "All running smoothly?"

Zen was slow to answer. "As smooth as it can with Psycho in charge. Romeo and Chaser are busting their butts. I'm back to work after my break."

"Do I need to speak to Psycho?"

"We're all about ready to speak to the boy," Zen said. "He's yanked everyone's chain at least twice."

The kitchen door swung open, and Psycho charged through, a plate of Rice Krispies Treats in hand. A white T-shirt stretched across his chest, printed with *TEAM EFFORT: A Lot of People Doing What I Say*. Buttery handprints marked his black-jeaned thighs. Marshmallow smeared one corner of his mouth.

Risk drew one hand down his face. "Treats aren't gourmet."

"But they're Psycho's favorite," Zen told him. "He badgered Jacy until she let him make one batch."

Risk caught Psycho stuffing his face. "He's eating the profits."

"Boy's got a tapeworm."

"Coffee's up." Stevie returned with their order.

Risk paid and tipped her, then left before *the blow*.

He crossed the room and came up behind Jacy. Curving his hand over her shoulder, he squeezed. "Time for a pain pill," he said, keeping his voice level.

Her hand shook as she took her last sip of coffee. The cup clattered on the saucer. "I'm ready to leave."

Frank Stall stood and volunteered, "I'll drive her home."

"I've got it covered," Risk returned evenly.

"Breakfast tomorrow, Jacy?" Frank looked hopeful.

Risk shook his head. "Tomorrow's too soon."

Jacy pushed herself off her chair, clutched her ribs, and winced. "Two weeks of breakfasts, Frank, if you let me slide a few days."

Frank beamed. "Definitely a deal."

Taking her by the hand, Risk drew her through the crowd. The clumping sound of her cast echoed on the tile floor. One step beyond the coffee shop and into the alley, and she folded against him.

"I hurt like hell," she moaned against his chest.

"Good."

She punched him in the arm. A puny little hit. "Mad at me?"

"I ought to beat you, babe, for sending me on a Snowball run so you could sneak out of the house."

"I didn't set you up, I swear. Frank called right after you left. I agreed to breakfast without thinking about the consequences."

"Consequences caught up with you?"

"I'm all beat up."

"Let's get you home." He gently turned her toward the Lotus. Once she was comfortably seated, he handed her his black coffee.

She dropped her head against the soft leather and closed her eyes. "Thanks for coming after me."

"Did you think I wouldn't?"

"You're taking on a lot of responsibility for a rebound lover."

He wanted the responsibility of being her husband. "I like taking care of you."

"I like you taking care of me."

Silence slipped in behind her words. Jacy didn't open her eyes until he pulled into her driveway.

"I'm hungry," she admitted when he'd cut the engine. "I sipped a chocolate caramel latte at the coffee shop, but didn't eat."

"There's a bag of Snowballs in the kitchen," Risk reminded her. "Unless you'd rather have an omelet or French toast."

"I'll go with the Snowballs."

He stripped her down and she crawled back into bed. All snuggly in his Rogues T-shirt, sans panties. Returning from the kitchen, he produced a glass of milk and a package of Snowballs on a wooden breakfast tray. He pulled up the rose leather armchair and watched her attack the Hostess treat.

Within seconds, coconut flaked one corner of her mouth and cream smeared her upper lip. Risk wanted to taste both woman and Snowball.

He stared at her mouth. "Can I have a bite?"

She set the tray to one side. "Take a big bite."

Risk bit. Taking her lip between his teeth, he licked and sucked, enjoying his own breakfast. She tasted of coconut and sugar. And sweet Jacy. He'd never tasted anyone so good.

Jacy let him taste her. Risk remained hungry long after he'd licked the coconut and cream from her lips. His mouth angled over hers, their tongues tangling, all the while feeding her hunger as much as his own.

She curved her hand around his neck, a strong neck. The muscles in his shoulders strained at the frustration of wanting her, yet being unable to take her. Her fingers stroked those shoulders, then slid into his hair. All thick and clean and soft to her touch.

She could touch this man forever.

His hand skimmed her body, over her breast, across her bare bottom, lingering on her thigh before finally settling on her hip. Where he squeezed hard. "Frustrated?" she breathed against his lips.

"I'm so hard my dick has track marks from my zipper."

Jacy rested her forehead against his, lowered her lashes. She was hardly able to breathe. "Time to stop?"

"Before I embarrass myself like a sixteen-year-old."

"I have two good hands." She ran her fingers over his blue-jeaned thigh, traced down his zipper. Felt the enormity of his erection.

He eased back. "Not the same as being inside you."

"It could be weeks."

"We'll wait, babe."

"If you change your mind"—she rubbed her hands together—"you know where to find me."

He shifted on the chair and crossed one ankle over his knee. "Choice of activity?"

"A little conversation."

"Cover yourself with the sheet first," he stated. "You're damn distracting."

She complied, tucking the ends beneath her naked bottom and thighs.

"What's on your mind?" he asked.

"Did you see Zen and Stevie at the coffee shop?"

Risk nodded. "They went horizontal."

She grinned. "Stevie had a hickey."

"Zen left his mark."

"Any sign of Aaron?"

"No one's seen him."

"Natalie Llewellyn really isn't his type."

"Natalie is who he's chosen."

She licked her lips and dared, "What's your type?"

He blinked, momentarily taken aback by her question. It took him several seconds to respond. "You know me better than any other woman, babe. You know what I like."

She grabbed a magazine off the nightstand and flipped through the pages. "There's paper and pen in the drawer. Let's take a *Cosmo* quiz."

Risk visibly flinched. "Too girly. Real men don't take *Cosmo* quizzes."

Jacy located the quiz. "It's on compatibility."

"Women take these quizzes far more seriously than men."

"We're not getting married. Let's take it for fun."

"I'd rather poke my eye with a fork."

"Plastic or sterling silver fork?"

"Pitchfork, Jacy. I don't want to play."

"Please . . ."

Damn. She had him. One simple word, said so sweetly. Her eyes all wide and her lips a little pouty. He was a total sucker for this woman.

"Heal fast, babe. I'm only taking one quiz during your recovery." That said, he searched the nightstand drawer for paper and pen. He found a die cut coffee cup notepad and a red neon marker.

Jacy chose a powder blue glitter pen to check off her answers in the magazine, then she began to read. "First question we mark separately. It's on body type. Men only: how do you like your woman? a) busty and brainless b) smart and sassy c) tiny tits and boyish hips d) pouty and dewy."

Risk rolled his eyes and shook his head. He wrote down a letter and nodded toward the magazine. "Read your choices."

"Women only," Jacy read slowly. "Do you like your man: a) primed and pumped b) tall and lean c) short and stocky d) beer belly and balding."

"What letter did you pick?" he asked.

" 'B'."

"I went with 'D'."

Pouty and dewy? Maybe she didn't know him as well as she thought.

"An athlete's body ages faster than that of a man with a desk job," he explained, perfectly serious. "A much younger wife can pick up the sexual slack, ride astride, when my body aches and my knees give out in my golden years."

Jacy went still. Ten months separated their birthdays. She was no sweet young thing. She'd wanted to grow old with this man, but apparently he was looking for a child bride.

She stared at him. Stared hard, until his smile broke and his laughter rolled over her, gut deep and husky. Holding up his paper, he pointed to the "B" penned and traced several times over. He'd gone with smart and sassy. "Gotcha." Amusement lit his gaze. "You're so gullible."

"You're not that funny," she sniffed.

"About as funny as this quiz."

"It gives us something to do."

"I'd rather watch you sleep."

"I'll take a pain pill once we finish."

"Sure you don't want it now?"

"Question two." Ignoring him, she read on. "First Impressions. Do you note a) eyes and hair b) smile and attitude c) style of clothing d) can't form an impression until I see the person naked."

Risk marked a letter, then said, " 'C'. You have your own style. Flamboyant and free. I do, however, like you best in nothing but your skin."

" 'B' for me." She tapped her glitter pen on the magazine page. "I've always loved your smile. The sensual twist of your lips. Your arrogance grew on me."

His brows drew together. "I'm never arrogant."

"You were cocky as hell in high school."

He indolently rolled his tongue into his cheek. "Hard to believe."

She returned to the quiz. "Say It With: a) flowers b) chocolate c) concert tickets d) sex."

"How about all of the above?"

"Pick *one*."

"Fine. 'D'."

"Ditto."

His gaze turned hot, his lips parted slightly. "Glad we agree."

"Next question, Foreplay: a) gazing deeply into your partner's eyes b) sex talk c) soft, sweet kisses d) sharing a six-pack of beer, no burping."

Risk drew his hand down his face. "Who thinks up these questions?"

"Write down your answer."

He did. " 'C'."

Jacy hesitated. "I like it when you talk sexy to me."

"I love your taste," he told her in a deep, dark voice that slid over her the way his body did in sex. "The way your nipples pucker, the way you go all breathless and moan, how your belly quivers when I penetrate. The way you dig your nails in my back. Sigh my name against my neck."

The man had a way with words. She fanned her face and swallowed hard, barely able to continue. "I Prefer Sex: a) in the morning b) at noon c) at night d) once a month."

He looked at his groin. "e) every hour on the hour."

"Favorite Release," she continued. "A) missionary b) doggie style c) hand action d) full Kama Sutra."

His jaw clenched and his nostrils flared. "Any questions that don't relate to sex?" he asked.

She scanned down the quiz. "Favorite Vacation Spot: a) beach b) mountains c) white-water rafting d) dude ranch."

" 'C'," Risk said as he jotted down the letter. "I like the rush of a wild ride."

"While I'm spreading on suntan oil in the Bahamas."

He changed his mind. "Nassau's good, as long as I can spread the oil all over your body."

"Dinner Date," Jacy moved on. "A) American b) Chinese c) Mexican d) French."

"Sweet and sour chicken."

"You said that 'cause you know that's *my* favorite."

"Did I score extra points?"

"A few." She returned to the quiz. "Two more questions to go. Afternoon Entertainment: a) movie b) shopping c) athletic event d) couch potato."

"I spend three-fourths of my life at a ball park."

"Baking, drinking coffee, and reading aren't even a choice." She sighed. "Moving on. Last question: Marriage Plans." She noticed that Risk grew tense. His male radar was on full alert. "A) in one month b) six months c) one year d) not in this lifetime."

He slowly crumpled up his paper, tossed the red neon marker back in the drawer, and stood. He was trying to act nonchalant, yet Jacy knew Risk and his tics. His eye twitch claimed him cornered.

She closed *Cosmo* and set it on the nightstand. "Silly quiz, means nothing—"

"I'd marry the right woman tomorrow."

Right woman. Jacy's heart stopped. Commitment was in Risk's future, once he found his life partner.

Silence filled the room as he snagged her breakfast tray off the bed and went for her pain pill. When he returned, she said softly, "Thanks for taking the quiz."

"It was a compatibility test. Rebound lovers don't exactly qualify for husband material." He paused. "Do they?"

"Depends if he has the qualities I'm seeking."

"Nudge, nudge." He appeared curious about her ideal man.

"Someone who understands that a wedding ring gives as much freedom as it does security. Someone who understands my quirks and craziness and is around when I need him."

"I'm here when you need me, babe."

"I'm talking forever."

Rebound to forever. Risk Kincaid needed to say his piece, stake his claim. Quickly.

"Pain pill, please." Jacy's request cut off his confession.

His window of opportunity slammed shut. "Right here." He handed over her medicine and a glass of water.

Once the pill was swallowed, she patted the waterbed. "Lie with me?"

"Sure." He'd never taken so many naps, been so well rested. Lying with Jacy was pure pleasure.

Removing his shirt and shoes, he crawled up beside her. She rested her head on his shoulder and closed her eyes. When he felt her body go lax, he kissed her forehead. "I love you, Jacy Grayson." Then he tested the words in the silence, words he'd been waiting to say. "Marry me."

She stirred ever so slightly. Her lips moved, her speech a bare whisper as she spoke in sleep. "Tomorrow too soon?"

* * *

"Any plans for Tuesday?" Risk asked Jacy following her two-hour nap. Any chance she remembered accepting his proposal?

Apparently not. "Nothing for tomorrow," she said slowly, squinting, as if trying to remember something she'd forgotten. "Don't forget my Bluebells later today."

He was supposed to coach her T-ball team. Little girls with pigtails and braces. All leggy and lacking coordination. "Can't wait."

She placed a soft kiss on his shoulder. "Maybe I could ride along—"

"Maybe not."

"—take a lawn chair, stretch out so my ribs won't hurt."

"No can do."

She nipped him then. "I've got cabin fever."

Jacy was restless. Not a good sign. Risk rubbed the spot where she'd bitten him. "I don't want you to overdo. The doctor ordered you to relax—"

"I'm sleeping sixteen hours a day."

"If I take you with me, will you promise to stay in bed all day tomorrow?"

"M-mmm, maybe."

Not good enough. "What plans have you made?"

She dipped her head. "Maybe bake at the coffee shop."

"No way in hell."

"You're not the boss of me."

"Childish, even for you, babe."

She rose on one elbow, winced, eased back down, and wrinkled her nose. "I could use a sponge bath."

Touching her would kill him. "How about a shower instead? We could wrap a trash bag from your knee down to protect your cast."

She contemplated his suggestion. "Can I have clean sheets too?"

He could change a bed. "No problem."

"Will you do a load of laundry?"

He could separate whites from colors. Delicates from denim.

"Water my plants?"

Also doable.

"Maybe you could dust and run the vacuum." Jacy hated housework.

"I don't do windows."

"Neither do I."

Risk pushed off the waterbed. "Sit tight. I'll be right back."

Sit tight didn't register in Jacy's brain. A plastic bag in hand, he returned from the kitchen to find her hung up on the waterbed frame, one arm and one leg dangling limply over the side. She was flat out stuck. "You moved," he accused.

"Getting in is much easier than getting out," she huffed.

"You need my help." He stood several feet from the bed, crossing his arms over his chest. "I should leave you in that position. You wouldn't go far."

Jacy struggled, then quit the fight. "Don't be a jackass."

"Jack *who*? Getting a little testy, babe?"

"Prepare to die when I'm back on my feet."

"I'm scared. I'll be looking over my shoulder, my knees shaking for four weeks." She went quiet on him. Her face was buried between the waterbed mattress and the bed frame. "You okay?"

Her voice was muffled. "I'm plotting your torture."

"Silken bonds and feather whips?"

"Knife and pliers."

The woman was vicious. Threats of castration sent him to her side. Tucking one hand beneath her shoulder and one behind her knees, he gently lifted her against his chest. She glared at him all the way to the bathroom. She was ticked off, and when he set her down, he tucked her into his body and kissed away her anger.

"Strip me down." Her words warmed his mouth.

Stripping her was easy. Seeing her naked made him hard. She stood before him, all soft and flushed.

He hunkered down, focused on covering her cast. Once the bag was secure, he made the mistake of looking up. Up over curvy thighs to a triangle of blond curls.

Sweet, sweet mercy. The urge to kiss and taste swelled within him, and his control slipped. The heat from her body signalled a longing to match his own. She needed release. He could make it good for her.

So good, she'd collapse from her orgasm, causing more pain than pleasure.

He wasn't going to chance it.

His hands shook as he got to his feet, turned her

toward the shower and adjusted the water to a comfortable temperature.

She hobbled into the shower. Water shot over her shoulders, steam building all around her. "Join me?" she asked.

He shook his head. "I'll be right here if you need me," he assured her. "Don't use the shower massager for anything but rinsing off."

She stuck her tongue out at him, then closed the shower door. The smoky glass soon fogged, making the outline of her body barely visible. Risk had showered countless times with her. He knew her bathing ritual. She'd shampoo and condition her hair, soap her body, then rinse fully. If he heard the shower massager flick from stream to pulse, he'd throw open the door—

Thump. Soft, but definitely a thump.

"I dropped the soap." Her voice rose amid the steam.

Risk flattened his hands against the door and rested his forehead against the glass. Hot, foggy glass. He began to sweat. "Pick it up, babe."

A low moan. "Too sore. Can't bend over."

"Try *really* hard . . ."

A second moan, louder, more strained. "Can't reach past my knees." Sounds of crumpling plastic. "Water leaked into my cast."

Crap! "Just rinse off and step out."

A deep, shaky sigh. "I'm not clean."

If he joined her in the shower they'd get down and dirty.

"Risk?" Her call hinted of panic.

He shucked his shirt, cracked the shower door, and spotted the bar of Ivory near her covered cast. Dropping down, he snagged the soap, only to have it slip out of his hand like a slippery fish. "Damn."

He leaned in farther, his hair and shoulders now completely wet. Water trickled down his chest and into the waistband of his jeans. Wet splotches spread across his thigh.

A second lunge for the soap, and he met with success. Squeezing the bar tightly, he left finger imprints. He straightened up and handed it over.

"Thank you." Her voice was barely audible over the spray.

"Can you manage now?" Risk asked, refusing to look beyond her eyes, wide and luminous, surrounded by spiky brown lashes.

"Can't reach my back."

Resigned, he stepped fully into the shower, jeans and all. He closed the door, trapped inside the steamy stall with a naked woman.

His naked woman.

Jacy wet was a sight to behold. Droplets gathered on her cheekbones and nose. Her breasts and belly were sleek and shiny. Traces of soap collected at her triangle of blond curls. A soapy stream slid between her thighs.

Risk could barely breathe, had no ability to talk. He motioned her to turn around.

She handed him the soap, gave him her back. The full view was soft and streamlined. The pale curve of her buttocks nearly did him in.

He moved in behind her. She was sweetly petite; the top of her head barely reached his collarbone. The scent of berries tickled his nose. Jacy loved fruity shampoo.

He clenched the soap as tightly as his jaw. The bar fit solidly in the palm of his big hand. She trusted him to wash her without getting carried away.

He skimmed Ivory over her shoulders, then down her arms. Cleansed the symmetrical sides of her spine. His callused fingers grazed her skin with each stroke. She felt damn good. Wet and slick. Sexy.

He ran the soap over her buttocks.

She leaned back into his palm.

His hand stilled.

She moved against the Ivory.

The slight sway of her hips drove him to his knees.

He needed to keep washing, not dwell on her soapy ass.

He gently washed the back of her legs.

She shifted slightly, parted her thighs . . .

He sucked air, taking a mouthful of spray as he shot to his feet. Coughing, he directed, "Rinse off, babe."

She eased around, took the soap from his hand. Massaged her palms into a lather. "Want me to do you?"

Did he ever. His erection swelled and pushed against his zipper. Throbbed for release.

However uncomfortable, he clutched a tiny thread of control. Jacy looked pale and tired. Her ribs hurt more than she would let on. Though he'd sell his soul to feel her hands on him, he'd suffer blue balls until they came together again. Fully together. With the passion and hunger that came after healing.

She'd better heal fast.

She rinsed her hands and he turned off the shower. Taking her hand, so small in his, he led her from the shower. "I'll dry you off."

She stood still, slumping slightly against the sink, as he briskly toweled her down. Her eyes were downcast, glazed. White lines bracketed her mouth. She had overdone it in the shower.

He dropped his jeans, toweled himself off as well. Pink terry cloth wrapped his waist as he stooped to tear the trash bag from her cast. Then he scooped her up against his chest, all warm and naked and fresh smelling.

Propping her against the dresser, he pulled out a black teddy and matching thong, which he twirled on one finger. "Rogues jersey's in the hamper."

"I'll go silky and skimpy."

"I'd prefer flannel gown and granny panties."

Jacy leaned on him as he slid the thong up her legs. She sighed softly when he slowly outlined the tiny satin triangle with his fingers, her tummy quivering when he pressed a kiss just above her navel. They both moaned when he circled her belly button with his tongue. Dipped the tip. Then pulled back.

The temperature in the room rose as hot as his sex. Her breasts bounced when he slipped the teddy over her head. She grimaced as she lifted her arms and the satin slid to her hips.

He stepped back, and with two strong tugs, stripped the waterbed of its sheets. Rustling through her linen closet, he selected navy satin. The last time he'd lain on those sheets, the waterbed withstood a full night of motion. They had invented positions, making love until exhaustion forced them to sleep.

He turned down the bed and settled Jacy on the clean sheets. She yawned. Blinked her eyes sleepily. "I'm drifting off."

"I'll wake you for T-ball practice."

"Promise?"

"I'd rather drive you than have someone else pick you up behind my back," Risk stated. "At least if you're with me, I know exactly where you're at."

CHAPTER 11

Jacy Grayson had to be related to Houdini. One minute she was sitting on a lawn chair near first base, watching her Bluebells; the next minute her chair was empty.

Her disappearing act was getting old. Fast.

Risk Kincaid was having a hard time keeping track of both Jacy and her twelve T-ballers. The little girls were everywhere they shouldn't be.

"Stay on third base, Hailey," he called to the blond ballerina in a red leotard and violet tutu now twirling between home plate and third base.

Hailey stopped in mid-twirl, thin arms spread wide, her hair a tumble of knots and curls clear down her back. "Jacy lets me dance until the game starts."

Jacy this and Jacy that. That's all Risk had heard from the girls. Jacy's word was their bible. She followed few rules in life or on the ball field. The Bluebells followed in her footsteps.

Dressed in unmatched colors, plaids and prints,

they modeled Jacy's style and behavior, imitated her free spirit.

Circling the bleachers, he caught Jacy hobbling toward him. Her scooped stretch top in neon yellow and burnt orange jeans made the sun blink. Amber and blue tourmaline hoops dangled from her ears. A large amber and gold broach was pinned over her right breast. Her arms were now loaded down with Gatorade from the parks and recreation concession stand. "Batters get thirsty," she breathed out heavily as she handed over the bottles.

He looked at her darkly. "There's a drinking fountain close by."

"Drink of choice is grape."

Risk took the Gatorade and nodded toward her lawn chair. "Sit." She complied. He crossed the diamond to the home team dugout and set out the drinks. "Ready, girls?" he called to the group. "Let's practice."

No one paid the least bit of attention to him. Three girls collected by first base, sharing a bag of M&M's. Half a dozen more chatted about school. One girl cuddled a golden retriever puppy against her chest. The rest stared at him as if they didn't speak English.

"Who bats first?" he tried again.

More stares. More silence.

He turned to Jacy. "I could use a little help here."

"Play ball," she mouthed to him.

He clapped his hands. "*Play ball.*"

"Do you want us to scratch and spit in the dirt?"

asked Cassidy, the tallest of the six-year-olds, as she approached the batting tee, an adjustable flexible tube on a moveable base.

"Not necessary," Risk assured her.

"Can we swear?"

"Keep it clean."

Wearing a stars-and-stripes batter's helmet on her head, Cassidy positioned herself left of the tee. She clutched her hands halfway up the bat, then put her entire sixty-five pounds behind her first swing. She knocked the ball a solid ten feet. Leggy and anxious, she took off for third base.

Risk watched her tennies kick up dust. "Wrong direction." He motioned her toward first. Cassidy shook her head. Gave the ballerina on third a high five instead.

He looked at Jacy, who perched on the end of the lawn chair, all smiles and applauding madly. "Super hit."

"She ran the wrong way."

"Doesn't matter," Jacy returned excitedly. "She connected with the ball today. It's usually whiff and miss until the sun sets."

So much for organized play. No one chased after the ball. Only the puppy took an interest. He stole each ball that was hit, dug a hole, and buried it in the outfield. The girls set up a new ball with each bat.

Redheaded Kayla, with a ponytail that spiked like a rooster tail, took the next bat. Taking her stance, she pushed her black-framed glasses up her nose, and dug in her red-fringed cowboy boots. The fringe on her brown cowgirl vest and skirt swung with her body as she twisted, then banged the ball.

Kayla jumped up and down, her boots leaving deep impressions in the dirt. She skipped toward first, fringe swaying. Her smile was so broad Risk was afraid the bands on her braces would snap.

"Good coaching," Jacy called to him.

"I've yet to coach, babe."

"We don't play by the rules."

"So I've noticed."

A girly scream raised the hair on Risk's arms. Just beyond first base, Brooke, with her short brown hair and preference for sitting in the grass and picking dandelions, now flapped her arms and ran in circles, screeching at the top of her lungs.

"Butterfly," Jacy shouted.

"*Killer* butterfly?" he shot over his shoulder as he jogged toward the little girl.

Tears streamed down Brooke's face. Grabbing him like a lifeline, her skinny arms snaked around his thighs. She squeezed tightly. Risk softly patted her back until she stopped shaking.

"Butterflies scare me," she sniffed, then wiped her runny nose against his thigh. So much for clean jeans.

"They can't hurt you," Risk assured her.

"Jacy says it's bees not butterflies that sting."

"She's right. Butterflies decorate the air."

Brooke blinked. "Like flowers decorate the ground?"

"Exactly," he agreed. "Next time you'll best the butterfly."

"You sure?" She looked as if she wanted to believe him.

"Gut feeling."

She patted his stomach. "Hope you're right." Slipping her hand in his, she said, "I'll help you coach for a while."

They walked back toward home plate. The little girl grafted herself to his side, secure in the belief that Risk would protect her from a second butterfly attack.

Ellie Rosen batted next. Smiling and a little shy in her new powder blue shirt decorated with pink hearts and her stiff denims, she took her stance at the batting tee and swung high. Missed. Then, swung again. This time the ball dribbled toward first. And Ellie ran her fastest.

Risk waved Kayla onto second.

Kayla shook her head. "I want to share first base with Ellie. We're best friends."

Two on first. Risk gave his head a shake. T-ball practice continued for the next hour. Every little girl batted at least twice, some three times. They took turns going for Gatorade, returning with purple-rimmed lips. Even the puppy came back with a purple tongue. Risk wondered which bottle the dog had slurped. He was sticking with water.

It was the most unorganized, utterly outrageous practice he had ever coached. If he could even call it coaching. Yet everyone cheered and did the happy dance, sometimes for no reason at all.

When it was over, the girls collected their bats, helmets, and tee stand, then huddled around Jacy, hugging her gently.

Jacy gave each one praise and encouragement. She recalled a specific swing, how fast each one ran, how much they had improved. Risk watched the six-year-olds blush and blossom. They adored Jacy. Absorbed her enthusiasm and warmth.

"What did you learn in school today?" Jacy asked the girls, killing time until their parents picked them up.

"Our teacher learned us about the sea," Kayla informed her.

"We have a new aquarium in our class," Ellie added. "Goldfish and guppies. No sharks. I get to feed the fish all week."

"I think sharks are ugly and mean, and have big teeth, just like Linda Mason," Cassidy said with all the indignity of youth. "She wouldn't share her crayons. She's not my friend anymore."

"We looked at picture books and saw a movie," Ellie added. "I like mermaids. They are beautiful with their shiny tails. How do they get pregnant?"

Jacy hugged Ellie close. "Mermaids aren't real, sweetie."

"Ariel had legs," Cassidy insisted.

"The Little Mermaid's a cartoon," Jacy said with unruffled patience. "Tell me more," she encouraged.

"An octopus has eight testicles," Kayla said proudly.

"Tentacles," Jacy gently corrected.

Risk swallowed hard and forced down his laughter.

"Jelly fish sting and electric eels can give you a

shock," Ellie added. "Eels live in caves and plug themselves into chargers every night. Bobby Talbott told me that on the playground."

Bobby Talbott, the classroom tease and storyteller. The kid sure had an imagination. "Not chargers, sweetie," Jacy explained. "Eels have organs that generate electricity. Like a power plant."

A few scrunched up noses, and several scratched their heads, as the girls took it all in. Bobby was their source of information. Some still believed him over Jacy.

Breaking the silence, Cassidy giggled. "A dolphin breathes through an asshole on the top of his head."

Bobby Talbott strikes again. "It's called a blow-hole." Jacy lightly pinched Cassidy's nose. "Similar to a nostril."

Risk admired how quickly Jacy corrected the girls, with humor and kindness. Attention spans were short, and the conversation skipped from one topic to the next with lightning speed. From starfish to the yucky taste of saltwater, then on to swimming.

"When boys swim in the sea, and it's cold, their willies get small." Brooke surprised even Jacy with her comment.

"Who told you that?" Jacy prodded the girl. Was it Bobby Talbott again?

"When me and Sarah went to the beach in the summer, we hid in the sand dunes and watched my big sister kiss her boyfriend. He told her he couldn't do it. He'd been out swimming. The ocean was cold and his willie shrunk. My sister called him a shrimp."

The girls covered their mouths and giggled.

Brooke darted a look at Risk. "Have you kissed Jacy?"

Jacy gave him a slight nod. He went with honesty. "Once or twice."

"My daddy says my mommy tastes like toothpaste when they kiss," Kayla said proudly.

"What does Jacy taste like?" Cassidy ask.

Sweet, sweet woman.

Before he could answer, Kayla jumped ahead. "Do you love her?" Her eyes were wide and innocent behind her glasses.

Twelve T-ballers stared at him. All wide-eyed and curious, along with their coach. A slight blush painted Jacy's cheeks. What to say? How to say it? Hell, he could propose to her now.

The arrival of several sets of parents stole his moment once again. After greetings and good-byes, the adults carted their girls off to dinner, homework, and an evening with family. Ellie Rosen caught a ride with her best friend Kayla.

The ball park had gone quiet. All laughter evaporated. Amid the light breeze and stillness, Risk extended his hand and eased Jacy to her feet. "Practice again tomorrow?"

"Can you handle another day?" She stood, a bit wobbly.

He folded up her lawn chair. "No rules makes for interesting play."

"We're skill building, learning as we go," she explained. "Not focusing on scoring, winning, or losing."

He slung an arm about her shoulders, snugged her close. "You do have fun."

"That's what it's all about. Enjoying the game." A slow smile spread. "Years ago, Stevie and I played T-ball. We were on the same team. The Violets. Stevie could hit like a boy. I ran like a girl."

"You are a girl."

"I wanted to run like the wind."

The ladies had a history, Risk well knew. He swore to never let them down again. His secrets were their secrets. He and Jacy would never fight again.

"Those little girls adore you," he stated.

Her steps slowed. "How about you, Kincaid? Adore me?"

"You're my best friend, babe."

A momentary flicker of disappointment darkened her blue eyes. "Take me for coffee, friend?"

"I'll brew a pot at home."

"I wanted to check on the coffee shop."

"You want to do anything and everything but stay in bed."

"Twenty minutes, promise."

He threw back his head. "I hate to cave."

She stopped beneath a poinciana tree at the edge of the parking lot. Branches of scarlet and orange flowers dipped low over the hood of his Lotus. "But you'll cave for me."

"Damn straight."

Beneath the flowery branches he slid loose tendrils of blond hair behind her ears, slowly driving his hands into her hair. He fully cupped her skull and skillfully angled her face to accept his kiss. "My caving is going to cost you."

He took her mouth then, gently at first, no more than a brush of lips, an exchange of breath. That was never enough. His tongue flicked, pried, and penetrated. She tasted of grape Gatorade and her own sweetness. Again and again, he mated with her mouth. Deep kisses that left him painfully hard.

Jacy clung to him, couldn't get close enough. She dug her fingers into his arms. Her nails scored his flesh beneath the short sleeve of his T-shirt. She was as greedy for him as he was for her.

He pressed against her, wanting her to feel him. Knowing her panties were wet, making her crave him.

They kissed until he'd stolen her breath and her chest heaved—until pain shot along her ribs and her low moan forced them apart.

Control returned, heartbeat by heartbeat. He rested his forehead against hers. He was still breathing hard and board stiff. But his concern for Jacy was foremost on his mind. "Did I hurt you?"

She met his gaze. Her eyes were glazed, her lips red and puffy. Her chin was abraded from his five o'clock shadow. "My only hurt comes from knowing you're not getting any."

"Neither are you."

"We're both suffering."

He kissed the tip of her nose and confessed, "I can live without sex, but I can't live without you."

She blinked and licked her lips, looking very uncertain. "We've lived a long time as rebound lovers. Sex has always been at the top of the list of why we get together."

"Time to rework the list, babe."

"Our time together has always been limited. You fly in, mend my broken heart, fly out."

"This time I'm staying a while."

"You'll survive without sex?"

He was about to take himself in hand. "Four weeks isn't that long." *Who was he kidding?*

"It will strengthen our friendship."

He wanted more than friendship. He wanted to make love to this woman as a man would to his wife. To mate with her soul. Forever. The damage to her ribs and ankle prohibited him from showing her how much he cared through kisses and caresses. He needed to find the words that would bind them for life. Make her believe she was much more to him than just a rebound lover.

"Friendship over a cup of coffee." He assisted her into his Lotus. Loading the lawn chair, he slid in beside her. "Then, bed."

"Beds are boring. I want to have sex in the alley before we leave town."

Natalie Llewellyn's demand sent chills down Aaron Grayson's spine. He'd climbed out of the limo and taken two steps down the alley toward the back door of Jacy's Java when Natalie came up behind him after sending the driver on his way.

Sex in the alley? His heart slammed so hard, it threatened a coronary. All that stood between him and the door was a dumpster and Stevie Cole's yellow Volkswagon. He would not have sex in garbage—nor anywhere near Stevie's car.

"Not the time or place, Natalie." He raised his hand, backed away.

Natalie came toward him, her strappy high heels clicking on the gravel, the sway of her thin hips seductive. Sliding her hands over her thighs, she slowly tugged her tobacco-colored skirt to her knees, then higher, soon proving she wore no panties.

Aaron's mouth went dry, as much from fear as arousal. The woman stood with her skirt hiked to her waist, one hip jutted at a do-me angle. His palms began to sweat. He was suddenly very much afraid.

"Not now." He tried to take command of a situation turned nasty. Very nasty once Natalie unbuttoned her ivory silk blouse and bared her breasts to God and the alley—and anyone walking along the sidewalk.

He ran a hand through his hair. "You're damn crazy."

She came to stand before him, ran one long nail down the front of his pressed shirt and screwed the tip into his belly. Then nipped his bottom lip hard. "Let me make you crazy."

He groaned as her fingers slipped beneath his waistband, tickled the tip of his sex, which stretched up to meet her.

"Against the wall?" She stroked inside his jockeys.

He couldn't breath. "Behind the Volkswagon."

"Trying to hide, lover?"

"Yesss." It came out as a hiss. She'd squeezed him so hard he saw black dots.

She released him. Taking his hand, she kissed, then bit his palm. Left a full set of teeth marks. She led him behind the yellow Bug.

"Don't touch the car." The words came out harsher than he'd intended.

Natalie ran her hand over the side panel. "You're precious Stevie's car. Take me on the hood."

He shook his head. "I couldn't do that to her." The car was an antique. Memories flashed back to a time when he and Stevie had made out in the VW. They'd had sex in the backseat and on the hood. That was their memory. Natalie wouldn't tarnish that for him.

Natalie flattened her body against his and insisted, "Do it for me."

The press of her breasts and hips, the distracting movement of her fingers down his back to his buttocks, nearly had him giving in. Nearly, but not quite. "No."

She dug her fingers into his ass. She shoved him back until his calves contacted the Volkswagon bumper. "Do it my way or—"

His temper broke. "Or *what*, Natalie?" He took her by the shoulders, his strength now dominating her. "You'll break off the engagement?"

Her lips twisted into an unpleasant smile. "I have options."

"So do I." He tugged her toward the back wall of the alley, pinned her with his body. They were no longer visible from the sidewalk, and he prayed to God no one from the coffee shop brought out the trash. "You and me against the wall." He kissed her then, with such force her mouth would surely be bruised.

Natalie responded, kissing him with a hint of anger and a lust so intense her body shook. Aaron tried to be gentle, yet the second he touched her with tenderness, she bit him, on the mouth, on the neck, on the shoulder, causing enough pain to drive him outside of himself. If she wanted it rough, he would oblige.

She encouraged his roughness, talking raw and dirty in his ear until he understood she could only get off by public sex. He wasn't certain how often he could go on *display*. It was downright frightening.

He fondled her breasts, pinched her nipples.

She continued to bite him. Marking him. Turning him into someone he no longer knew.

He found her wet. Slick. Ready for him.

His sex stood rigidly upright. Fear kept him stiff.

She scored a condom from his pants pocket, fitted him.

He clutched her bottom, lifted her until they locked.

She bucked wildly, nearly knocking him off his feet.

He ground against her once, pulled out, streamlined in.

She screamed. So loudly he covered her mouth with his hand.

The woman was a biter. She clamped down hard on his fingers.

The spasms of her orgasm milked his own. He came, his chest heaving, his body sweating, his moan guttural. Almost unrecognizable. He was on the verge of becoming someone else. A man on the edge of getting caught, almost challenging someone to catch him. Did he want to be this person?

Natalie had showed him the pleasures of being

edgy and exposed. Taunting and tempting, she fired his blood.

Sliding down his body, she licked her lips and smiled. "I liked."

Aaron's fingers shook as he adjusted his clothing.

Natalie was much quicker. Her experience with public sex gave her a quicker recovery time.

The limo pulled up to the curb with the slide of his zipper. Talk about perfect timing. Natalie had her sex down to a science.

He glanced at his watch. "I need to say good-bye to Stevie. Give me ten."

Natalie looked bored. "I don't understand why—"

"You never will," he cut her off. "Stevie and I have a history. We both need closure."

"Close the door for good," Natalie directed. "Frostproof is a part of your past."

The thought of never returning gave him pause. Never was a long time. He had friends and family here. Cutting them out of his life seemed severe.

He watched Natalie stroll to the limo. She looked slim and beautiful and momentarily satisfied. Her scent lingered on his skin. He needed to wash his hands and face in the bathroom sink before locating Stevie. Ditch the condom as well.

It was time to face the woman he'd loved as a boy.

And get on with his life as a man.

Stevie Cole's radar tracked Zen Driscoll as he worked the coffee shop. Good-looking and personable, he charmed customers into smiling and sampling slices of orange-cranberry pound cake and black-and-white cookies, along with Psycho's Rice Krispies Treats—Treats that contained more sticky marshmallow than actual cereal.

Stevie had witnessed firsthand how personable Zen could be and right after lunch they'd gained first hand insight into Jacy's fascination with the cooler. She'd gone in for cream. He'd appeared for raspberries. They had stared at each other for a very long time.

Until Zen threw the deadbolt and she hit the lights.

They'd enjoyed a quickie.

Afterward, he'd flipped on the lights. Her blue coffeehouse polo had hiked up to her nipples. Her white cotton panties and khakis were caught mid-thigh.

Once Zen had adjusted himself, and she'd tucked in her shirt, he caught her by the shoulders and pulled her close. He rested his chin on the top of her head. "Next time I want candlelight. One tiny candle. I want to see your freckles. Trace them with my tongue."

Stevie would light a candle for this man.

"Black coffee with my cream."

Aaron Grayson's voice cut through her thoughts. Stevie turned slowly and faced the man she'd loved for so many years. She found not a trace of the man she once knew.

Aaron appeared unusually unkempt. The hair over his forehead shone with sweat, the strands finger combed. His light green long-sleeve shirt was rumpled, his white chinos wrinkled. His belt hung loosely, hooked in the wrong notch.

"Planning to sit or should I make the coffee to go?" she finally managed.

"I'll sit if you'll join me."

She felt Zen's eyes on her and glanced his way. He'd grown thoughtful. Concerned. And considering the clench of his jaw, Stevie decided he was not overly pleased.

"Place is full. We're incredibly busy," she hedged.

Business hadn't let up the entire day. The line for coffee still stretched out the door and wrapped the corner of the building. Customers were clustered about tables, some sharing a single chair.

Truth be told, she wasn't all that certain she wanted to sit down with Aaron. He'd shattered her world. She was slowly picking up the pieces—with Zen's help.

He nodded toward the kitchen. "Five minutes, Stevie. I need to talk—"

"Talk is cheap." Psycho pushed between them. All rough and tumble and looking criminal in his black T-shirt with half a dozen tears, jeans bleached white at the knees and seams, and his day-old stubble. Yet it was the glitter in his eyes that marked him dangerous. "Actions speak louder than words. What's left to say, buffet boy?"

Aaron's face turned red. "Stick it, Psycho."

The young power hitter hung a protective arm about Stevie's shoulders. "Stevie's like a sister. You hurt her, you hurt me."

"And we hurt back." A shuffle of feet and Romeo and Chaser backed up Psycho. They looked relaxed,

Romeo even smiling, yet Stevie could feel the hostility in the air. Hostility that could turn into a fight.

The coffee shop had gone quiet. The customers were probably placing mental bets on three-against-one odds. The hometown boy might not come out on top this time.

"Let her speak to Aaron."

Zen. He'd joined the group, a man of self-control and logic. His hands were jammed in his pants pockets. His gaze was on her. "Do what you need to do." He handed her over to Aaron.

Her heart swelled. She would always be grateful to this man. Zen understood she had to hear Aaron out, to understand why he'd dumped her. She needed closure.

Zen turned to face Psycho. "I respect Jacy and her coffee shop. There's no need to take Aaron and the place apart. As *manager*, I expect you to back off and keep order."

"I can do order." Psycho slowly released Stevie. "Free coffee all around." Customers quickly filed to the counter for refills.

"Profit margin, Psycho." Zen nudged him toward the register. "Those freebies come out of your pocket."

Psycho reached for his wallet and headed off to pay.

"Let's go." Aaron nodded toward the kitchen.

Stevie hesitated.

"Greatest baseball novel," Zen quizzed softly.

His calm washed over her. "*The Natural* by Bernard Malamud," she returned.

245

Zen shook his head. "No, has to be *Shoeless Joe* by W. P. Kinsella."

"Something to debate."

"Perhaps later over dinner."

"You're on."

She took his nod of encouragement with her, knowing Zen trusted her. That trust brought a tightening to her nipples. In the worst of situations, the man turned her on. The curve of Zen's all-knowing smile stuck with her as she followed Aaron into the kitchen.

Alone with him, she stood stiffly, waiting for him to speak. The silence proved painful. In one short weekend so much had changed. They'd once talked over each other, finishing sentences; now neither of them knew what to say.

Blowing out a breath, Aaron hiked himself up onto the butcher block counter, shoulders slumped, his legs splayed. Natalie's expensive cologne clung to his clothes. Had he come to the coffee shop directly after sex with his fiancée? The thought turned her stomach.

He looked down at the floor, then up to her. "I'm sorry, Stevie. Honest to God sorry."

Tears for what might have been pressed the back of her eyelids. But didn't fall. "Yeah . . . me too."

"I'd planned to tell you."

"When, Aaron? After the wedding? Following your firstborn child?"

"The night of the auction."

The night Natalie had shown up and outbid her.

"I never meant to hurt you," he went on.

"I never wanted to be hurt."

He ran his palms down his thighs. Sweaty palms, judging by the damp streaks they left behind. "I've outgrown Frostproof."

Stevie would die there.

"I never, however, meant to outgrow you."

But he had.

"At one time, I'd wanted you to join me in Tampa," he confessed.

A time before Natalie Llewellyn came into the picture.

"Once Natalie and I met, my life changed."

Changed to public sex.

"Natalie is different from any woman I've ever met."

She was very, very naughty.

"Natalie sees life on a big scale."

And Stevie was small town. "Are you happy?" she forced out.

His brow furrowed. "I think so."

Think so? This from a man about to marry.

He shifted on the counter. "I'll always love you."

As a friend, not as a wife. The pain she'd expected never came. Her heart tightened just a little, more dull ache than stabbing pain. The ache would fade with time. Zen would see to that. The very thought of the shortstop cleared her heart of sadness. "Have a good life, Aaron."

"You too."

He hopped off the counter and came to stand before her. Without warning, he wrapped her in a farewell hug. She splayed her hands on his chest and kept a distance between them. She was no longer comfortable in his arms.

The kitchen door swung open the exact second Stevie closed her eyes and Aaron pressed a good-bye kiss to her cheek.

Her eyes flew open.

Zen stood stiff and staring, his expression hard.

Stevie cringed. Heat shot into her cheeks. She wanted to explain, but Zen came, saw, and retreated.

Back in the coffee shop, Zen Driscoll silently swore. A picture told more than a thousand words. This picture was now embedded in his brain. Stevie didn't need saving. She and Aaron had been pressed together intimately, looking guilty. The renewed color in her cheeks spoke of newly fanned flames. Her parted lips awaited Aaron's kiss. She still wanted Aaron, despite Zen's lovemaking. Aaron was responding as he should, once again engaged in memories that tied the two of them together.

Zen was jealous as hell, ripped apart with envy. He'd fallen for Stevie Cole. Aaron now had the woman Zen wanted. He'd been stupid to believe he could erase Aaron from her heart in a few days. The pitcher was ingrained in her soul. Forever.

Pain pulsed around his heart.

A sense of loss cut deeply.

He'd yet to see her by candlelight, yet to trace her freckles with his tongue. He was infinitely disappointed.

He didn't do vulnerable—refused to crash and burn.

He had no desire to hear Stevie's explanation. She was returning to Aaron. He couldn't take her sympathy.

It was time to move on.

He suddenly needed out. Out of the coffee shop, out of this town. His out came with the appearance of Natalie Llewellyn. She stood in the doorway of the coffee shop, looking poised and bored.

In that moment, he knew what he had to do. He had the power to steer Natalie far enough off Aaron's path to give the childhood sweethearts time to recover what they'd lost. Without Natalie in the picture, Aaron and Stevie would be home free.

He caught Psycho's eye. "I'm done for the day. I won't be back."

Psycho looked from Zen to Natalie and shuddered. "Bad move, dude. I'm a nudist, and the chick scares me. Might want to rethink—"

"My mind's made up."

"Thought you'd started with Stevie?"

"She's not finished with Aaron."

Psycho cast him a get-real look. "You're not as smart as you think, Einstein. Major misunderstanding—"

"You didn't see them in the kitchen." They'd stood as close and tight as their memories. He couldn't compete with their past. He could, however, give them a future.

He took his first step toward Natalie. Then a second. Slow, steady, formidable steps that told her he was coming for her.

Her eyes flashed. The pulse at her throat throbbed visibly. She flicked her lips with her tongue, now slick and ready to taste him. She looked hungry. He took advantage of her hunger. Natalie still wanted him. He could distract her long enough for Stevie and Aaron to reconnect.

Taking her by the hand, he led Natalie to the limo and slid in beside her. The darkly tinted windows and dim interior lighting clasped them in intimate shadows. The supple leather seats swallowed them in softness. Zen knew how to survive in her world. He'd done it once. He could do it again. He cut to the chase. "Break off your engagement. I'm back."

She slid the diamond off her finger with a seductive slowness, a slowness she reserved for her garters and stockings. She dropped the ring in the ashtray on the car door. Her eyes glittered with sexual expectancy as her hand slid along his thigh, tapped his sex with one bloodred nail. "It's about time."

CHAPTER 12

"There goes the limo." Jacy pointed to the black stretch taking the corner, turning west onto Wall Street. "Aaron and Natalie must be leaving town."

Risk stood beside her on the sidewalk outside the coffee shop. "With Aaron gone, Stevie can get on with her life."

She hobbled toward the door. "Let's see how she's doing."

There was no immediate sign of Stevie, but she found the Bat Pack lounging at a corner table. The coffee shop was momentarily empty. "Take a load off," Psycho called to them.

Jacy and Risk wound between tables to join the men.

Romeo scooted his chair closer to Jacy. "How're the ribs and ankle, sweetheart?"

Risk's scowl set him back a few inches.

"Surviving," she said. "Quick cup of coffee and I'm out of here. How's business been?"

Psycho grunted. "I busted my balls."

Chaser patted his jean pockets. "Big tips."

Jacy knew the ladies found Chaser enigmatic. He was seldom without his Oakleys, so few knew the color of his eyes. The diamond stud in his ear and the turned-up collar of his shirt added to his edge. His lazy grin labeled him lethal.

Psycho did a drum roll on the table. "Sold every last one of my Rice Krispies Treats."

"We ran out of baked goods," Romeo told her. "Psycho dashed to the grocery for bags of cookies. Oatmeal raisin, ginger snaps, and chocolate pinwheels."

Store-bought cookies in a gourmet coffee shop? Jacy made a face. "I need to bake—"

Risk shook his head. "I'll bake. Once you're settled at home, I'll return and whip something up for tomorrow."

"We'll hang and help," Psycho offered.

Risk declined his offer. "Four cooks in the kitchen ruin the batter."

"Batter that comes from a recipe," Jacy reminded him. "You can't throw ingredients in a bowl and hope for the best."

"I've watched you bake."

"You've sampled more than you've sifted and stirred."

"You give good samples."

"I can cook," Psycho tried again. "As a kid, I spent summers at BoBo's on the Boardwalk in Atlantic City."

"You flipped burgers and spun cotton candy. Nothing gourmet," Risk stated.

Looking smug, Psycho slapped a fifty-dollar bill

on the table before Risk. "You and me, pops. A bake off at eight," he challenged. "Bring your best spatula and rolling pin."

Risk lifted the fifty. "I'll consider this payment for all the eggs you'll break. All the flour you'll sift on the floor."

"You two bake," Romeo said approvingly. "Chaser and I will babysit Jacy."

"She doesn't need babysitting." Risk glared at the third baseman. "She needs to sleep."

"Three on the waterbed—" Risk's glare grew so dark, Romeo retreated. "Is three too many."

"Coffee anyone?" Stevie approached their table, looking pale and grim. Flat down in the dumps.

Jacy ordered a vanilla latte and Risk black coffee. The Bat Pack had already downed banana-berry smoothies.

Stevie headed off before Jacy could question her mood.

Psycho stretched his long legs into the aisle and slouched down low. He looked perfectly comfortable as he conversed in a civilized manner about the weather, dirt bikes, and then baseball. "Favorite moments as a kid?" he asked his teammates.

Romeo grinned. "Skipping school to attend Opening Day at the park. Making preseason predictions."

"When they used to play Sunday doubleheaders," Chaser added. "Fireworks Night."

"The whiteness of the baselines and bases at the beginning of a game," Jacy joined in. "They were so bright they'd blind you even from the nosebleed seats."

Risk planted his elbows on the table. "On-deck hitters swinging several bats. A slugger comes up with the bases loaded."

"A nail-biting, extra-inning game," again from Jacy.

"Booing the umpire." Typical Psycho. "Most hated pitches?"

Chaser was first to answer. "A two-seamer fastball that sinks."

Romeo groaned. "A split-fingered fastball—like a changeup, but with the bottom falling out," he explained for Jacy's benefit.

Bottom falling out? Jacy didn't quite grasp the concept.

Risk steepled his fingers. "A wicked slider that breaks parallel to the ground."

The men moaned in agreement.

"Best upsets?" Psycho asked.

Romeo rubbed his hands together. "When the worst player on the team gets the biggest hit. When a last place team upsets the best team in the league."

"Pennant races that go down to the final day," Chaser said.

"A leadoff walk that turns into a home run. The winning run of the World Series," Risk stated.

Jacy loved listening to the men talk baseball. Here sat a fraternity of major league players. Their memories combined to form vivid pictures of the sport.

"Worst moments?" Romeo tossed out.

"First time at bat in the majors. I slid into first base and missed the friggin' bag," Chaser bemoaned.

"Off the field," Psycho admitted. "I was showing off. Got hit in the head by a ball from a pitching machine. Had my eye on the girl and not on the ball. My date laughed her ass off."

Neither Risk nor Romeo could top Psycho's mishap.

"How about you, Stevie?" Psycho asked when she returned with the two ordered coffees. "Worst moment in baseball?"

When Aaron dumped her for Natalie Llewellyn. Jacy shot Psycho a killing look. How insensitive could the man be?

Psycho thumped his forehead. "Damn, hon, I'm sorry. I'd never, ever—"

Stevie patted his shoulder. "You'd never purposely hurt me, I know." She then set out Jacy and Risk's coffee in matching English china cups patterned with the King and Queen of Hearts. "Anyone seen Zen?" she asked.

All but Psycho shook their heads. He dipped his instead, fidgeting with the edge of the table.

"Ps-y-cho." Stevie drew out his name.

"Fool man climbed into the limo."

Jacy blinked. "The Tampa Bay limo that left town?"

"*Left town?*" Aaron Grayson swung through the kitchen door. "Impossible. Natalie wouldn't leave without me."

Jacy was confused. She looked at Aaron. "If you're here—"

"She left with Zen," Psycho affirmed.

All color drained from Stevie's face. "You saw them leave together?" she questioned Psycho.

Psycho nodded. "They split right before Jacy and Risk arrived."

Risk held up his hands. "I didn't know. Swear."

Jacy was beside herself. "Did Zen go willingly?"

"Zen said—"

A cell phone rang, cutting Psycho off. Aaron recognized it as his. "Talk to me." Sixty seconds of listening and his face heated. A blistering red. "You can't be serious?" Followed by, "You told me you were over him." A sequential, "You never loved me?" A long pause. "Bitch." He closed the cell phone and threw it against the wall with all the power of his pitching arm. It shattered and the pieces went flying. Jacy ducked.

With fire in his eyes, Aaron looked around for something else to throw. Risk was off his chair in a heartbeat. He grabbed Aaron's arm before a vase of sunflowers joined his cell phone. Blind anger had Aaron swinging on his longtime friend.

Risk blocked the blow. "Stupid son of a bitch. Never punch with your pitching arm."

He then strong-armed Aaron into a chair and stood over the pitcher until Aaron's breathing slowed and his thoughts were less murderous.

Jacy sat on the edge of her chair. She was awed by Risk's quick reflexes, yet dismayed by Aaron's anger. She'd never seen him so mad. "Natalie Llewellyn?" she dared to ask.

Aaron jammed his hands through his hair, spiked the ends in a pull of frustration. "She's broken our engagement. She's back with Zen Driscoll."

"Holy shit," Psycho said, voicing what everyone thought.

"Shit is right," Aaron growled. "I should have

seen it coming. Zen showed up in Frostproof to steal my woman."

"Wasn't planned," Risk said, sticking up for Zen. "I kidnapped the man. He had no plans to attend the weekend events. Besides, no one knew Natalie would show."

"They have a freakin' history," Aaron growled. "Apparently Zen couldn't stand to see her engaged."

"Apparently . . ." Stevie's voice was barely audible.

Jacy pushed back from the table. Rising, she pointed Stevie toward the kitchen. Once out of earshot, she earnestly said, "This can't be happening. You and Zen—"

"Spent the night together." Stevie sagged against the sink. "A night I took to heart and he took as a one-night stand."

Jacy's heart fell. "He seemed so straightforward and honest. Not the type to steal another man's fiancée. Especially one into public sex."

"Appearances can be deceiving."

Jacy crossed her arms over her chest and winced when her ribs throbbed. She swung her arms at her sides instead. "Something's off."

"My judgment in men," Stevie said ruefully. "I've been dumped twice in five days."

"Let's close up shop and call it a day," Jacy suggested.

Stevie glanced at her watch. "It's near closing."

"Come by the house," Jacy appealed. "Risk's going to try his hand at baking here, so I'll be alone. I could use the company."

"Odds are good Romeo and Chaser will show up."

"They'd better be gone by the time Risk returns."

"The boys have entertainment value."

"They're all play." Jacy knew this for a fact. "Romeo only flirts when Risk is around. He loves a reaction. Alone, he treats me like a sister."

"Let him flirt," Stevie said. "Romeo's not as hot as Risk, but he'd give any man a run for his woman."

"I'm not Risk's woman."

"The look in his eye says you're claimed."

Jacy didn't believe that for a second.

Stevie slapped her palms against her thighs. "Think I'll hang with Risk and Psycho. Do a little baking myself."

Jacy knew her friend wanted to stay busy. When she slowed down for the night, thoughts of Zen would catch up with her.

Of all the ball players, Zen was known for his solid and sane decisions. He wouldn't walk away without a damn good reason.

Not like Psycho and his knee-jerk reactions.

Or Chaser going cold and confrontational.

Or Romeo leading with his dick.

Einstein thought things through. Something was off. Way off. Something that needed to be corrected.

The kitchen door swung open, and Risk strolled through. "Time for bed," he announced as he took her hand, and tugged her toward the back door. "Say good-bye to Stevie."

"Bye, Stevie," Jacy mimicked.

"I'll be back in a few," Risk told Stevie. "I might try my hand at caramel rolls."

Jacy and Stevie exchanged a look.

"They couldn't be any worse than Psycho's Rice Krispies Treats," Risk insisted.

The ladies swallowed their laughter.

Risk Kincaid baked until he could bake no more. Even under Stevie's direction, his attempt at caramel rolls bombed. Baking was harder than it looked. He would savor every bite Jacy baked from this moment forward.

Psycho proved to be a total nuisance. A baking lunatic, he hadn't measured one ingredient—just added a pinch of this or that, then cupped his palm, using it as a measuring cup. Yet he'd lined the counter with key lime bars and raspberry tarts, along with two pans of Rice Krispies Treats, dripping in marshmallow. A tray of Psycho's own creation—peanut butter-macadamia nut cookies—cooked in the oven.

"Bow to the master," Psycho taunted.

Risk scanned the kitchen. "Master of the Mess."

"Looks like a flour storm came through," Stevie agreed, taking in the white dusting on the counter and floor.

Risk glanced at his watch. Almost midnight. "Let's clean up."

Stevie turned on the tap and squirted lemon Joy into the sink. "Go home to Jacy. I'll wrap up here," she said as she grabbed a sponge.

Psycho slipped off his white cook's apron. "Time to see our girl."

"Think again." Risk blocked his path. "She's sleeping. I don't want her disturbed. You stay and help Stevie."

A cocky smile curved Psycho's lips as he pulled a second fifty from his pocket and slapped it on the counter. "Bet Romeo and Chaser greet you at her door."

Risk's jaw worked. "They'd better not."

"Town's small. There's not much to do," Psycho defended his friends. "A beer at the Silver Dollar Saloon, then kicking back with Jacy makes for a nice night."

"I told them to leave her alone."

"We listen to you on the field. Off-season—"

Risk slammed through the kitchen door. Son of a bitch. If Romeo and Chaser were at Jacy's, blood would flow. She needed her rest. He'd left her tucked in tight beneath the sheets in his Rogues T-shirt sans panties. Bare-assed Jacy belonged to him, not two of the Bat Pack.

His Lotus responded to his urgency to get home. He whipped into the driveway and cut the engine. No lights came from the front of the house. He entered through the unlocked door. The sound of deep male voices and light female laughter came from the bedroom.

Risk moved to the bedroom and stared.

"Old man's home." Romeo raised his beer in greeting. Propped against the headboard, he leaned shoulder to shoulder with Jacy, looking through a sports magazine together.

Chaser lounged in the pink leather armchair. Headphones secluded him in his own world of music.

Jacy looked worn out. Pale and rumpled. Glassy-eyed.

Risk's blood pumped and muscles rippled beneath his shirt. He felt like the Incredible Hulk, ready for the seams in his gray T-shirt to stretch and split.

Heads were about to roll.

"Out." One word. Ominous and barely controlled.

His tone caught Jacy's attention. She nudged Romeo.

Romeo cut Chaser a look. Chaser removed his headphones and nodded.

Both men rose, kissed Jacy on the cheek, and cut for the door. They skirted Risk by several feet. "Tomorrow," Romeo called over his shoulder.

Risk glared at his back. Once the click of the door announced their departure, he growled, "I left you to rest, not to entertain the Bat Pack."

Jacy yawned, snuggled low into her pillows. "They arrived shortly after you left. When the bell rang, I thought you'd forgotten your keys. I answered the door—"

"You should have told them to get lost."

She clutched the navy satin sheet. "They're your teammates, young and bored, and doing me a favor at the coffee shop. I didn't want to be rude."

"Rude works where they're concerned." He glanced at the waterbed, the armchair. "You allowed them in your bedroom."

"Where I'm the most comfortable. Neither the barber chair nor the church pew was an option. Besides, they spent time here on Sunday. You didn't mind then."

"I was here with you on Sunday. Tonight you were alone with them." He knew he sounded like a jealous ass, but didn't give a damn. "Romeo's way too attentive. No one belongs in your bedroom but me."

"An ultimatum?"

"Damn straight."

She rolled her eyes.

He stared at the outline of her body under the sheer satin sheet. "You wearing panties?" She hadn't been when he'd left.

"Romeo helped me into a thong."

His hands fisted. He stared at her so intently, she burst out laughing. "Baking sucked all the fun out of you," she teased. "When I went to answer the door, I tugged on a pair of cutoffs. Not an easy feat."

He approached the bed. "Need help getting them off?"

"Assistance is always welcome."

He assisted. She was soon naked from the waist down. His callused hand ran the length of her thigh and curved over her hip. His thumb rubbed her belly. Soft and supple, with enough tremble to know he affected her.

He bent, circled her navel with his tongue.

Jacy dug her fingers into his hair. Lifted her hips ever so slightly.

Risk nipped and sucked, marking her with his mouth. Then he slowly leaned back.

She scrunched up her nose. "You smell like burnt caramel."

"I lived burnt caramel," he confessed. "Made a major mess of the rolls. To Psycho's credit, the boy can bake. You're stocked for tomorrow."

She patted the sheet. "It's time for bed."

"I'll shower and crawl in beside you."

"Wish you could slide inside me."

"Not for another three weeks, babe."

"I'm counting the days."

He'd begun counting the minutes.

"It's after one in the morning. You should be home," said a slurred male voice. Stevie was on her hands and knees, sponging the last of the flour from the baseboards. Aaron's appearance surprised her. Insomnia shone in his eyes. Bright and restless. Even from a distance, she could smell whiskey on his breath. "I saw your Volkswagon in the alley. Stopped to check on you. The door was unlocked."

"Psycho just left." Stevie turned toward the sink and rinsed out the sponge. "He helped clean up, but his idea and my idea of clean clashed greatly. I sent him home after he'd tracked flour back and forth a dozen times. I'm on my way out as well now."

Aaron swayed, somewhat tipsy, looking lost. "I have nowhere to go."

She wasn't sure she wanted him here. She didn't, however, want him driving drunk. "Coffee?"

He looked instantly relieved. "Black, no cream."

Untying her apron, she entered the main shop with Aaron on her heels. The overhead lights were dim. The star-studded sky shone through the windows. A half pot of a Cuban blend stood strong enough to stand a spoon in the middle of a cup. Stevie poured the brew into a sun yellow china cup decorated with cobalt blue butterflies.

Aaron slumped against the counter, took his first

sip and choked. "Tastes like tar. It'll put hair on my chest."

Stevie had always loved the smooth lines of Aaron's torso. But after being naked with Zen, she'd taken to hair-roughened pecs.

He looked at her, his expression sour. "Can't believe I got dumped."

She wasn't feeling overly sympathetic. "Not fun, is it?"

His face went from sour to sheepish. "Pretty ironic, wouldn't you say?"

Aaron had dumped her. And Natalie had dumped him. In Stevie's eyes, it was his just reward. While Aaron moped and grumbled, her thoughts were focused on Zen. She'd taken to the man. And she missed him terribly. Aaron was unaware of her feelings for the shortstop. She kept it that way.

He finished his first cup of coffee and took his second with cream. "Did you ever think our lives would take such a turn?" he asked.

Stevie ran her hands over her hips. She had always thought them wide, yet Zen had called them womanly. "Some things weren't meant to be."

He averted his gaze. "I can't go back to Tampa."

He'd feel awkward and vulnerable seeing Zen and Natalie together Stevie realized. The same feelings she'd had when Aaron announced his engagement at the auction. "Stick around a while then."

"You wouldn't mind?"

"Town's as much yours as it is mine."

"Maybe we could get together—"

"I'm very busy."

"Busy every minute?"

Not *every* minute. But most minutes.

"Having coffee with a friend takes little time," he suggested. "Pencil me in."

Coffee and small talk. A short hookup. The thought should have thrilled her. Yet her heartbeat held steady. No tingle in her breasts. No pointing of her nipples as there had been with Zen. She shrugged. "One cup wouldn't hurt."

"For old time's sake."

Old times might not be as good as she'd initially expected.

Aaron Grayson stared at Stevie, at the woman he'd once thought he'd marry. Life had thrown him a major curveball. His taste in women had gone from small-town sweet to city slutty.

He realized now that Natalie was a slut. She'd hopped from their alley sex into a limo with Zen Driscoll. The soft leather seats cupped a body better than the human hand. He was certain Zen was being cupped—by both seat and Natalie's palm.

The urge to strangle her fought with his need to seduce her. His dark side desired her still. Desired a date for public sex.

He was one depraved man.

Zen had no desire to touch Natalie Llewellyn. Even now as she curled against his side, making cat noises deep in her throat. One hour and they'd reach Tampa. The trip had been long and tiresome. Avoiding her hands was an all-out battle. She had a fascination with his crotch. He'd needed to devise ways to distract her.

At the moment, he allowed her to snuggle. She snuggled so close, she nearly crawled under his skin. To keep his charade alive, he'd wrapped an arm about her shoulders and lightly stroked her arm. Just enough touching to keep her happy, but not enough to trigger sex in the backseat.

He couldn't get it up for this woman.

Natalie didn't turn him on. Not like Stevie Cole.

His softly rounded, wonderfully freckled Stevie.

His do-it-in-the-dark Stevie.

He'd foolishly considered her his. He wanted to take her by candlelight and during the day. He wanted to prove to her how beautiful she truly was. Unfortunately, that door had closed.

Aaron and Stevie's rediscovery would take them to the altar. The people of Frostproof would approve and applaud.

His sense of loss settled heavily over him. Depressingly so.

Natalie shifted beside him. Her long dark hair spilled onto his chest, her palm pressed to his sex. Her body went lax as sleep overtook her.

Zen finally let down his guard. He looked back over his time in Frostproof: From the moment Stevie had first served him a double cappucino and a blow, to their sexual exploits in the cooler. The thought of her freckled belly made him smile. The thought of her puckered nipples caused his sex to twitch. He prayed to God Natalie hadn't felt his stirring.

Natalie Llewellyn was in a deep sleep, dreaming darkly. It was nearing midnight, and she was being chased. Chased fully clothed by an unknown man through Frostproof. As she darted around each street corner, a piece of clothing disappeared, ripped from her by the stretch of the man's hand.

He wanted her naked.

She lost her designer shoes near the coffee shop. Her white silk blouse shortly thereafter. Then her tobacco brown skirt. She nearly tripped when it slid about her ankles. Barefoot, she sprinted on in her wispy bra and panties.

The man drew closer.

She could hear him breathing.

Deeper now, close to panting.

She wanted him to catch her.

But she wanted him to sweat for her first.

He did. His scent rose around her. Musky and dark.

The air was sexually charged.

The crescent moon became her midnight guide.

Her footfalls suddenly shifted from pavement to grass.

Her bra and panties disappeared. Now she was no longer in Frostproof.

The man had chased her to Carver Stadium. Home of the Tampa Bay Bombers.

Naked as the night, she rounded the dugout, darted onto the diamond. The grass was dewy beneath her feet. She skirted first base, took a second to look over her shoulder . . .

He caught her near the pitcher's mound.

His hands were firm. His body dominating.

He'd chased, caught, and now claimed her.

He never gave her a chance to catch her breath.

Clutching her waist, he lifted her against him.

She snugged her thighs about his hips.

Pulsing and sweat sheened, they came together with an urgency that scared even her. She clung to him. The pleasure inside her mounted.

His rocking thrusts, white-hot and raw, communicated his restless passion. A male's passion that stormed her senses.

She clawed his back. Drew blood. Demanding release.

He swatted her bottom. Reminded her she was at his mercy.

He would allow her to come.

When he was ready.

He wasn't ready . . .

Pop.

Pop, pop.

Pop, pop, pop.

One by one the stadium lights flashed on. Blinding lights that lit the baseball park as bright as daylight.

Natalie Llewellyn climaxed amid a cheering crowd of eighty thousand fans. The man's face finally became visible. Her spasms were so shattering, she screamed his name, *"Aaron!"*

Her body jerked. Her eyes flew open. Yet she couldn't see. The dream dominated her like the man who took her.

She fought for reality. When the present again settled about her, she came nose to nose with Zen Driscoll.

One corner of his mouth twisted. "Not Aaron, Zen," he said calmly. Knowingly. "Lady, you've got the wrong man in your limo."

Natalie Llewellyn silently agreed.

CHAPTER 13

"Let's agree to disagree." Jacy Grayson glared at Risk Kincaid. "I'm feeling better. The Bat Pack plans to leave town at the end of the week. The coffee shop needs me."

Risk glared right back at her. "It's only been two weeks. You're up and moving, but not moving fast. I see you wincing when you move abruptly. You still need to take it easy."

How to get around this man? She'd be stark raving mad confined to her waterbed. "I'll work in the mornings, rest in the afternoons," she bargained.

Arms folded over his chest, he rested a lean hip on the corner of her dresser. A big frowning man, not giving an inch. "Take a nap and I'll think about it."

"You've *thought* about it for days," she reminded him. "Same subject, different day."

"I'm looking out for your best interests."

Jacy knew that for a fact. Risk really cared about her. He'd proved it in so many ways. Clean sheets daily. Freshly polished toenails. He'd massaged her instep with a sensual slowness that was almost orgas-mic. Then he'd gritted his teeth and taken another *Cosmo* quiz. This one was for married couples on children and pets.

The outcome surprised Jacy. Risk wanted three children and two dogs. Whereas she'd gone with five kids and six dogs. Big families appealed to her. Had they been an official couple, Risk admitted, half the fun of having children would come in trying to get her pregnant. Jacy agreed.

Country living appealed to them both. A two-story brick house on ten acres. Risk needed breath-ing room away from baseball. She liked his idea of furnishing the house with overstuffed furniture. They both envisioned a fireplace, hardwood floors, and woven scatter rugs. Walls in every color of the artist's palette.

Sadly, it was no more than a *Cosmo* quiz. Some-thing to do for fun. To kill time. Nothing permanent or overly serious.

No matter Risk's attention, Jacy had grown irrita-ble and testy. A bit irrational. And very horny.

Looking at him now, and being unable to make love to him, made her nuts. The man was hot. From his bed-tousled hair and sexy mouth, to his bare chest and low-riding jeans, he had a body women would die for. Jacy desired seduction.

"How about a shower?" she suggested.

"You had one last night."

She patted the apple red satin sheet. "Come snug-gle."

"Not with that look in your eye."

"What look?" she asked innocently.

"The look of sex. I know what's on your mind. And it's not going to happen."

"Surely there has to be a position—"

"That won't cause you pain?" He shook his head. "I'm not taking any chances."

She slapped her palms against the sheet and ripples spread beneath her fingers. "Then what?"

"Ride with me to my parents' house," he suggested. "With Zen gone, I need to check on the place. I'd planned to exercise, swim laps in their pool. You can sit in the Jacuzzi. Enjoy the healing jets."

"Will you heal with me?"

"Sure, the Jacuzzi seats six." He opened the bottom drawer of her dresser, searching for a swimsuit. "Tank or bikini?"

"Bare skin?"

"Not an option." He snagged a metallic purple tank suit that would cover more of her body than a bikini.

Risk's parents resided in a sprawling ranch-style home on the outskirts of Frostproof. He had bought it for his folks after his second season with the Rogues. As they drove to the house, Jacy remembered how proud Ben and Mary had been of their son.

Risk now provided them with vacations too, including this month's Alaskan cruise. He was good to his family.

Jacy wanted to be part of that family. She just didn't know how to convey her need. Risk had shown her every consideration during her recuperation. But he'd never touched on love in their many conversations.

His time in Frostproof was coming to an end. Less than a week remained of his stay. She needed to act or let the opportunity of a lifetime pass her by.

"I'll turn the Jacuzzi on," Risk said as they entered his parents' house. "Give it twenty minutes to heat."

Hunger hit her. "Anything to eat?"

Risk motioned her toward the kitchen. "Zen might have left food in the refrigerator."

Jacy hobbled behind him. The kitchen faced east and welcomed the sun each morning. French doors led out to his mother's garden. "Does Mary still garden to feed the rabbits?"

Risk grinned. "Nothing from the garden ever reaches the table. Dad says it's a waste of time. Mom says God's creatures need to eat too."

He pulled open the refrigerator door and scratched his jaw. "Fully stocked, as if Zen planned to stay awhile. Pretty damn strange, given his spur-of-the-moment departure with Natalie Llewellyn."

Jacy came up behind him. "Something's not quite right."

"Zen always thinks things through. Hits both sides of any issue. He must have had a reason for doing what he did."

She reached around Risk, snagged a bag of green grapes, then grew thoughtful. Slowly, she fitted the pieces of the puzzle together. "He put himself between Aaron and Natalie."

"Which threw Aaron and Stevie together again."

Jacy popped a grape into her mouth. "A calculated move?"

"It's what Stevie wanted."

"It's what she wanted going into the auction weekend. By Monday, she and Zen were pretty chummy."

"Zen looked damn happy at the coffee shop."

"So did Stevie."

"Then Aaron arrived . . ."

"And Zen and Natalie took off in the limo."

Jacy scrunched up her nose. "We're missing details."

"Talk to Stevie."

"I will. Later today."

Risk checked the time. "Ready to Jacuzzi?"

Jacy returned the remainder of the grapes to the refrigerator. "What about my cast?"

"Plastic bag just like in the shower. You'll have to elevate your foot on the side of the whirlpool."

Once he'd secured her cast, she shuffled toward the screened outside patio. "Are you going to change into your trunks?"

Risk Kincaid slipped on a pair of Hawaiian-print trunks, navy blue with emerald green palm trees. He found Jacy by the Jacuzzi, dipping her toes into the swirling water. She looked small and vulnerable. Yet he knew the power of the woman beneath the striped handkerchief top and pleated plaid skirt.

She was strong-minded, with a dedicated heart and a potent body.

The jiggle of her breasts got to him as she struggled with her top. He moved to assist her. She wore her tank suit beneath her clothes.

When she stood before him, all sweet and sleek, his brain shut down and his erection stood up. So much for swimming laps. He'd never be able to kick his legs.

He caught the slightest curve of Jacy's smile and knew she was pleased. Pleased she could arouse him.

"Let me get you positioned," he said.

Keeping her ankle suspended on the edge of the Jacuzzi was not an easy feat. Clasping her shoulders, he eased her into the warm water. Only to the first ledge. Beneath her suit, her breasts bounced in the bubbles, full and perky, the nipples pebbled.

Damn. Risk sank into the water and looked everywhere but at Jacy. Rust at the base of the patio table caught his eye. He'd replace the table later today. A leaf was stuck in the corner of the screen, one he could easily remove. The ceiling could use a fresh coat of paint. The grout at the base of the Jacuzzi—

"Risk?" The sound of his name on Jacy's lips was soft, uncertain.

He focused on her face, noticing the dampness of her hair, the flush in her cheeks. Her slightly parted lips, the flick of her little pink tongue.

"Tell me about Richmond."

He rested his head against the curve of the Jacuzzi, forcing his muscles to relax. "Great city. Lots of history and nightlife. I've invited you to visit a thousand times."

"I never wanted to interfere with your work."

"I'd have found time for you."

Jacy believed him. His offer stood. Maybe someday she'd take him up on it. Someday before he got married.

She closed her eyes and let the jets ease the soreness from her body. Bouyant and blissful, she grew as liquid as the water.

Risk was equally quiet until he nudged her thigh with his foot, and she met his gaze through lowered lids.

"I've been thinking."

"About me?"

"Always about you." He ran one hand down his face, his expression suddenly serious. "Richmond might be a good city to franchise Jacy's Java."

"Franchise?" A most surprising and exciting thought.

"There's a historical building near the ball park with space available," he continued. "Newly renovated and a bit avant-garde—right up your alley. An art gallery and photography studio have leased the second floor. Three shops remain open on the lower level."

Jacy's heart kicked. "Wild idea, Kincaid."

"Not so wild," he said. "You've built a loyal following in Frostproof. Richmond would give you an even wider demographic for customers."

"I never thought about expansion." She gnawed her bottom lip. "If I had, I'd have gone Tampa or Jacksonville."

"Richmond is closer to me. Closer means more accessible."

"As my rebound lover." Not her husband. Could

she live with the possibility of running into him every day? Risk stopping in for coffee every morning? Greeting the day with his smile and sex appeal. Could she live seeing him arriving after a night with another woman? Buying that woman coffee and a caramel roll? "I'll give it some thought."

"Some intense thought, babe. You're looking at a ready investor."

"*If* I franchise, I'll take out a loan to set up."

"You're too damn independent."

"You'd prefer me batting my eyelashes and drooling over you?" she asked.

"A little drool never hurt."

"Get a dog."

"I'd rather get you." He slid toward her then, ran his hands up her thighs, pulled her to him. He kissed her softly. Soft soon turned deeper, more passionate. Downright hot. After dropping a final kiss on the tip of her nose, he drew back. "I'm going for a swim. Do you want a lounger on the deck or would you rather stay here?"

She looked along the deck. A turquoise air mattress caught her eye. "I want to float in the pool."

He pointed to her cast. "Not safe, babe. You fall off and you'll sink. I'm not pulling you from the drain."

"I'll hold on to the side of the pool."

"At the shallow end."

Once she agreed, Risk assisted her from the Jacuzzi. After several tries, he managed to position her on the air mattress without soaking her cast. She stretched out on her stomach, propped her chin on her hands, and watched Risk swim laps.

Whether he was swimming freestyle or butterfly, the man cut through the water. The muscles across his back bunched and released. The power in his legs was a driving force.

She wanted to get a little bit closer. . . .

"You're in my lane." Risk broke his stroke and tread water. "You promised to stay in the shallow end."

"I, uh, must have drifted."

"You paddled, babe. I saw your hands under water."

Busted. She sighed heavily. "I'll paddle back."

"Paddle fast." He gave the air mattress a subtle shove and returned to his workout.

Jacy paddled back to three feet of water. She skimmed her hands across the surface, letting her fingers dance with the sunshine that filtered through the pool cage. Eventually Risk joined her.

"Ready to dry off?" he asked.

She yawned, nodded.

He rolled her off the air mattress and into his arms without mishap, then snagged her skirt and top and carried her to his bedroom—a room reserved for his stays in Frostproof. Snagging two towels from the linen closet in the hallway, he gave her body his full attention.

She soon stood before him, naked and dry, and slightly sunburned. He ran a hand over her shoulder. "Sweet pink, do you need lotion?"

She shook her head. "Doesn't hurt."

He helped her into her clothes, then wiped himself

dry. While he raided his closet for a cream-colored polo and khakis, Jacy wandered around his room. His parents had dedicated it to his high school memories. On view was the shaping of a boy into a man.

A king-size bed stood in one corner, made up with ecru cotton sheets. Two leather club chairs and a dresser faced each other. Her attention was soon drawn to his trophy shelf.

She ran her fingers along the polished mahogany edge. Risk Kincaid had excelled in both football and baseball. She touched each trophy, lifted and read each inscription. Behind a marble plaque, she found two ticket stubs set within a picture frame.

Prom tickets. May 1994.

"You saved our tickets?" Her voice caught ever so slightly.

"Worthy of my trophy shelf." He toweled his hair. "You wore a skintight black dress and stilettos that night. A dress I peeled down your body."

Peeled down in the backseat of his Cougar. She'd been a virgin. He, highly experienced. After that night, Jacy had never wanted another man.

"Check this out." Risk lifted a second picture frame from behind a skyscraper trophy.

Jacy looked into her past. A collage of her and Risk the summer before he'd left for college. Together at the lake. Him jogging. Her on a bicycle. Him grinning. Her laughing so hard she'd fallen off the porch swing. The two of them embracing, his chin resting on the top of her head. Petite and slight, she was barely visible in his arms. He'd been a man at eighteen.

Awed, she asked, "Who made this for you?"

"Stevie," he said. "She had plans to be a photographer that summer, remember? Everywhere we turned she'd blind us with a flash. She made the collage, told me straight out not to forget you."

"We were so young . . ."

"And incredibly happy."

Could she make him happy for the rest of his life? This she contemplated as Risk moved to the dresser and selected a CD.

She arched a brow. "Elevator music?"

"Mood music."

Soft and mellow. Meant for slow dancing.

Risk pressed his right palm to the base of her spine, then folded her hand in his left and settled it over his heart. Jacy tucked herself in close, one hand splayed on his shoulder.

Formal, yet intimate, they danced barefoot in the middle of his bedroom. Their bodies brushed just enough to excite, yet Risk tempered the heat between them.

He kissed her forehead. "Dancing is nice."

Damn nice, Jacy agreed, enjoying the shift and sway, the pure pleasure of being held. She sighed. "I'm sorry November was lost to my cracked ribs and broken ankle. The month brought little sex and a whole lot of doctoring on your part."

"I've spent time with you. That's all that mattered."

She leaned back slightly. Met his gaze. "You sure?"

He nodded his head. "No complaints."

Neither had she.

They continued dancing, silent and content. Their bodies engaged in the sensual press.

Eventually the late afternoon sun shifted behind a cloud, casting Risk's bedroom in shadow. He slowly released her. Removed the CD. Then dropped a light kiss on her lips. "You need to talk to Stevie."

That she did. "She's at the coffee shop."

"Call and leave a message for her to come by your house. I want you back in bed resting."

"I needed a caffeine fix. Stopped by the coffee shop. Took Jacy's call. She wants to talk with you. No emergency."

Stevie had heard Aaron approach long before he spoke. She knew the weight of his footsteps on Spicer's Dock. The way the boards creaked. His voice was followed by his reflection in the clear blue lake as he stood over her, smiling.

She'd sought privacy and peace on the weathered wooden planks. The lake had called to her, offering a place to clear her head.

Red paddleboats bobbed all around her. They represented old man Spicer's seasonal trade. He rented the boats during the summer and took them out of the water after Thanksgiving. It was almost time to store them for the winter.

Aaron had known where to find her. He'd known her his entire life, after all. He knew the hiding places she frequented.

She leaned back on her hands. Her feet dangled in the water, cool for this time of year. The breeze gently stirred her bangs as she looked up at him. "I'll call her later."

He jammed his hands in his blue slacks and asked, "Mind if I join you?"

Such formality. Not so long ago, he wouldn't have asked permission. He would have grabbed her by the shoulders, pinned her to the dock, and kissed her senseless. Then dived into the lake to cool off. That time had long passed. "Have a seat."

He dropped down beside her, placing his coffee between them. All gelled hair, starched shirt, knife-sharp creases in his slacks. Tasseled leather loafers. He was overdressed for sitting on a dock.

She closed her eyes and inhaled his scent. He smelled of soap and light cologne. She felt nothing. Not a single tingle. Her pulse remained as calm as the lake.

She cut him a glance. "Missing Natalie?"

He nodded. "Go figure."

"I miss Zen."

"You *and Zen?*"

He looked so surprised, Stevie couldn't help laughing. "After your announcement at the auction, Zen was nice to me. We became friends." And lovers. She missed Zen's humor. His honesty. The way her body came alive to his touch. The fact he humored her about making love in the dark.

"I was never fond of the man," Aaron admitted. "He and Natalie had a history. I, uh—"

"Felt threatened?" Stevie supplied.

"She talked about him all the time."

"Maybe she wanted to get a rise out of you."

Aaron ran his palms down his thighs. "She got a rise all right. Woman knows how to get what she wants wherever she wants it."

"She wanted Zen."

"Shit."

A small fishing boat cruised the shoreline. A young boy waved to them. They waved back. A dog barked in the distance.

Aaron sipped his coffee. "Life is so laid back here."

"I can't imagine living anywhere else."

"Perhaps if you experienced a bigger city—"

"Frostproof fits me fine." She lazily swung her legs, lightly splashing water. The spray cast rainbows on the mirror surface.

Aaron scooted back, not wanting to get wet.

Years ago he would have kicked off his shoes and tried to outsplash her. They would have both gotten soaked in the process.

"What will you do?" she asked him.

"Who the hell knows?" he muttered darkly. "Eventually I have to return to Tampa. Investments. Off-season workouts. How 'bout you?"

She needed to stop thinking about Zen and throw herself into her work. Between parks and recreation and the coffee shop, she'd force herself to stay busy. Zen had chosen Natalie, a fact of life she couldn't deny. Or change.

"I plan to swear off men." She scrambled to her feet, stomped wet footprints on the planks.

Aaron rose as well. "Would you make an exception for dinner with a friend?"

She had no desire to dine alone with Aaron. "Let's order a couple of pizzas and eat with Risk and Jacy."

He flipped out his cell phone and dialed. "I'll connect with Risk."

Stevie stood in the twilight as Aaron conversed with his longtime friend. Memories of shared pizzas lifted her spirits.

Tonight they would return to a time when the choice of toppings was the toughest of life decisions. No stress. Just sharing a slice. She poked Aaron, mouthed pepperoni and extra cheese.

"Feels strange, the four of us eating pizza, reminiscing," Jacy said to Stevie.

Seated at Jacy's kitchen table, the two of them split the last slice of ham and pineapple. Aaron and Risk had removed themselves from the kitchen, choosing football on the fuzzy black-and-white television over gossip and girl talk.

Jacy sipped her Pepsi through a wildly curving orange plastic straw. She had to wait awhile for Stevie's reply.

Her best friend shrugged. "Aaron found me at Spicer's Dock. Delivered your message. We talked a while. When he asked me to dinner, I decided pizza with you and Risk was a better choice than being alone with him."

"A month ago, you wanted to be with Aaron."

"That was before Natalie Llewellyn. And . . . Zen."

"Einstein." Jacy scrunched her nose. "Thought he had more sense than to take off with the queen of public sex."

Color crept into Stevie's cheeks. "Natalie and I are opposites. I prefer the dark, she wants to be seen."

Jacy pushed aside her paper plate. "Did Zen say good-bye?"

Stevie shook her head. "Aaron showed up at the coffee shop. Zen knew I needed closure. He insisted I speak to Aaron in the kitchen. When Aaron got ready to leave, he hugged me. Zen walked in just as Aaron was about to kiss my cheek. One startled look, and Zen was gone."

So that's how it went down. Jacy suddenly understood Zen's departure. Zen had interpreted that hug as an embrace.

Jacy tapped a plastic knife on the table. "What if Zen thought you and Aaron had reconciled?"

"That's ridiculous."

"What if Zen, knowing Natalie still had the hots for him, removed her from the equation so you and Aaron could reconnect."

Stevie's jaw dropped. "Pretty far-fetched."

"Zen is noble. *And*, he must really care. Care enough to see you happy."

"I was happiest with him."

"He doesn't know that."

"When Aaron hugged me, I realized I wanted new memories, not old. Zen never gave me the chance to tell him so."

"Instead he sidetracked Natalie so you'd have a clear shot at Aaron."

Stevie sighed. "If only we were sure that's how it went down."

"I say we confide in Risk, have him get in touch with Zen."

"What if we're wrong?" Stevie was suddenly apprehensive. "I'd feel twice the fool."

"I'd play the fool to learn the truth."

Stevie narrowed her gaze on Jacy. "Speaking of fools, how much longer can you play Risk?"

Jacy pretended not to understand the question, but Stevie's hard stare forced her response. "I have a few days left. Confession isn't easy."

"You love him, Jacy." Stevie's voice dropped to an insistent whisper. "*Tell him.*"

Jacy cut her glance to the living room. Risk was reclining in the barber chair, sipping a beer. Wearing a white T-shirt, jeans, socks, no shoes, he looked at home. "I'd thought to tell him in bed, while having sex, at the point of climax."

"You're not normal."

"He'd either fire like a bazooka or go utterly limp."

"I'm thinking major explosion."

"Since we're not having sex, no moment's been right."

"Make a moment," Stevie insisted. "You're creative."

Jacy licked her lips. "Risk asked me to franchise the coffee shop in Richmond."

"He wants you close."

"Me or my coffee and caramel rolls? The man has a hunger—"

"For you. Trust me. You're his sugar fix."

Kate Angell

* * *

"What's the score, Aaron?" Risk asked, following a Miami Dolphin field goal. The Fins had moved ahead of Buffalo; the score was now ten to seven.

"Score?" Aaron shifted on the church pew.

"Do you even know who's playing?"

Aaron shook his head. "Haven't a clue."

"Get a clue," Risk stated. "Go after Natalie."

A choked laugh escaped Aaron. "No one *goes after* Natalie. She determines the man she wants and where she wants him."

"Change her mind. Wear the pants. Dominate."

One corner of Aaron's mouth twisted. "She's into domination."

Which was more than Risk needed to know. Natalie Llewellyn wasn't his type of woman. He'd never liked kinky or bitchy. He enjoyed soft and sweet, yet someone independent enough to put him in his place. "Do what you have to, man, but do it fast."

Risk had seen the sadness in Stevie Cole's eyes. Zen and she deserved a chance. If Aaron went after Natalie, Zen might return to Frostproof—might bring a smile to Stevie's face once again.

"Before I leave, there's something I need to know."

"Shoot."

"What are your intentions toward Jacy?"

Risk took a long, slow sip of his beer. "You're asking this because . . . ?"

"You've been her rebound lover since high school."

"By mutual consent."

"Maybe it's time to make things permanent."

"Maybe it is, maybe it isn't."

"She's bound to get involved with another man sooner or later. Why let her go through another disastrous relationship?" Aaron met his gaze squarely. "I know you care about her. Act now, don't lose her."

Lose her? Unthinkable. He'd been trying to find a way to propose for weeks now. But the opportunities kept slipping through his fingers. Taking that damn *Cosmo* quiz should have secured his future with her. He'd spilled his guts. Laid out his designs for a house, discussed children and pets. If that wasn't permanence, what was? "I'm on it," he assured Aaron.

Finishing off his beer, Risk got off the barber chair. He crossed to the kitchen. Stevie and Jacy had their heads together. Their voices were soft, yet intense.

Sock footed, he came up quietly behind Jacy and smooched her on the neck. She nearly jumped off her chair. Goosebumps broke out on her arms as she swatted him. "You scared me."

"It must have been a pretty deep conversation for you not to hear me."

Jacy blushed.

He knew that blush. "You were talking about me, right?"

"Don't get cocky," she returned. "A word or two, never a complete sentence."

"Bullshit, babe."

He kissed her then, in front of Stevie. A hard, deep kiss that had Jacy curling her fingers into the short sleeves of his T-shirt.

Stevie fanned her face. "I need a cold shower."

"Me too," Aaron said from the doorway.

Stevie shoved back her chair and stood. "I'm out of here."

"Right behind you." Aaron followed Stevie to the door.

Risk was left alone with Jacy, just as he'd wanted to be.

They needed to talk.

Jacy rubbed her stomach. "I'm full and tired, and ready for bed."

Bed was good. He could hold her, get his feelings off his chest. He needed to see where things stood between them. Do or die.

Marry me, Jacy. The words itched to be said.

He stretched out beside her on the waterbed, relaxed and ready to propose. She rolled to his side with a soft smile and a kiss to his cheek. She fell asleep before her head hit the pillow.

Disappointment socked Risk like a punch to the gut.

He wanted to shake her. Wake her.

Make her listen to him.

Yet he knew she needed her rest.

Another opportunity lost.

CHAPTER 14

Zen Driscoll lounged against Natalie Llewellyn's bedroom door in a gray T-shirt and black pajama bottoms. He took in her bedroom, designed in gold and silver and accented with vases of champagne roses.

He cut her a glance, a hint of a smile on his lips. "Did you dream of Aaron or of me last night?" he asked.

Natalie propped herself up, then punched her silver-cased pillow. She gave an unladylike snort. "Aaron, you ass. Happy?"

Damn happy. Zen strolled toward her and stopped at the foot of her canopy bed. He smiled to himself. Her succession of dreams had affected her greatly. Totally shaken her up. Her sexual partner was always Aaron, a fact she couldn't deny. "It's time you ditched me and dialed his number."

She plucked at the thin satin straps of her French blue nightgown and moistened her lips with her tongue. "I still want you."

Zen scratched his belly. His pajamas were bunched at his groin. Natalie's gaze lit on the bulge. He smoothed down the material. No morning erection. Not for this woman. "Don't be mistaken," he told her straight out. "You only want me because I once walked away. Aaron won't leave you. Go back to the man."

Her face free of makeup, her hair pure bed head, Natalie lacked pretense and looked almost human this morning. Her attitude, however, needed work. She sniffed. "I refuse to grovel."

"For better or worse, for public sex, the man planned to marry you," he reminded her. "Once you're available, Aaron will circle around. He willingly played your games."

"He played them so well."

"So apologize."

"I'm not yet ready." She pouted. "I thought we'd sail to Key West tomorrow. Maybe take in the Caribbean."

Every minute with Natalie had felt like a lifetime. "I'd thought to return to Frostproof."

"Return to Stevie Cole?"

"That was my plan."

"Let's discuss this over breakfast." Natalie reached for her bedside phone and punched in several numbers. "Eggs Benedict, English muffins, fruit cup, served on the terrace," she directed.

Zen went to dress. When he returned, he found her seated on the terrace of her villa overlooking Tampa Bay. She'd started eating without him—a sure sign she wouldn't miss him when he was gone.

He'd distracted Natalie for two weeks, until the night Risk Kincaid called. The second he'd learned Aaron and Stevie were no longer an item, he'd planned his retreat.

He needed to return to Frostproof and his woman.

Natalie had let him go. Without a fight. Her future belonged to the man in her dreams. Thank God Zen was her past.

He pulled up a chair and poured himself a cup of coffee.

Across the table, Natalie dabbed her lips with a linen napkin. She stared openly at Zen as he read the *Tampa Bay Tribune*. He was clean-cut, intelligent, sexy, but reserved. He'd showered and shaved, and dressed to catch a plane—white dress shirt, dark slacks—a plane that would take him back to Frostproof. To reunite with Stevie.

A small part of her still craved this man. The fantasy side where wishes were made but seldom came true. Her reality lay with Aaron Grayson, a handsome, daring man she could mold to her sexual preferences. Aaron was phenomenal. The man had large, amazing hands and an even larger—

"Eat your breakfast, Natalie," Zen said, without looking up from his newspaper. "You've called Aaron, sent your private plane for him. He should be arriving within the hour. You'll need all your strength."

Make-up sex. Nothing was more delicious. She attacked her meal with the same vigor she would soon attack Aaron.

Zen departed with no more than a handshake.

Natalie sighed. A kiss would have been nice, but the man was saving his kisses for Stevie Cole.

She took a long hot bath and pampered her skin with imported bath salts, then toweled dry. She spread lotion until her skin was baby soft.

A loud impatient knock on her bedroom door announced Aaron Grayson. He had a key to her villa and had let himself in.

Her hair still damp, she greeted him in no more than her mascara and Paris pink lipstick.

The reunion did not go as planned.

His gaze raked her body. Disgust twisted one corner of his mouth. "Put some clothes on."

The sharp edge of his voice frightened her a little. She snatched her satin robe from the end of the bed and slipped it on. "Better?"

"Tie the sash."

She did as he requested, leaving enough cleavage showing that he could glimpse her breasts. Her nipples poked the black lace lapel. The outline of her hips and sex were visible beneath the delicate fabric.

Aaron didn't seem to notice. Anger stamped his features. Tension made tendons tight across his shoulders. His hands fisted.

Natalie slowly took him in. He didn't look like the Aaron she'd left in Frostproof. Gone was the well-groomed, sharply dressed man. In his place stood someone unrecognizable. Someone in ratty jeans and a ripped T-shirt, in need of a haircut, shave, and a trip to the tailor. He'd swapped his Cartier Panther for a Timex. The laces in his tennis shoes had broken and been knotted. Not replaced.

Not a bad look . . . if she liked rugged and earthy.

His scent hit her the hardest. No Gucci cologne. Only male heat and raw power. This she liked. A lot.

"You look different," she finally managed.

"This is the real me, Natalie," he stated without apology. "I've had two weeks to reevaluate who I am. Who I want to be. I like casual. Feeling at home in my skin. I'm done being someone I'm not."

A man with his own mind. Better and better. "I rather like the real you."

"Look hard and look long." His tone was still harsh. "You've got twenty minutes to state your case, then I'm gone."

"Gone?" She started, taken aback.

"I'm not here to be played," he stated. "I don't do threesomes. It's either me or Zen."

"Zen has already left."

Aaron's jaw shifted, along with his stance. "Left on his own or under your direction?"

"I . . . I told him to go." A little lie that served a bigger purpose.

His gaze flicked to her canopied bed, took in the rumpled gold comforter and silver-cased pillows. "Zen stayed here all week?"

"Stayed in a guestroom. We never had sex."

Aaron threw back his head and laughed, a harsh bark of disbelief. "Liar."

"Zen didn't want me after—" She hesitated.

"After *what?*" He forced her to continue.

"After I dreamed of you."

"Tell me about the dream."

She relived it in vivid detail. Her nipples peaked and she grew wet. The dream turned her on.

"You dreamed the day you left Frostproof," he contemplated, unconvinced. "Yet you took fourteen days to contact me."

"Zen wouldn't let me near a phone," she said. "The man's insane. He saw you and Stevie in the kitchen at the coffee shop and thought you'd reconciled."

Aaron went utterly still. "So Zen cut you out of the picture."

"He didn't want me interfering in your future." She sighed. "A major sacrifice on Zen's part. He tolerated me. But he's taken with Stevie."

"Zen wanted Stevie happy." Aaron pinched the bridge of his nose between his thumb and forefinger. "It's finally coming together."

"Where does that leave us?" Blunt, but she needed to know. "Are we back together?"

Aaron shrugged. "Maybe, maybe not."

Maybe not scared her spitless. Yet she couldn't let her fear show. She turned on her heel. "When you decide, let me—"

He snagged her arm and jerked her back against him. She slammed against his chest. A cut and defined chest that rippled with tension. "Don't walk away from me."

Aaron had issued an order. His first order to her ever. The sharpness of his tone made her tingle. "Or you'll what?"

"Force you to stay."

She didn't need to be forced. She wanted this man. She let him take her.

A long, slow taking on her canopy bed.

Stripped down, he took her in the missionary position. All dominant and sexually driven, he controlled each kiss, every touch, the depth of his penetration.

Alone with Aaron, she found a new freedom. For the first time in her life, Natalie Llewellyn allowed the searing sweet friction to build and build, without fear of getting caught.

The rise was both pleasurable and painful. Her throat burned and her breath caught. A low moan escaped her. She rocked against him in a hot restless rhythm. In response, he slowed his pace, withdrew, almost stopped.

Her skin slick, she shattered with his next entry. The soul-robbing climax bound them together. For an unguarded moment she embraced a future with this man. Treasured the thought.

Aaron Grayson spilled inside her.

Pulling out, he bemoaned the fact he'd taken her without a condom. Natalie hadn't objected. Always the one to insist on protection, today she'd kept silent. Merely spread her legs in liquid welcome.

He didn't know where they stood. They'd had slow, phenomenal sex. The best he'd ever had. But that didn't mean they were on speaking terms.

Rolling off her, he lay flat on his back. His body jerked when she eased alongside him. She wasn't one to snuggle, to share in the afterglow. Yet at that moment, her hand splayed over his heart. Her bloodred tipped toes stroked his calf.

"My corporal went into battle without a helmet," he finally said.

"I know . . ."

"You could be pregnant."

"Possibly . . ." said softly, without concern.

"Guess I'll have to make an honest woman out of you."

"You're under no obligation."

"*If* we marry, I've a few new rules."

"I like playing by my old ones."

He clenched his teeth. "No more public sex."

She stiffened. She bared her teeth. He thought she'd bite him. "I like exposure."

"Not as my wife," he said firmly. "I'll install monkey bars and a swing set in our bedroom if you like. Even a stripper's pole. But I won't take you in public, in front of God and any chance passerby."

She patted her fingers against her lips, yawned. "Sounds boring."

Aaron showed her boring. He took her again. This time with thrusts so red-hot and hungry, they both felt on fire.

Tangled in the sheets, they slid off the bed and landed on the carpet. It was so plush, the deep pile cushioned their fall. They rolled around. Each seeking domination. Until he exerted his strength. Rose above her.

Lust ripped through his senses. Tore at his heart.

His climax slammed through him and into her. So powerfully, she screamed. His name.

Sprawled on the carpet, he covered them both.

She slept, all flushed and sated. With a smile on her face.

Aaron knew she dreamed of him.

"Double cappuccino and a blow."

Zen Driscoll had caught Stevie Cole daydreaming. His voice embraced her, his very presence stunned her speechless.

Her throat worked, but no words came out. She could only stare. He stood across the counter, tall and handsome. Scrutinizing her with an intensity that drew her nipples to points.

She shivered, crossed her arms over her chest.

He seemed satisfied.

"I missed you," he confessed.

"Missed me while you were with Natalie?" She found that hard to believe.

"I made a mistake."

The most logical man on the planet had miscalculated?

He nodded toward a deserted table in the far corner of the coffee shop. "We need to talk. Join me?"

The afternoon crowd had dispersed. The Bat Pack conversed with those few still seated. Stevie had free time. "Have a seat and I'll bring your cappuccino."

"And a blow," he reminded her.

She served his double cappuccino in an off-white china cup with dark brown pheasants. She took a seat at his table, brought the cup to her lips and softly blew. The foam swirled in lazy circles.

His gaze lit on her mouth. Eyes narrowed and focused. "Sweet," he finally managed.

She handed him the cup. "My specialty. Pucker and blow."

He took a sip of his cappuccino and shifted on the lavender retro stool. He rubbed his hamstring.

"Leg still hurting you?" she asked, concerned.

"A little. It's better than it was."

Silence sliced between them until Zen said, "I owe you an explanation. For leaving Frostproof so abruptly."

Stevie sat perfectly still. Her hands were clutched in her lap. She was afraid if she moved, Zen would disappear. Again. Her heart couldn't take his leaving a second time.

"Backtrack a month," he began. "When I first met you, Aaron was your man. Even after his engagement, after you and I'd slept together, I still wasn't certain you'd be able to move beyond him to be with me."

"I was certain."

"I didn't know that at the time. The day Aaron stopped by the coffee shop, and I saw you in the kitchen—"

"You jumped to conclusions. You never gave me a chance to explain."

"Logic's my strong suit. But with you, I lost my mind."

"I was just putting the past behind me that day," she told him. "Aaron hugged me, kissed me on the cheek. You read too much into his good-bye."

"It looked . . . intimate."

"So you split, took off with Natalie."

"I went with Natalie so you could be with Aaron."

Foolish, foolish man. "I didn't want Aaron. I wanted you."

"So I now see." He held out his hand, an offering. "Forgive me?"

She locked her fingers with his. "Tell me about your time with Natalie."

He sipped his cappuccino. "Not much to tell. The days dragged on and on. She shopped. I worked out in her gym. Nights, she went to bed early. She kept having sex dreams about Aaron. The dreams convinced her that her future lay with him."

He hadn't quite answered—

"I didn't sleep with her. No desire whatsoever."

Satisfied, she breathed easier. Leaning across the table, she whispered, "I get off shortly. Want to do it in the dark?"

His gaze skimmed over her. "You look thinner."

"You left and I dropped five pounds." Five pounds from her waistline. Once she shed ten additional pounds, she'd light a room full of candles. Twenty pounds total, and she'd parade around naked.

Zen cupped her chin. "I like you curvy."

She'd keep her curves, just count calories.

"Bat Pack," Zen called to Romeo, Psycho, and Chaser. "Stevie's leaving early. Cover her shift."

Psycho grinned. "Einstein's seen the light."

"Trivia buffs together," Chaser groaned. "Unbeatable team."

"Go play, children." Romeo motioned them on their way. "Coffee shop's covered."

"Coffee shop's closed," Romeo's voice carried from the kitchen.

Jacy pushed through the swinging doors. She found Romeo at the sink, his sleeves rolled up, elbow deep in sudsy water. She lifted a brow. "Washing cups and saucers?"

He rubbed the back of his hand across his brow. "Stevie said not to put the china in the dishwasher. Psycho and Chaser aren't into dishpan hands. I told them I'd lock up."

She hobbled over to him. "Want some help?"

A sexy grin split his face. "I like the idea of your hands in my dishwater."

The man was pure tease. She submerged her hands in the warm water, then put him in his place. "Find a woman. Settle down."

"*Settle down?*" From the tone of his voice, her recommendation sounded like a death sentence to him. He cut her a look. "You taken, darlin'?"

Jacy thought of Risk—how she'd snuck out of the house when he'd stepped into the shower. He wanted her to rest. She'd wanted to check on the coffee shop. They hadn't reached a compromise.

Unable to shift her car with her cast, she'd stripped the gears on her Mazda Miata. When Risk discovered her gone, there would be hell to pay. He'd drag her home, dead or alive.

She rinsed the suds from a red china cup decorated

with white orchids. "Not taken, Romeo, but involved." She resumed washing the matching saucer.

"Heavily involved?" He found her hand under the water, rubbed his thumb across her palm. "Or can you still fool around?"

Romeo was coming on a little too strong. "I'm—"

"Taken." Risk Kincaid stood in the doorway, the calmness in his voice deceptive.

Romeo held up her hand. "No ring, no commitment. Open season on Jacy Grayson."

"Taken." Risk said it a second time. This time with a force that laid claim.

"Jacy?" Romeo pressed. "This true, sweetheart?"

The muscles in Risk's jaw flexed hard. "She's not your sweetheart."

Romeo snagged a dish towel and dried his hands. There was pure challenge in his gaze. "Until she tells me different, she's fair game."

Fair game? Jacy gaped. What the hell was wrong with Romeo? Provoking Risk could be detrimental to the third baseman's health.

Risk rocked back on his heels, then forward on his toes. A fighter's stance. "Why are you here with Romeo?" His question hinted at knocking heads and breaking bones. "Was this a planned visit?" The faintest hint of uncertainty. "You left the house without a note."

"I came to check on the coffee shop," she explained.

"And to check on me." Romeo raised and lowered his brows suggestively.

"Psycho and Chaser?"

"Don't wash delicate china," she informed Risk.

"I'd do anything for Jacy." Romeo encircled her waist, rested one hand possessively on her hip. "Wash china. Scrub floors. Anything at all."

Risk took in their closeness. Didn't like what he saw. His fists balled. "Get your hand off her."

"Jacy's free to leave," Romeo insisted. "But she's not moving, pops."

Not moving because Romeo had dug his fingers into her hip. Jacy tried to pull away from him, yet he held her so tightly, she couldn't move.

Tension vibrated between the two men. The air was thick with testosterone.

She swatted Romeo's hand just as Risk took one giant step forward. His green gaze was dark and dangerous. Murderous. "Too damn chummy." He scowled.

"Not chummy enough." Romeo in his stupidity did the unthinkable. He kissed her full on the lips.

Jacy pushed at Romeo's chest. Whimpered.

Romeo's kiss was warm, but short-lived.

Goaded to the breaking point, Risk reacted. He grabbed Romeo by the front of his shirt and cocked his arm, ready to pound the man's pretty face.

Romeo spiked a brow, raised his chin and sneered at Risk, asking to be hit.

Panicked, Jacy grabbed Risk's arm. She tugged with the little strength she could muster without hurting her ribs. "No blood! Romeo's a harmless flirt."

Romeo covered his heart with one hand. "Harmless? I want you, sweetheart."

The muscles in Risk's arm flexed, and his forearm

shook as he tossed Romeo aside. He took a step back. "Touch her again—"

"And you'll what? Pull another punch?" Romeo taunted. "I'd fight for you, Jacy."

"Fight for her?" Risk stared a hole through Romeo. "I'd kill for her. You could be the first man I bury."

Risk could lay Romeo out, leave him as no more than a chalk outline on the kitchen floor. She'd pulled Risk off the young power hitter once, but doubted she could do so again.

"Harsh, old man." Romeo shook his head. Then he scratched his jaw. "What's she to you anyway?"

"Soon to be my—"

"Your *what?*" Romeo drove the question home.

"Wife."

"Your *wife?*" Jacy repeated, wide-eyed and bewildered.

Risk ran his hands through his hair, then jabbed a finger toward the door. "Take a hike, Romeo."

Romeo didn't budge. "So you can propose?"

"That's none of your damn business."

"I'm making it my business."

"Romeo . . ." Risk threatened.

"Squeeze play." Romeo had the balls to grin. To grin big. "I had to bunt to bring you home. Jacy's home plate, pops." He swaggered toward the door. All full of himself and his accomplishment. "Marry the woman. Name your firstborn after me. Jesse, boy or girl."

Risk Kincaid stared after Romeo. Romeo had set him up. His evil flirting had been done for good. He owed the young power hitter an apology. Romeo wouldn't, however, be getting one tonight. Maybe not even tomorrow.

Jacy broke the silence that followed Romeo's departure. "Marriage?" Her tone was incredulous. "Romeo and his wild ideas."

"Not so wild," Risk said slowly. "My body loves your body. That's a strong basis for any relationship."

"I want more than sex."

"So do I. A whole lot more. I want you in my future."

Her eyes went wide. "You do?"

"I've tried to tell you several times over the past few weeks," he admitted. "But every time, we were either interrupted or you fell asleep on me. I want you forever, babe. Which means no more boyfriends. No more broken hearts. No more rebound lover. I want an exclusive in your bed."

She blushed looking more than a little guilty. He nudged her with his elbow. "Spill, Jacy."

She wet her lips and stared at the base of his throat. Her confession came softly. "There's never been anyone but you. Only imaginary lovers and breakups to keep you in my life."

Un-friggin'-believable. "Only me?"

"Since the backseat of your Cougar."

Risk took it all in. Jacy Grayson was his and his alone. Had been for twelve years. In his heart, he'd been married to her for a very long time. He didn't feel the least bit tricked. His chest and sex swelled simultaneously. "Marry me, babe."

She caught the rise in his Levi's. "At Christmas?"

"I want to jingle my bells long before then."

"My ribs are almost healed."

"Maybe if we took our time . . ."

"Went very, very slowly . . ." she agreed.

They both grinned. After four weeks, they'd finally agreed on something. Something that would bring them both pleasure.

Risk was immensely creative.

Six months later

May, and spring was in the air. It was opening day at Jacy's Java in Richmond. The coffee shop was bursting at the seams. Businessmen, housewives, and ball players all sipped their favorite blend. A few enjoyed gourmet bars and brownies, including Psycho's now-famous Rice Krispies Treats. The man promoted the treat at every opportunity. Even during television interviews after Rogues' games. He promised to send lots of business Jacy's way.

She looked over the crowd and searched out her main squeeze. She found Risk Kincaid at a table against the far wall, sipping a black coffee, his cream puff untouched. He'd wanted a caramel roll, but the batch had sold within an hour of opening. She would bake for him shortly.

He looked up from a sports magazine, caught her staring, and winked. A sexy wink that always set her heart to beating faster. She loved this man.

The Richmond branch of Jacy's Java would bring in big bucks. The restored landmark was a prime piece of real estate. She'd decorated with a flourish of wild color and Tiffany lighting.

Seated at the counter, Frank Stall and Walter Tate

discussed the weather. Risk had flown in a group of Frostproof's best customers to celebrate the Richmond opening.

"A little of your sugar, Jacy," Frank Stall requested.

Jacy added two pansy-decorated sugar cubes and stirred with the tip of her finger.

"And a blow." Walter Tate held up his china cup for her to cool his coffee.

Jacy blew gently on the French Roast.

Both men smiled broadly.

Life was good.

Risk rose from his chair and crossed to where she stood. He leaned against the counter. "I've business to catch up on. Can I work in your office?"

"My computer is your computer."

"Same password?"

She'd broken down and told him that *LoveRisk* would link him to the Internet. Knowing her password always made him smile. A warm smile that left her body hot.

Risk departed as Zen and Stevie Driscoll entered. They had married during spring training, having decided weekend commutes from Richmond to Frostproof didn't satisfy their need to be together.

Jacy had offered Stevie stock in the coffee shop, which gave them a chance to work together again. Stevie waved as she and Zen located a table.

Jacy held her smile even when Aaron and Natalie Grayson came in for coffee. They'd flown to Richmond for her grand opening. Aaron's desire to stay in contact with both her and Risk was quite touching. He'd become his own man—a man of casual dress and little pretense.

Jacy had yet to warm to Natalie, although she found a pregnant Natalie almost human. Natalie was due around the time of the World Series. The woman would have her baby in the owner's box if Tampa Bay again faced Richmond.

The Bat Pack trudged in. Psycho, in a red T-shirt with *Black Belt in Crazy* printed across his chest, gave her a high five. Chaser, with his Oakleys and diamond stud, hugged her tightly. Romeo greeted her with a gorgeous blonde on one arm and a sexy brunette on the other.

"Hello, sweetheart," he greeted. "Still married?"

"Happily married," Jacy returned easily.

"Always hopeful." He grinned.

Jacy looked from one woman to the other, then back to Romeo. "You'd have no time for me."

"I'd find time. Just give me the word."

Romeo continued to tease her. Around Risk, he openly vowed he'd be the first suitor at her door should Jacy ever divorce the old man.

Risk no longer felt threatened. Jacy saw to that. She took him to bed each night and loved him with every passionate bone in her body.

She left the Bat Pack to fend for themselves. They'd once worked her coffee shop and knew their way around the counter.

She went after Risk and found him hunched over the computer in her office. He was scrutinizing a piece of real estate.

Coming up behind him, she pressed herself against his back.

He leaned back into her body.

"Prime acreage." He pointed to the screen. "Plenty of room to raise children."

"You're tired of your condo?"

"No pet clause."

"You've got kids and dogs on the brain?"

"Kids and dogs and you."

"Glad I'm part of the package."

He swiveled the chair, pulled her down on his lap, and kissed her hard. "You were part of the package from the day I kissed you on the high school bleachers."

"The day Danny Rhodes ditched me."

"His loss. My gain."

She kissed him lightly. "I'm about to make caramel rolls."

His eyes lit up. One corner of his mouth curved. "Dough's in the cooler."

"The cooler with the deadbolt."

He skimmed his fingers down the ruffled edge of her green top with the turquoise polka dots, then tugged a strand of her hair, dyed to match the dots. "I'm in need of something sweet."

She hopped off his lap, moved two steps ahead of him out the office door. "Time for your sugar fix."

CRAZY FOR YOU

KATE ANGELL

From the moment she spots his hamburger-and-French-fry emblazoned boxers with the word *supersized* on them, Bree knows Sexton St. Croix is trouble. Here is a man with just one thing on his mind, but Sex has hired her to do a job, and she'll let nothing get in her way.

Sexton St. Croix's luxury ocean liner is haunted—by the ghost of an unflappable flapper named Daisy. Now, in an effort to persuade Daisy to "cheese it," he's opened the ship to a veritable psychic circus. He is counting on Bree's "clairsentience" to save his bacon. Her exquisitely sensitive fingers can detect the emotional vibrations of an 80-year-old love triangle, while her tender touch unlocks secrets in his own heart.

Dorchester Publishing Co., Inc.
P.O. Box 6640
Wayne, PA 19087-8640

_____52616-6
$5.99 US/$7.99 CAN

Please add $2.50 for shipping and handling for the first book and $.75 for each additional book. NY and PA residents, add appropriate sales tax. No cash, stamps, or CODs. Canadian orders require an extra $2.00 for shipping and handling and must be paid in U.S. dollars. Prices and availability subject to change. **Payment must accompany all orders.**

Name: _____

Address: _____

City: _____ State: _____ Zip: _____

E-mail: _____

I have enclosed $_____ in payment for the checked book(s).

CHECK OUT OUR WEBSITE! *www.dorchesterpub.com*
_____ *Please send me a free catalog.*

KATE ANGELL
DRIVE ME CRAZY

Cade Nyland doesn't think that anything good can come of the new dent in his classic black Sting Ray, even if it does happen at the hands of a sexy young woman. He is determined to win his twelfth road rally race of the year.

TZ Blake only enters Chugger Charlie's tight butt competition to win enough money to keep her auto repair shop open. What she ends up with is a position as navigator in a rally race. All she has to do is pretend she knows where she is going. All factors indicate that the unlikely duo is in for a bumpy ride . . . and each eagerly anticipates the jostling that will bring them closer together.